To save her own life, Elena must save Hana, whose mission is to protect her tribe. They're stronger together. The problem is they're 4,000 years and 6,000 miles apart.

Wounded during a terrorist attack, NYC police commando Elena Labat wakes aboard a Phoenician boat on the Mediterranean Sea to find a young girl lashed to the mast. The girl is Hana, who has trekked across ancient Lebanon to prevent a king from destroying her tribe. Elena knows she must save her. Hana must escape the barbarians who abducted her before she can go home. Slipping in and out of consciousness, Elena teaches Hana everything she can. But Elena's family needs her, and she can't stay in the past. Hana will have to succeed on her own.

KUDOS for *Blue Girl on a Night Dream Sea*

In *Blue Girl on a Night Dream* Sea by Ginny Fite, Elena Labat is rescuing hostages from terrorists in NYC when she is badly injured. She loses consciousness, and when she wakes, she is on board an ancient Phoenician ship on the Mediterranean Sea. Elena realizes that she there to rescue Hana, a girl who is lashed to the ship's mast, and help her save her people. But Elena is needed in the present and she has very little time in the past to teach Hana everything she can. Expertly combining the past and present, science fiction, and suspense, Fite weaves a tale that will keep you enthralled from beginning to end. ~ *Taylor Jones, The Review Team of Taylor Jones & Regan Murphy*

Blue Girl on a Night Dream Sea by Ginny Fite is the story of Elena Labat who is a lieutenant with NYC's counter-terrorism unit. She is injured while rescuing hostages from terrorists and ends up in a coma. As she slips in and out of consciousness, she finds herself in ancient Phoenicia, trying to help a girl tied to the mast of a ship. The girl's name is Hana, and Elena tries to protect her—first from kidnappers and then from a priestess, and finally from a king. Hana thinks Elena is a goddess, helping her to save her tribe. *Blue Girl on a Night Dream Sea* is a combination time-travel fantasy, a historical thriller, and a modern-day suspense. Well written, fast paced, and intense, this one will keep you glued to the edge of your seat all the way through. ~ *Regan Murphy, The Review Team of Taylor Jones & Regan Murphy*

Also by Ginny Fite

Cromwell's Folly

No Good Deed Left Undone

Lying, Cheating, and Occasionally Murder

No End of Bad

ACKNOWLEDGMENTS

To all the people who came before and left their marks for me to see and read, my humble thanks. To all whose minds and hands helped build this mosaic, my deep appreciation.

Always to Carolyn Bross for seeing every word, to Carmen Procida for reading everything written by women, to Dr. Gregory Mestanas for Cyprus history and images, to Dr. Tisha Gallanter for her medical expertise, to Sanford Holst for the rich detail of his book, *Phoenician Secrets*, to Kat Howard for insightful comments when the story was still finding its legs.

Thank you, Tara Bell, for wonder, Catherine Baldau for the brilliant cover idea, K.P. Robbins for seeing what isn't needed, Solveig Eggerz, Leslie Rollins, Linda Morefield, Deb Barger, Michael John Barron, and Cathy Baker for thoughtful questions, Frank Joseph for being in my corner, and archaeologist Ticia Verveer for posting splendid inspirational photos of ancient artifacts, mosaics, and murals. I'm grateful, as ever, to the entire Black Opal Books team who make my dreams into reality.

Namaste to my sons for their infinite patience. To all children, and especially my grandchildren, who look at the world with clear eyes and true bravery, my love. To the women warriors who take bullets for us, a humble salute. And to the universe, for serendipity, synchronicity, and just waiting for me to catch up, my deepest gratitude.

Blue Girl
on a
Night Dream
Sea

Ginny Fite

A Black Opal Books Publication

GENRE: SUSPENSE/PARANORMAL/TIME TRAVEL

BLUE GIRL ON A NIGHT DREAM SEA
Copyright © 2019 by Ginny Fite
Cover Design by Ginny Fite
All cover art copyright © 2019
All Rights Reserved

Print ISBN: 9781644371855

First Publication: SEPTEMBER 2019

Published by Black Opal Books **http://www.blackopalbooks.com**

DEDICATION

For my children and grandchildren. Dream deeply.

"Who is as fair as the goddess Anath, who is as comely as Astarte, whose eyes are lapis lazuli, whom El has given in my dream, the Father of Man in my vision..."
~ The Rapiuma

"Hiraeth: homesickness tinged with grief for a home you never had.
~ Welsh word with no English equivalent

Chapter 1

ELENA

Lieutenant Elena Labat put her team's chance of surviving somewhat north of fifty percent. *Not too bad.* They approached the skyscraper from the southwest. From helicopters a mile above them, the rescue team was a pre-dawn shadow moving beneath trees in the plaza. *We're here to save the world*, Elena reminded herself and half-smiled. Humor was where she retreated when all seemed lost. Today it wasn't really a joke.

It was late May, still cool at six-thirty in the morning, ten minutes until dawn. Light rising from the east would reflect off the skyscraper's thousands of windows and send indecipherable signals flashing across the sky. Despite the cool, Elena was sweating—pre-op anxiety. It would abate when they got going, replaced by the sweat of physical exertion.

Dressed in black garments meant to wick away sweat, with sleek oxygen masks, backpacks, climbing shoes and harnesses, eight elite officers took a knee and held in place—anonymous, ready, and waiting for "Go." Hidden in the shadow of the giant building, they geared up mentally. They had the skills and training for this operation. Tested under fire during the last five years, they were good at their job. This wasn't the time for misgivings, although each of them had their own. Elena certainly had hers.

She scanned the environment for anything out of place. All streets around the entire World Trade Center complex in lower Manhattan were closed to traffic and pedestrians. SWAT teams assembled on the north side of the building waited for a signal to storm the front, back, and side doors on the ground floor simultaneously. National Guard troops were in place around the entire perimeter and throughout the below-ground visitor and retail space. Social media transmissions were blocked within a square mile to prevent civilians from posting images of their impending strike. Press, cordoned off two city blocks back from the building and barricaded by police, were embargoed from reporting on this mission until it was completed. Media had been warned: anyone breaking the police line would be treated as a terrorist.

Elena tucked an errant black curl back under her helmet. In spite of the cool weather, sweat trickled down the back of her neck. Inside her mask, the world smelled empty. She patted her utility belt for one last check: knife, Ruger LCP semi-automatic pistol and loaded backup clips, taser, truncheon, ropes, carabineers, oxygen concentrator, nearly forty pounds more weight in weapons than she carried on her bones. Touching the shoulder straps of her emergency parachute, she reminded herself BASE jumpers had climbed up the building in 2013 before it was completed, opened their chutes, jumped, and survived. If she slipped, she could survive also.

Her problem was waiting. It was now half an hour since they took their places. She wasn't good at waiting. Waiting opened the wormhole of fear, fear that rendered her either inert or bent on a rampage. Waiting preceded the death of people she cared for. Waiting was what you did before your buddy stepped out from cover into a sniper bullet or your vehicle rolled over an IED.

Elena snapped her mind back to the task at hand. Her squad had trained in buildering, climbing up the face of skyscrapers, but never under this kind of pressure, never for real, and never this high. It was 1,268 vertical feet to the top floor. They would climb two-thirds of that distance, ascending in pairs, scaling first the special grooved glass that encased the concrete and steel podium at the base of the building. The first one to reach a steel cross beam would lash a rope to it and so on up a thousand feet. No looking down. No time for fear. No second-guessing.

They had no illusions about the feasibility of this mission. It just had to be done. They deliberately quashed memories of the beautiful September day two decades before when two commercial planes flew into the twin towers: the flying debris, the smoke, the sudden collapse of thousands of tons of steel, glass, and concrete that stunned the world. They called only on their fury from that day. Fury fed resolve. Grief they left at street level.

Elena's sister, Alissa, was one of the hostages who did not escape from this skyscraper yesterday. Alissa told her family she needed to complete a brief before she knocked off for the long weekend. She'd now been out of contact for twelve hours—no texts or calls to or from her cell phone since four-thirty p.m. yesterday. Elena refused to believe her sister was dead.

It doesn't matter what the terrorists demand, Elena thought. It doesn't matter, either, what the hostage negotiator is saying to the terrorists, or that the US Attorney General is claiming these criminals would be brought to justice. That was all smoke. Any negotiation was only performance. *We're going to find them and kill them.* The directive was simple and clear.

Their advantage is that they don't value life the way we do. Elena's thought startled her. In spite of everything she'd seen as an Army medic under fire, she'd never allowed herself to admit indifference to life was a tactical advantage.

Her mind flashed frame by frame through the video and slides the squad had been shown to acquaint them with the skyscraper's interior: three-million square feet of space, miles of corridors, thousands of doors. Alissa must be hiding somewhere in all of that space, in an overlooked closet that wouldn't be checked by the terrorists in a rapid search. She had to hope that was true. She had to get to her sister before the terrorists found her, before any bombs went off, before the building collapsed.

Minimal information gave Elena a kind of claustrophobia. She felt boxed in, only knowing what she was told by her supervisors. They knew only what was happening after the fact, after it was reported to them. Everything else was speculation. Anything could go wrong and probably would. That was the norm. That was the way it went in Iraq and Afghanistan.

In the early morning briefing, the Captain told them the operation was risky. They might die. They might lose civilians. RANGE-R radar devices mounted on drones flying circles around the building had taken infrared images through the windows. Individual red and yellow blobs that roamed freely through the structure were presumably terrorists moving around to control their hostages and patrol the building. Hostages were huddled together on five floors from the seventeenth to the eleventh, making rescue more difficult. But terrorists would expect a police incursion from ground level, not from above them. A first rescue attempt to rappel down from stealth helicopters hovering above the building was scuttled when wind shear slammed the lead jumper into the building's four-hundred-foot spire.

Elena's team would make the second attempt. After the ascent, their job was to clear the top portion of the building floor by floor from the observation deck to the twentieth floor. From the twentieth floor, they would rappel in pairs down four different elevator shafts to the floor directly above where a group of hostages were held. They would take the seventeenth floor first, kill the terrorists, save the hostages, and proceed to the next floor. That was the plan, and it had to be executed perfectly or the terrorists might blow everyone in the building to kingdom come.

On her earpiece she heard the voice of the deputy commissioner for counterterrorism. "We've got a go!"

Holding her hand up to get the squad's attention, Elena pointed to the building. "Move out."

She raced forward and leaped up to grab a handhold on the highest angled glass fin protruding from stainless steel panels she could reach. For however long the climb took, her complete focus would now be on her hands, feet, breathing, and pushing her body up the face of the building to the platform above.

Her fingertips gripped the thin edge. She pushed up to the next tiny ridge, looking for toe holds in the slimmest rim where glass window plates had been fitted together. Creeping up the side of the building as if it was laid horizontal and she could simply push with her legs and reach with her arms, she crawled across its surface section by section. It was less than a quarter of a mile to their destination, a distance she could do in under a minute running on the ground. All thought fled.

Chapter 2

HANA

Hana had climbed halfway up the mountain and paused to look back and catch her breath. The world she knew lay far beneath her, undulating in green and blue. Great heights of snow-covered mountains hugged depths of dark blue lake surrounded by white sands. Black earth littered with tiny gems glinting red, green, white, and blue was behind her.

At this height, the wide river wound out of the lake like a loose thread from a spool of silver. Home was the world wrapped in a glowing blue cloak. In the other direction, the direction she climbed, lay nothing familiar, a landscape as foreign as the first was known, a place where ground devoured stones and earth shifted under her feet at every step.

Hana swallowed the loss in her throat and stepped forward, hard ground meeting her foot halfway, jarring her. The ground tilted upward. She lost her balance and tottered like an elder, who, at twelve grain harvests, she was many seasons from becoming. She looked ahead and saw rain-starved trees writhing skyward in the distance like a wandering charcoal mark made by a gnarled hand moving shakily across sandstone. She sighed and inhaled scorching air. Her mother said she must make it across this wasteland to save her village.

"You must go," her mother said when Hana objected to being sent away from her home. "You are our tribute to the king, and you must deliver that gift yourself. He has demanded you, and your obedience is required if our tribe is to continue."

She held Hana's face between two hands and looked into her eyes. There was something else in her eyes: a warning, a message. Her face, usually the color of fresh apricots, was tinged pomegranate-seed red. Her brown eyes tried to tell Hana what she couldn't say out loud. Hana could barely take in the words her mother said. She couldn't guess what she meant to say but didn't.

"This is a test of your courage, my dearest. You are braver than you think you are." What was her mother forbidden to say out loud, bound by the laws of their clan?

Her words made a small tremor start in Hana's belly and continue down her legs. She gripped her mother's hand. "What do you mean, Ouma? I don't want to go anywhere. I want to stay here with you."

She wanted to wrap her hands up in her mother's long black hair as she'd done as a child. She wanted to climb into her lap, lean against her breast, and be comforted by the rhythmic beating of her heart. Instead, tears burning her eyes, she turned away from her mother, defiant. "I won't go! I'll run away to another clan."

Strong hands clasped Hana's shoulders and spun her around. "My sweet girl, we must comply with the clan's demands. You've been sent for by the king. If you don't go, everyone here, our entire clan, will be killed." She swept the air with her hands as if to erase everything in

their path. "The world is small. The king's men will find
you wherever you go. They will kill you. You must obey.
It's our only hope."

As if her parents had piled stones on her chest and
placed her on a raft in the river for her death ceremony,
Hana was suddenly too tired to run. She wanted to lie
down and never get up. A bird flew by on blue wings.
Bird song lilted from nearby trees. How could she leave
this place?

Her mother smoothed the hair away from Hana's
face and embraced her. "We have made arrangements
with members of our tribe," she whispered in her ear.
"You will have a guide, but I don't know who has been
chosen. He cannot be seen here lest someone betray us.
He will meet you in the wasteland and take you to
Batnoam's house in Sidon and from there to the Matron.
She is one of us and serves the queen. We hope she can
find a way to prevent the worst."

She broke off and kissed Hana's cheeks and forehead many times, holding her close, breathing with her.

Hana pushed her mother away. "What is the worst?
Why are you doing this?" Her skin felt turned inside out,
burning rippled along her arms and legs. Her vision
blurred. "Why is it me? Why can't the elders send someone else?"

"It is you, my dear one, because you are the one spoken of in dreams of our ancestors, the one with eyes of
lapis lazuli. The king has demanded that you go to him.
We must comply."

Hana shook her head until her black curls tangled. "I
don't understand how you could do this to me." She
looked away. Hurt in her chest stopped words. Questions
lodged in her throat. Her mother was sending her away.
That was all she could comprehend. Nothing else mattered. She closed her eyes. Nearby, the river swished

against the rocks on the shore. Grass in the meadow rustled in the breeze.

No one would tell her what the worst was, or what would happen after she completed this journey. The elder brushed away Hana's many questions with a swipe of her hand. "You will not see this village again." The old woman's head shook, the cracked clay of her face breaking into tiny fissures as she spoke. "It is no matter. This village is just a collection of sticks and lumps of clay. You will not miss it."

Hana was affronted by this description. Her home was the people in these huts, the songs they sang as they worked mud from the riverbank into pots, the murmur of their voices as they spun yarn and wove cloth. Her home was the rustle of reeds at the river's edge, the splash of fish surfacing to snatch a fly out of the air.

She didn't believe the elder who said she must save her village. If the village wasn't important, why should she leave everything she loved to save it? There was something they weren't telling her. It couldn't be her fate never to return. Would she never see her mother and father again? Questions exhausted her.

She had now walked farther than she had ever gone before, more than four times the length of the river from her village to the waterfall and back. Her heart was hungry for home. She left behind safe shelter, a comfortable bed, layers of wool carpets beneath her feet, bowls of grapes, olives, and figs she could nibble on any time she was hungry. She already missed the people who brought her cool water and kissed her cheeks, who filled the air with the sound of flutes and strings.

As instructed, she had climbed the green mountain until she reached snow and stepped onto a path the elder described to her. It took her from dawn until dusk to reach the path. She looked ahead for the next marker.

"At the mountain's apex, there are two large rocks as black as the river at night," the elder explained to her, gray head nodding as if in agreement with her own words. "They are as tall as your shoulder and shine in the moonlight if you arrive at night when the moon is high. You cannot miss them. They flank the path you must take. At the top of one of the rocks is carved the shape of the feather you carry. Even in the dark, you can feel the carving with your fingers. You will know you are going the right way if you stand between the rocks and the stone with the carved feather is under your right hand."

Her parents nodded but she saw loss in their stricken faces. This was not their choice for her. They wanted her to stay with them in their village, marry, make her marks on the sides of clay pots, weave baskets, have children, and sing with her mother. Her father gave her a bronze dagger he forged in his fire and beat into shape. He placed it in a small leather pouch he hung by straps from the leather girdle that held her tunic and blue scarf secure to her body.

"As a last resort, to save yourself, you must jab this dagger into your attacker's neck just here." He placed his fingertips at the spot on her throat and kissed her forehead. "Push the blade in with all your strength." His face was the color of hot metal. "Do it quickly." His anger singed her skin. He didn't want her to go.

"Why don't you run away with me, Aba, take me away from this village and this horrible king?" she whispered. "How can the village be more important to you than I am?"

He didn't answer her questions.

Her mother slipped a ring with a flashing blue stone onto Hana's finger. "This is our bond," she said, holding up her hand to show Hana the matching ring on her own finger. "Wear it always." Her voice rasped. "It will guide you on your journey as if I were there whispering in your ear. If you look into its many surfaces, you will see me."

She held Hana's hand as long as she could.

Hana's entire clan accompanied her to the foot of the mountain. She ascended the grassy slope, from time to time looking behind her. Her mother stood where she had left her, her hand still outstretched as if to grasp Hana's. Soon, her mother was only a speck of purple in a sea of green grass. Hana turned to wave one last time and then gave her full attention to the steeply rising mountain, scrambling on all fours, grasping the roots of trees and the edges of small boulders to ascend.

By the time Hana reached the marker rocks, the moon was riding high in the sky. Soaked in sweat and chilled by the sudden cold, she was surprised the stones the elders described were really there, the ground between them tamped down where a slight depression marked many footfalls of people who had passed through before.

When had all this coming and going occurred? She had been completely oblivious to anything but her own child's life. Her days had been filled with singing and dancing, fishing and weaving baskets from fronds she and her mother picked near the river's edge. She chased butterflies and raced along the river with her friends.

Spellbound, she had watched sparks flitting around her father as he melted ore in the fire and beat out heated metal into spear heads, swords, daggers, bowls, and once an orb of bright yellow metal for someone's head. A gold crown, he told her, for a prince.

Her father was a god to her, strong and all powerful. His arms around her were all the protection she needed. He talked to her as he worked. "Something inside me reaches out into the molten ore and sees the shape it must be. It is as if I had other eyes that saw what was not yet there. We breathe together, the rock and I. We become one for a time."

His words are a kind of magic, Hana thought. They bring something new into being that is not yet there. The words made her think she could do something that had never been done. When it was time for her to take on her adult task, Hana wanted to make clay pots. She imagined special marks she would paint on them and practiced drawing them in the sand at the riverbank, swirls of stars and wavy lines for the river shining in the sunlight. At night, she fell asleep to the sound of her mother's voice telling about her clan's beginnings. She dreamed of making designs that would tell their story.

Hana pulled herself away from the tug of memories. She selected a round white stone from among many small rocks strewn along the ground and placed it atop the black rock next to the engraved feather to indicate she had arrived at the crossroads. In case anyone climbed the mountain to see if she had made it this far, they would see the stone and know she not been eaten by lions or blinded by the claws of an eagle enraged that she stumbled near its nest.

The moon lit her way as she walked through the night, her eyes on her feet to make sure she stayed on the path. Twice she thought she heard a large-winged bird fly overhead but when she looked up, she saw only an endless sky of stars. Her ears were playing tricks on her. Now, with the sun rising ahead of her, the wind whistled in her ears and worried her scarf. Sand burrowed into the folds of her clothing. All else was silence. No birds, no animals, at least none that she could see. The world was the color of clay and dust.

For a few heart beats, she closed her eyes. In the self-imposed darkness, she saw her people, a chalk outline on a sandstone wall with some parts painted in—a hand emerging like an offering of help, a sandaled foot, a small yellow coin being held aloft. A picture formed itself in her mind, the story of who she was, where she had been, where she was going. She couldn't see the end of the painting from here. She sank to a crouch with her back against a large rock and slept.

Chapter 3

ELENA

When Alissa's firm moved to the new World Trade Center building in 2016, she had joked, "If the power goes out, I can still walk down twenty flights in heels, even at nine months pregnant. I'm a New Yorker."

Elena, her sister, had worried no one was that fit. "At least take your shoes off," Elena said. Alissa grimaced now, remembering.

The first mild contractions began at four-thirty p.m. on Friday, the day before Memorial Day. She put on her superwoman face and continued to plow through one last review of the brief she was preparing for her most important client. She could do this, she told herself. Labor was normal. That's what her Lamaze instructor said.

This was Alissa's first child and it could be hours before contractions were ten minutes apart and strong enough to make her groan. At least, that's what it said in the book. Just in case, though, she texted her husband: *I think it's started! See you at home seven-ish.* No need to tell him what "it" was. There was only one long-anticipated "it" in their lives.

She got up from her desk to walk off the sensation, breathing deeply to relax herself. One turn around the office, two, and as the mild pain dissipated she stopped to admire the view from her window, not high enough to see all of New York City, but just the right height to see what was important—the life of the city flowing along the streets like blood through veins. That's how she thought of it. If she wanted to see forever, to remind herself she was a small cog in a very large machine, she could go up to the Observation Deck. She went back to her desk and settled in.

She looked up next when the flashing lights for the deaf accompanied by an annoying, loud blatting began. Of the fifty or so colleagues in the two-hundred-person firm who had come in today, a few ran by her open office door. Tom stopped in the doorway. "Alissa, get out, that's the alarm. We've got to get out of the building. Remember the training? Run first, then hide. You're in no condition to fight. Come on."

A flash of heat ran through her. *Get out*, her brain instructed. Muted, frozen, she slipped off her shoes, remembering her joke to her sister three years before, never thinking it would ever be true. Her mind was in overdrive, issuing instructions too fast for her to evaluate their usefulness, too fast for her to follow any of them. A contraction gripped her, and she gasped. Tom waited one beat, two, and then he fled, leaving her alone.

She took the cell phone off her desk and instinctively opened Twitter. The first five posts on her feed were about a terrorist attack on her building. She put a hand on her belly. She had to protect the baby. In rapid succession she considered crushing into the nearest elevator with everyone else or heading down seventeen flights of stairs at her ponderously slow pace and into the arms of waiting terrorists or hiding under her desk and hoping she wouldn't be found. None of those were good options. There had to be another way.

She texted her sister. *Elena, what's happening?* She waited five seconds for a reply—an eternity—and then realized Elena would be offline, mobilized.

Oh, maybe she'll come for me. Please, Elena, please come for me, she prayed. She couldn't wait for a rescue. She couldn't risk being found by terrorists. Think, Alissa, think, she urged herself. Upstairs, I can go up a flight, find a place to hide. The terrorists would expect her to go downstairs. Everyone was fleeing out of the building. If she went up, maybe she would be undetected. She would find a place to hide. Forgetting her phone on the desk, she walked barefooted through the empty space of the usually bustling office, out into the corridor, and up the stairs.

સ્જ

Commissioner Kwame Mfume of the New York Police Department fielded reports of bomb threats and massacres from all over the city, some true, some spurious. The moment he was sure the One World Trade Center attack was not a hoax or some stupid tourists with a box of firecrackers, he convened the pre-designated executive action team that included high-level representatives from the mayor's and governor's offices, mass transit, the National Guard, Coast Guard, FBI, and the Army's Special Ops for tactical advice. While they were talking—their specialty—he implemented the first phases of the city's established terrorist response plan. As far as he was concerned, these experts were all in the way, but optics, as the mayor was always reminding him, were important. For the after-action report—because there would be one, because his people were going to win—he had to be seen as having gotten the best possible advice.

The hotshots argued, the sound of their heated voices washing over him like waves at high tide. He didn't need more opinions about what to do. He needed more people to do what he told them to do. He ran a hand over his head. He could feel his hair turning white. Just yesterday he allowed himself a moment of joy, watching kids playing in the park across from his Brooklyn townhouse. He had made his city safe. Today, he had failed. If he lived through this day, it would be the worst in his life.

His mind roiled with history, tactics, and politics. It didn't help that he wasn't alone in having to manage a city-wide response to terror. Mumbai, 2008, nearly simultaneous terrorist attacks at hospitals, movie theaters, hotels, and cafes killed over two hundred people. It took three days and an army to quell that assault. Multiple, simultaneous attacks in Paris, 2015, completely undetected by intelligence agencies before the first pop-pop of a gun—a warning to anyone tasked with protecting a city.

Mfume stood up, walked out of the conference room, and paced the length of his operations room, pausing to look over the shoulders of officers tracking activity on their computer screens. On the long wall, monitors showed him what cameras were picking up live all over the city. He didn't know if the trade center building was the only target or if this hostage-taking was the smoke screen meant to pull all units downtown while terrorists attacked the subway system or hospitals.

One thing Mfume was sure of—they weren't taking any prisoners today. The argument about whether police forces should be militarized ended years ago when homegrown and foreign terrorists made it clear that they would use anything they could get their hands on to kill innocent civilians. Any weapon could be bought out of the back of someone's old Chevy van or purchased online and delivered by UPS. For that matter, these criminals were happy just to use their vehicles to murder innocents. The police had to be equally equipped. They would find out today if they were.

No one intended to arrest the terrorists. They had declared their guilt on the world's stage, announcing in a series of tweets that they'd taken the building and were holding hostages at gunpoint. This wasn't Norway. There would be no day in court for these monsters, no cushy private room with access to television and the internet, Mfume promised himself, regardless of what the attorney general was saying on television.

He stopped the many-voiced conference going on in his head, went out into the corridor and called the mayor. "We've got to shut down the subway system," he said without preamble. "That's probably the next target."

The mayor groaned. "What are your experts saying?" she countered.

"I can't wait for them. We'll all be dead of old age before they agree on anything."

The mayor snorted. "Okay. I've got your back. I'll call the governor. He'll send an order to the Metropolitan Transportation Authority."

Over the shortwave came a report of a bomb blast at the Grand Hyatt Hotel, adjacent to Grand Central Terminal, the heart of the city where thousands of tourists flocked to gawk at neon lights and buy knock-off junk from vendors on Forty-Second Street. Mfume felt he was viewing a head-on collision from behind the steering wheel. Time moved in slow motion as his brain caught up to the information coming right at him.

"Fuck them," he said out loud to no one in particular. "They're running the same game plan as Mumbai. Let's go get those fuckers. Show 'em we're as good as the Indians and the French in taking back our city."

"Yes sir," his aide said.

"Any word on the Trade Center?"

"Still running silent, sir."

Mfume looked around the command room. Hundreds of people were scurrying around doing something that seemed important, phones at ears, fingers on keyboards, engaging in quietly urgent communications. Through the bullet-proof glass enclosure around the conference room he saw his high-ranking colleagues arguing the finer points of the posse comitatus law.

At this moment, all of that seemed trivial. He had people scaling a building at one end of town and he had no sense of whether they were still alive. Police officers were trying to control panicked crowds streaming out of the subways all over the five boroughs. And the body count coming from the hotel at mid-town had already reached two hundred in the short time since the blast was reported.

Advantage the bad guys. In addition to the thousand people the terrorists were holding in the tower they now had another few hundred hostages. Fury engulfed him. For the first time in his life, Mfume pictured himself standing behind a blindfolded man and shooting him in the head. He wanted to weep but there was no time for moral dilemmas.

"Get the tunnels and bridges closed to car traffic," he said. "Get the FAA to shut down helicopter traffic into and out of the city, except for us and the military. That means press also. I don't want to see a single goddamn news chopper in the sky.

"Stop all train traffic into or out of the city at its origination point. New Jersey, Connecticut, Westchester, Long Island. I don't care where they're coming from.

Shut down the ferries. Set up roadblocks on all the roads leading out of the city.

"I want credential checks on all pedestrians at bridges. I don't care how goddamn long it takes or how long the lines are. Put enough officers out there to control a mob at every bridge. Arrest anyone who doesn't have a legal U.S. ID. Let's see how these bastards like being trapped like rats."

A chorus of "Yes sir" came from five aides who scurried away to get it done.

☙❧☙

The terrorists chose the Friday of Memorial Day weekend when a third of the city's 36,000 police officers were on leave at the beach or mountains. Elena got the text alert to report in, on duty or not, an hour after the first strike. She drove the one-hundred-fifteen miles back into the city from her father's place in the Catskills at ninety miles an hour. She'd wished she could fly.

It took hours until everyone reported in. Mustered in the early morning, they were greeted by the New York City police commissioner for counterterrorism and intelligence—never a good sign. Within the next few minutes, as his terse voice filled them in, Elena watched his white lips move in a gray face, all hope drained out of him.

"Fifteen men dressed in suits carrying briefcases entered One World Trade Center early yesterday evening, signing in for meetings with various businesses on the first ten floors."

Commissioner Mfume paused, wiped his lips with a handkerchief, and continued. "At the elevators, they turned around and shot the guards at the door and all other visitors and workers who were entering or leaving the building at that moment. Then they shot out the cameras.

"We got lucky," Mfume said. "Before he died, one of the guards triggered a whole-building emergency alert by pushing the button on his console. Thousands managed to flee using the fifty-four elevators that go from the observation deck to ground in sixty seconds."

Elena imagined thousands of people screaming, running from all exits of the building, in spite of gunfire and shouted commands, running down stairwells, packing into elevators that zoomed to the bottom of the building, pouring out onto the plaza, running, pointing, weeping. Chaos. Civilian panic was as useful to the attackers' propaganda as the terror of those left inside.

Mfume went on. "We don't know what they're going to do next. We don't know if One World Trade Center is their only target. We're deploying resources across the city to be ready. But taking this building is their statement action, this is their goal dance, their 'fuck you, USA.' We're going to wipe that smirk off their faces."

"Do we know who they are, sir?" Elena asked.

"They're calling themselves the Sons of Breivik after that Norwegian white supremacist who single-handedly killed seventy-seven people, most of them kids, in 2011." Mfume wiped his lips as if the name had dirtied them.

"But it doesn't matter what they call themselves. Fifteen criminals got by our security systems, killed civilians, took a thousand people hostage, shut down the building floor by floor, and then bragged about it on social media, complete with a video link showing them shooting an unarmed woman. It took them only an hour. It's our job to take that building back from these bastards."

Mfume saluted his officers. The room rustled with the sound of a thousand people returning the salute. Chief Carmen Ruggierio stood before the thirteen-hundred strong counterterrorism force. Dark eyes burned in her fierce face. "The hostages could be your aunt visiting from Georgia, your neighbor, or your stock-broker brother. Chances are, you know someone who's trapped in there. They could be pregnant, old, or disabled. They're in peril and scared. They've been held hostage for twelve hours now. They're exhausted and praying for you to save them. This is your family and they're counting on you. There's no way of knowing how many are really left inside, but we need to proceed as if a thousand terrified people are being held inside the tallest building in New York."

They got their specific assignments. Elena's squad was the sharp end of the stick. Cliché or not, that was the fact. Their job was to find the enemy and drive stakes through their hearts. These attackers weren't people, Elena told herself. They're just the enemy, plural or singular, dehumanized, demonic, unrelenting. Her task was to be relentless in return, to attack first, hard, and never stop until the other guys were dead. She didn't question her training.

After the chief's briefing, Elena walked into a stairwell and called her father. "I'll get her out, Dad," she said, her throat constricted by fury, "I'll get her out alive."

Her father said nothing. Aden Labat wasn't the kind of man who bargained with fate. He knew she would keep her word. Elena imagined her father sitting on his front porch in the white wicker rocker, his hands gripping the arms, staring into the sky, willing God to protect his daughters.

Chapter 4

HANA

Hana shook herself awake. She had walked steadily through two sunrises, but she shouldn't sleep. Ahead of her, a few hundred paces from where she had stopped, a small wooden structure, half aslant, clung to the ground. The door was open a crack, to let in air, she thought, or let out cooking smoke. Unlike her clan's curved, thatched roofs, this building had a flat roof. An open wooden platform with a flimsy railing topped the shelter. A ladder led up to the roof. She walked toward the hut and hoped the rule about welcoming strangers prevailed in this dry country as it did in her lush one.

"Of course, you're welcome," called an old woman emerging from the narrow opening as smoke did from a chimney. Her voice creaked. Stooped over, back parallel to the ground, her black robe swept the earth as she moved. The old woman had to lift her face to speak or she would have been talking to the dirt. She reminded Hana of the turtles who lived along the river. The old woman's scarf, the color of sand, was wrapped twice around her head and covered her nose and mouth. Only her gray-clouded eyes were visible. They didn't seem unkind.

"Come in, come in," the old woman said. "My name is Osnot. I live here alone in this outpost. All my children are gone. I'm glad of company."

Hana entered the structure and waited for her eyes to adjust to the darkness. The smell of burnt herbs filled her nose and an odor below that spoke of age and things long used. Objects took on solidity—a low wooden table, two piles of pillows on the floor, a low bed of pelts from animals Hana didn't recognize, a clay basin of water on a table, a large loom threaded with red, gold, and blue fibers of varying thicknesses. Hana wondered where the goats or sheep whose hair formed the thread in the loom were kept. There were no animals in the hut and none around the shelter. A brief memory of standing up to her knees in a field of blue flowers came to her. Flax. Could that be what the old woman was weaving? But what could grow on that vast moraine that surrounded the hut and where did the old woman get those bright pigments?

"Wash, wash," Osnot gestured to a clay basin and unraveled her head scarf. "You must be covered in sand."

Hana unwrapped the blue scarf from her head and neck. Sand drifted from it onto the woven rug on the floor. Sand sifted through her clothing as she stepped toward the basin. "Oh, I'm sorry," she said, looking down in dismay. She looked for a place to put her scarf and not finding one, wrapped it three times around her waist and tucked the end in to keep it in place. She touched the place where the blue bird's feather was secured by her girdle against her skin to make sure it was still there.

Osnot shook her head. "That is how it goes here," she said, "I have a broom, for all the good that does. The sand and I co-exist. It falls through the rug and I ignore it."

Hana dipped her hands into the cool water twice, rubbed them together and rinsed them again. She leaned over and splashed her face and neck. The water refreshed her, and made her think of home, of standing knee deep in the river in the early morning, the rising sun painting the surface pink and gold, her hands in the water, waiting for fish. She longed for water. She longed to lie down on the pebbled bottom of the river's edge and let the water wash over her. If she lived here, she would dream of water.

Osnot handed her a cloth to dry herself and pointed to pillows. "Sit, sit, have something to eat with me. I rarely have someone to talk to."

"Where does the water come from?" Hana asked. "I didn't see a river or creek as I approached."

"There's an underground spring. It comes down from the snow on the high mountain. My sons tapped it for me. I fetch water from it at night when it's cool."

Sitting where she was told, Hana watched Osnot busy herself at another table and within a short time a shiny green plate holding fruit, olives, and cheese with slabs of flatbread was placed on the floor near her. The old woman sat with a sigh on the pillow opposite Hana. Her face was a mass of wrinkles as thin as fissures in river ice at the beginning of spring. When she sat, the old woman was upright. Nature, it seems, wants Osnot to sit rather than stand at this point in her long life, Hana thought.

She touched the smooth, solid edge of the plate and ran her finger along it. "The plate, I've never seen a material like this. What is it?"

"That is glass," Osnot said. "We melt the sand that is all around us. Our makers shape it into plates, bowls, goblets, beads. Something in the sand turns the glass green in the fire, many different greens. It's beautiful, isn't it?"

Hana nodded, noticing there were bubbles caught inside the plate, as if someone's breath was captured in the glass.

"Now," Osnot said, breaking off a piece of the bread and putting it into her mouth, "tell me where you have come from."

"Why did your children leave you here by yourself?"

"You are a curious girl for someone who has walked a long way without eating or drinking." Osnot took another bite of bread. "This is my place. I'm supposed to be here. They are supposed to be somewhere else." Her eyes closed for a moment, praying, or sleeping.

Hana wondered how old Osnot was. Women who were this wrinkled and stooped in her village would be considered ancient and perhaps holy, particularly if they had visions or told stories about the old times. How could Osnot's children have left her to fend for herself in the middle of nowhere?

"Come now," Osnot said, "I'm waiting for your story. I already know my own. I am bored with it. Begin." She chewed slowly, watching Hana's face.

"Where does your food come from? I feel guilty eating any of it."

"A boy brings it once a week from the city beyond. That is his purpose. It takes him two days to cross the wasteland to me and two days to return to his city. He rests for three days and begins again."

"Why do the city folk send you food?"

She put her gnarled hand over Hana's. "I am a blessing to them, but you should know this. I see your eyes. Like you, I belong to the wise lord."

Hana shrugged off the comment. She didn't know what Osnot meant. Surely, she belonged to her parents and her clan. The wise lord, as far as Hana could tell from her mother's stories, was a god they all vaguely remembered but no longer worshipped. "What is the lookout tower for?"

Osnot laughed, her entire face brightening, her wrinkles smoothing out across her cheeks and catching in folds near her eyes. "To watch for you, of course!" Her laughter ended with a dry cough. "Now, begin. I have waited here in the silence of this desolate land for long enough."

Hana made herself comfortable on the pillow, folded her legs, took a bite of cheese and began her story. "I was born in the small village of Andulat, near the blue river beside the green mountain. My parents call our village paradise. They came to paradise after running from the fire that ravaged the land where they had been living, the fire that followed the shaking of the world, the shaking that broke apart the earth, heaved up stones, and continued for three days." She took a sip of cool water, licked her lips, and resumed.

"Their village was high on the hill to which their ancestors had fled many generations ago after the great flood. Now that home on the hill was destroyed. They fled, although leaving drove a grief through their hearts that lasted for years." Hana turned her face away from Osnot. That was how she felt in her own heart right now.

Osnot rocked, nodded her head, and sighed. "I remember this time. The world shook."

Hana continued. "The sky was full of fire, my mother said, and they had to leave. A wall of fire came toward them burning everything in sight. The ground shifted under their feet as they ran, yawning open into darkness they had to leap over not knowing if the next footfall would meet solid ground or they would fall into the mouth of the earth."

Osnot rocked, her hands folded in her lap. "Yes, yes."

"They ran as far as they could, as fast as they could, the breath in their chests on fire, until they could only see the flames in the distance. Then they walked for sunrise after sunrise until they found the spot where they knew they should stay, where they felt safe."

Hana took several bites of food before she continued. "My grandparents saw paradise from afar, my mother said, standing at the top of a hill in the early morning with the dew still beading the green and yellow grasses and the morning sunlight making small rainbows all across the plain. They wept when they discovered the place, overcome that there was still beauty in the world, that colors so different from the fire's orange and red and the black of the earth's maw still existed.

"Everything we needed was in the paradise they found. They walked to the river and waded in to wash and drink. A fish kissed my grandfather's ankle. They knew they were home. Over time more people arrived and stayed to live with them there. My father is the clan bronze maker. He mines the rocks, heats them, and shapes the molten metal. My mother has always been the clan's story keeper."

Hana took another sip of water. She thought if she lived here, she would have to drink cool water often. The hot air penetrated her skin. *This must be the way a clay pot feels being fired in a pit.*

"Our village is surrounded by a small forest that gives us fruits and nuts and animals we hunt. We use its fallen trees to make shelters. We pull fish from the river. Birds of every description wake us in the morning with their chatter and song. Red and yellow birds call out our names. A bird with blue feathers comes and goes as it pleases, flying into our hut, fluttering around and flying off again."

Osnot laughed and clapped her gnarled hands. "Such a wonderful place."

Hana smiled her agreement. "I was born in the village. When I was little, my mother told me I laughed and danced with our blue bird. Our lives are full of color. My mother put blue feathers into my braided hair. She says I knew the names of colors before I walked but my favorite color has always been blue. My father calls me his blue girl, because of my eyes. He says I am the only person he has ever known with blue eyes. I have been on earth more than twelve harvests and I have known only blessings."

Hana paused to examine a strange looking piece of fruit she had chosen from the glass plate. She put the tip of her tongue on the fruit to test whether it was sweet or bitter in the way her mother had taught her to determine whether something she had picked in the forest was safe to eat or poison. It smelled delicious and the yellow flesh was sweet. She took a bite, closing her eyes to concentrate on the flavor. Color exploded in her mouth, sending ripples of a strange sensation across her tongue. The fruit tasted yellow to her, both sweet like an orange and tart like a lemon. It also had another flavor entirely, one that tickled her throat. She bit into the flesh again and waited to see if she would die.

When she opened her eyes, she was still alive, still in Osnot's hut. This was her life, then. She would not leave the earth today or at least at this moment. Her journey, the one on which her father had warned her she might die, would continue. She looked up to see Osnot watching her. There was a glint in the old woman's eyes she had not noticed before, as if Osnot knew something that Hana did not. But since she knew nothing, that wouldn't be a surprise. Perhaps Osnot knew what would happen next.

"Do you know where I'm going?" Hana asked.

"I have been told you will go to the city on the plain below called Sidon on the sea," Osnot said. "The boy who brings my food will take you there. You have a long, hard walk through the wasteland ahead of you. There will be dangers. You will need to be alert and brave. Now you will sleep. You can start off on your journey in the evening when it's cooler."

Osnot pointed to the bed. Suddenly tired beyond words, Hana walked over to the pile of furs, lay down, and was instantly asleep.

Chapter 5

ELENA

On the security landing, the squad silently high-fived each other, relieved they'd lost no one in the ascent. Elena checked her watch. The climb had taken them an hour. Grim about the lost time, they gathered for any last-minute update on their mission before they split into pairs to reconnoiter and clear the building.

The three restaurants at the top of the Trade Center tower were deserted. Napkins had fallen from laps, water glasses were tipped over, liquid puddled on the floor. The kitchen had an odd sweet and sour reek of lobsters, burned butter, wine, and caramelized pears combined in a new kind of stew. They checked all storage spaces for bodies, bombs, and combatants, and then turned off the gas and water at the main switches.

In every office suite they entered, computer screens were blank, desk drawers open, purses left on chairs, papers scattered on floors near copiers. But no damage had been done. People had either been able to flee in express elevators that dropped to the bottom floor in gravity-suspending time, or they were efficiently rounded up and moved to another floor.

The squad moved like shadows through every floor until the twenty-fifth, eight flights above where tactical told them hostages were being held. Elena listened for the "Clear, clear, clear" over her secure comms as each pair in her squad followed procedure, looking for terrorists, bombs, or stray hostages. Silence meant the squad found nothing. She hoped they missed nothing. The process took two more hours. *Too long*, she thought, now eager to confront the enemy head on.

Eerie quiet prevailed inside the elevator shaft. Elena took several deep breaths of oxygen. The pause gave her time to think, to worry. Every extra second ate away at her. *People could be dying. My sister is here somewhere.* Blood pulsed in her ears reminding her of waves beating on a shore. Her breath was ragged. She was ready to rappel down the elevator shaft in the southeast corner.

Descend first, her partner, John Westmore, signaled. He would belay her.

She slung her rope onto a steel cross beam and attached the rope's end to an anchor using a single-loop figure-8 and a locking carabiner. She slipped the other end through her climbing harness, placed one gloved hand on the rope in front of her and, with her other hand, held the rope behind her body.

Leaping off the platform, she let gravity carry her back to the wall ten feet below as the rope slipped through her hands, her feet and knees ready for the impact and to push off while descending again. She dropped until the number painted in red on the wall read TWENTY-ONE. *So far, so good.* Just below her feet was the top of the elevator door. Inching down the last few feet, Elena balanced herself on a girder on the side of the elevator opening and rigged herself to belay John. She looked up and signaled for her partner to descend.

John pulled the doors apart. They waited a few breaths. Only the HVAC system inhaled and exhaled along with them. Fluorescent lights in the ceiling buzzed. Simultaneously, they unhooked their safety ropes and stepped into the corridor.

Go right, Elena signaled.

They crouched, sidling down the corridor, hugging the wall toward the first door ten feet from them. At any moment they could come face to face with a terrorist, or a bomb. The trickiest part of this mission was to avoid killing a civilian by mistake. Elena held the fear of accidentally shooting an innocent person tight in her chest. Her brain would have to communicate instantly with her hands: *Friendly, don't shoot.* Faster than words, a millisecond-long leap across synapses from one neuron to another, the message would have to communicate with her hand, her trigger finger. On high alert, it was hard to overcome the training to kill.

John opened the first door, a closet, did a quick visual search and closed the door. They moved on to the next door that opened into an office. Elena pushed ajar the glass entryway, both of them ready to shoot anything that moved in the large, loft-like space, but the office was in the same state as those they'd cleared in the floors above this one, with one exception. A middle-aged woman lay in a pool of blood in the kitchen area. A broken porcelain mug lay fractured on the marble floor near her body; spilled coffee mingled with her blood. She had taken a spray of bullets to the chest. This was the woman the terrorists killed in the video they posted.

Elena's heart clutched. *Bastards.* Did the dead woman say something bold that infuriated them or did they just make an example of her, showing the others how easy it was for them to kill a random hostage?

They checked through the entire office and moved on. The story was the same in every office space on the floor. Empty. They went down the stairwell to the next floor, opened the door to the corridor and checked their movement. Elena's pulse thudded in her ears. A man with a black balaclava covering his face and black clothing similar to Elena's was standing in the center of the corridor, not ten feet from her, apparently listening for something.

For a fraction of a second, Elena thought the man was in her squad and then she looked more carefully and saw the bulk of the bomb vest. The man raised his weapon to shoot her. A jolt of adrenalin raced through her. She braced herself against the wall and fired, hitting him just above the nose, square in the middle of his forehead. He dropped to the floor. Her heart pounded in her chest.

At the soft *whift* of her silencer's retort, another man ran around the corner toward them, wildly shooting his M-16 automatic combat rifle. John fired. The man's head jerked back, he sank to his knees and keeled over. Elena and John ran to the men and kicked away their weapons. They each took another kill shot to make sure the bastards were dead.

That is for the lady with the coffee mug.

Elena and John crouched and held their breaths, anticipating the bomb vests might detonate, and exhaled when nothing happened. John searched the terrorist's pockets, found the detonator, and disarmed it by cutting the wire from it to the vest. Elena did the same to her would-be assailant. That would have to do for now. *The bomb squad could make sure these damn things would never go off.* She hoped there was no secondary remote firing mechanism, or a timer embedded in the vest.

"Two out of fifteen," John said. "Not too bad."

Elena couldn't see his smile under his mask, but she knew it was there. "Save the glee," she whispered. "They might've had people inside waiting for them. There could be more than fifteen."

She stood still for a few seconds listening. That's what the now-dead guy had been doing. She could hear whimpers. A door marked "Women" was to her right. *Was a terrorist torturing someone in there?* Elena signaled to John she was going in; he should cover her. She breached the door and swung her gun around. She heard someone gasp. That didn't sound like a terrorist, but she'd have to clear each stall to make sure. She tried not to calculate the odds against her as she pushed open each stall door. Any assailant inside would have a clear, first shot at her. She held her breath. She threw open the last door, saw a body hunched over on the toilet, feet drawn up. On automatic, adrenalin coursing through her, she aimed.

"Please," the woman said. She kept her head down and put her hand out, palm flat, as if that could stop a bullet. "Please. I'm in labor. I'm having my baby. Please."

Elena stopped. Her eyes unglazed. Her sister, Alissa, was doubled over in labor.

Chapter 6

HANA

Osnot cleared the table and put the remaining food into a small drawstring sack. She poured water from the pitcher into a skin container, wrapped the top with cord to seal it, and tied the water skin to the sack of food.

Looking over her shoulder at the girl sleeping peacefully on a bed of lion skins, Osnot thought of all the futures the girl could have, might have, and shook her head. The perfect symmetry of the child's face—long, black lashes curling against cheeks the color of new-found gold—was as much a danger to her as a blessing. There was no way of knowing what would befall the child.

Somehow, she must try to protect her from that unknown future. She was no magician, no god, not even a priestess. Still, she was human and that was something. She could do the one piece of magic she had learned from the wise lord's priest—she could write words that might keep Hana safe. Words, those crooked, round, and straight marks inscribed on a surface, had power. If she wrote the right ones, she might invoke the voice of god.

From a wooden box on the table Osnot withdrew a thin piece of papyrus, the priest's gift to her before he was killed, and she was exiled for clinging to a god who had been replaced. She crushed four black berries in a small clay bowl, dipped the nib of a feather in the dark blue juice and wrote the marks on the papyrus that spelled out, "Give her safe passage." She took a small stone on which cross-hatched marks and the symbol for life were etched, dipped the stone in ink, and pressed the seal onto the paper. Osnot blew on the page until the ink was dry, then rolled it up and tied it into the end of Hana's scarf. If fate intended, the girl would find the passport when she needed it. This was the best she could do.

☾☽

Hana woke to find an impatient boy standing over her. His dark brows met in thunderclouds over his long nose. Lightning leaped from his black eyes. "Get up, get up," he demanded. "The sun has gone down behind the mountain. It's time to leave."

Hana swung her feet to the floor and leaned over to tie on her sandals. "Where did you come from?"

She looked around the room for Osnot. The old woman was nowhere to be seen. In front of her, the boy shook his head of dark, curly hair, stamped his foot, and glowered at her. Hana had time to admire the bronze color of his skin before he broke through her observations.

"I came from where I always come from, and now it's time to go back. The old woman has her food and now I must also get you safely to Sidon." His face twisted into another scowl. "We don't have time for your questions."

Hana began to wind her scarf around her head, covering her long, dark curls while the boy stared at her. "Who are you and why are you in such a hurry?" Hana asked. "It's the same two cycles of the sun, if Osnot is correct, whether we leave now or ten heartbeats from now."

Her impatience with rudeness rose to meet the boy's. She stopped herself short of stamping her foot in imitation of him. Her mother had warned her that different people would have different customs. She was the one who must adapt.

"I am Danel, son of Batnoam of Sidon." He waved his hand in a circle between his chest and face. "And we are in a hurry because," Danel leaned down toward her as if she were a little child who must be sternly chastised, "we must get to the caves in the Aliat plain before the sun reaches the middle of the sky or we will be burned to a crisp. It is too hot there even for lizards." He backed away from her and turned toward the door. "If you need to empty your bodily waste, there's a place for that purpose a short distance away. I'll wait for you in front of Osnot's hut."

Blood rose in her face to the roots of her hair. Danel was as crude as he was rude. She checked to make sure her scarf was securely tied, her dagger was still in the pouch, and that the feather she carried was safe against her skin. She was to present the blue feather as proof she came from Andulat, the elder had said. She must not lose it.

"The entire world," Hana recalled her mother saying, "knows that the beautiful blue bird comes from Andulat. The feather will establish your identity." It had never occurred to Hana before to wonder how her mother knew what the entire world knew. She brushed past Danel at the doorway and walked to the latrine. He was right. She should make use of it now. The indignity would be much greater when they were walking through the wasteland with nowhere to shield her from his eyes.

When Hana returned to the front of the hut, Osnot was there with a bundle of food and a water pouch. "Water for you and Danel." Osnot handed the bundles to her. "Drink sparingly but frequently and you will have enough for your journey."

Hana draped the tied bundles around her neck and thanked the old woman. "I will stop to see you on my way back."

Osnot turned her head sideways and looked up at Hana from her perpetual bow. "You will not be coming back this way. And, at any rate, I will no longer be here. I have completed my last task. Go with the gods."

Hana felt a small tremor. Her face chilled. A sob caught in her throat. If she didn't return this way, how would she see her parents again? The village elder had told her she wouldn't be coming home but she hadn't believed it. Now Osnot also said she would never see her family again. She looked at Danel. He seemed unconcerned. Her return was apparently not his task.

"The gods be with you, old mother," Danel called to Osnot as he walked away from the hut.

Hana hurried to follow him, turning back once to wave to Osnot. She was startled by what she saw. The old woman stood with her hand in the air above her head. In her black robes, with her hand raised and her body stooped, the shape of Osnot's body looked to Hana like the symbol for life, the *C'hai* that her mother had drawn on the ground before she left her village.

"Watch for this symbol, Hana," her mother said. "It signifies those you can trust. They will help you if they can."

Hana wondered if Osnot was Danel's grandmother. There had been no demonstration of affection between them but who else would care for an old woman abandoned in a desolate place but a grandson. She didn't have time to ask questions, though. Danel was moving swiftly away.

After they'd clambered over sand-colored rocks jutting up through the ground and were briefly on a flat path, Hana looked back, hoping to catch another glimpse of the old woman. She could see neither Osnot nor the hut. Both the woman and the structure had disappeared in a whirl of sand. She turned back to concentrate on walking. As far as she could see ahead of her, the world was strewn with rocks of all sizes turned at all angles. In the quickening dark, she had to watch her feet.

ↂↄ

"Come on, girl," Danel growled at her. "It's not long now until we reach the caves. Take a sip of the water and let's go. You can rest there."

The straps of Hana's sandals had broken, snapped apart the fourth time she twisted her ankles stepping between stones. They had traveled only a short distance, but it seemed to Hana they had been walking through two cycles of the sun. Clouds obscured the moon and it was so dark, she couldn't see her feet. Finally, she had tied the sandals onto her feet with the rope Osnot used to attach the water pouch to the food bag. Since then, she had carried the water pouch in one hand and the food bag in the other. Her hands were tired. She thought she might never be able to unclench her fingers. Her wrists were tired. Her feet hurt. Her ankles were sore from all the times her feet twisted the wrong way stepping among the rocks.

This journey was a huge mistake. The wise lord must have thrown the rocks down in this part of the world to keep people from crossing it. Surely there was another way to go from her village to her destination. Why did the elders choose the hardest way? From time to time, a tear streaked down her dusty cheeks. She dared not waste the water to wash her face. She tipped the water pouch up to her lips and took two sips. The water was still cool. She should count her blessings, as her mother would have told her.

She handed the water pouch to Danel. "How much farther to Sidon?"

The boy took a long swig of water, wiped his mouth with the back of his hand, and retied the top of the water pouch. "I can carry this in my sash."

Hana was grateful. She nodded and flexed her fingers in relief. It hadn't occurred to her that she could carry the bag of food in her own tunic secured by the straps of her girdle. She rearranged her clothing to accommodate the bag of food.

"Hah!" the boy exclaimed. "Now you look like my mother when she is large with child."

Hana frowned at him and wondered how old he was. He seemed too immature to have been given a dangerous task. On the other hand, on the path they had been following, she had not seen any animals that might have harmed them and there were certainly no people. He didn't carry a weapon, although rocks were plentiful and a well-aimed one could kill a poisonous snake. The enemies here were the sun, the wind, and the rocks. Maybe the trip was simply arduous and boring, something any able boy could accomplish. Danel was only her guide, not her protector. Remembering the dagger, Hana realized she would need to protect herself.

"How far?" she asked again.

"We'll sleep in the cave during the day. It will be dusk when we wake. After we eat, we will continue our journey, walking through the night to arrive at an escarpment above the plain just before dawn. The steep drop after the caves takes us to the plain below. This is the fastest way and the light is necessary to get down the mountain without falling to our deaths. The descent will be short, but it will seem long to you, since you've never done it before and you're a girl with little strength."

Hana huffed at his comment about her strength but didn't interrupt him. His description of what would happen next made her mute with fear and then angry. How did he know she wasn't strong? She might be. She would prove to him that she was.

Danel seemed to understand her fear without her saying anything. "There's a rope for you to hang on to. We'll climb down with our faces to the mountain wall. You'll be fine if you don't look down. Then we'll walk through the plain. You'll like the plain. The grass is high and sweet, the ground is level. Many birds of all colors fly above it. They make a fine clatter, better than all the silence of the wasteland. It's a short walk from there to the city. We'll arrive in Sidon in the early morning, before the guards at the gates fully recover from their night of drinking. It will be easier to enter the city without being detected then."

Hana leaned down again to secure her sandals. "Why did the elders select this difficult route to Sidon? Wasn't there another way to go?"

"This is the safest route, the one where there is the least likelihood of other people on the path." When Hana looked at him perplexed, Danel said, "No stranger is to see you. Do you understand?"

She shook her head and sighed. "Aren't you a stranger?"

"You silly girl. Don't you know anything? I'm from your tribe, even if you look different from me with your blue eyes and golden skin."

His answer was more proof that the elders did not tell her everything she needed to know about her journey. Everyone knew more than she. Ignorance, Hana feared, might be more dangerous than rugged terrain, sheer cliffs, and strangers.

"Where is Sidon?" Perhaps she wouldn't be so silly if people told her what she needed to know.

"It's by the sea where the sun goes down, to the west of here. Sidon is much larger than that small village tucked between the mountains you call home."

How could he know how big her home village was? She had never seen him there.

When they reached the cave, Danel built a small fire in a pit that had been dug some time ago for that purpose. "To keep animals away," he said. Hana wondered if he was afraid of something more fearsome than animals.

Strewn around the cave were a stone spear tip, a few cutting stones, and a small clay bowl. Others had been here before. Danel said nothing about the objects. Perhaps many people passed this way during hunting seasons, Hana reasoned. Her mother had told her that many clans migrated from place to place in search of more food or safety, although what anyone would hunt in the wasteland was a mystery. Maybe Danel's fire let others know someone was sleeping here in this cave and they should move on. She curled up on the ground near the fire, cushioned her head with her scarf, and slept, too tired to wonder if the people who had left their tools behind would come back.

Chapter 7

Elena removed her mask. "Can you wait until we get you to a hospital?" she asked her sister.

"Thank God it's you." Alissa moaned. "But not likely. I'm in transition."

Into her comms device Elena said, "This might take a while."

"I'll wait," John said.

Elena kneeled on the floor and lifted her sister's skirt. Maybe the birth wouldn't take long. She pulled off her gloves, leaned forward, and forgot everything else. Alissa groaned through gritted teeth, her brow furrowed, her eyes squeezed closed. Elena placed Alissa's bare feet against her shoulders for balance. Alissa's hands gripped the handicap railing around the toilet. Elena put her hands under the baby's head and shoulders. "Push," she said and waited, breath held.

The infant was covered in iridescent mucus. She fit in Elena's two hands. Her own tiny hands were closed in fists. She took a breath and before she squalled, she opened her deep blue eyes and stared for a few seconds at Elena without blinking.

Oh my God, oh my God. This. Elena felt her soul make a quarter turn in her body and look back at her. *Is this what I'm meant to be doing?* She looked up at Alissa, who had ignored her own terror and pain as she pushed the baby out. She was weeping silently, a smile of joy so bright on her face that it was hard to look at her.

This birth, this baby, that this could even happen, did happen while death and fear were all around them, the building stinking of the threat of it, there was something here Elena was supposed to notice. *A baby. Is that all it took?* Was the act of birth the singular miracle it was chalked up to be? All her hard-won crustiness fell away. Cynicism was no defense against a newborn child. A chasm of yearning opened in Elena. She only had a few seconds for this kind of thinking. She wondered if there was a bumper sticker with the words *"I'd rather be a Mommy."* And then she was back to her hardcore self.

"Lis," she said in a tense whisper, "we've got to get you out of here and I've still got twenty floors to clear. Can you stay here with the baby while we do that?"

Alissa nodded. She removed her blouse, reached for her child, wrapped the baby in her blouse, and held the infant against her breast.

It looked to Elena like her sister and the baby needed some time together anyway. They had a lot to figure out. Maybe this wasn't the best day to come into the world, certainly not the best place, but now that she'd assisted at this birth, Elena could only think of it as a miracle. The baby's arrival somehow made her hopeful that they would win today. The birth made her understand what she was willing to kill for. *Propitious*, that was the word she was looking for.

While the baby figured out how to suckle, Elena tied the umbilical cord with a narrow piece of cloth she tore from her sister's skirt and cut the cord. She couldn't wait for the delivery of the afterbirth and hoped Alissa would be okay until she got her to a hospital. At least her emergency training for baby delivery hadn't been wasted. A thought hit her as she looked at mother and child. She needed a coat or blanket to cover them. Alissa's skirt was a mess and she was now topless. Elena's usually carefully dressed sister didn't seem to notice her disarray.

"Hannah," Alissa said.

Elena looked at her. "What?"

"I'm going to call her Hannah, after Mom."

Elena nodded. *Of course.* She stood, leaned over her sister, and kissed her forehead. "I'm going to find you a coat, or something to wrap around you. I'll be back soon, and then I'll be gone for a while. I don't know how long. Stay here."

Alissa nodded, completely absorbed in counting her infant's fingers and toes.

Elena pulled her mask down over her face and exited the bathroom. John stood sentry in the corridor. She touched his shoulder. "A girl," she whispered. He nodded and gave her a high five. It was a good thing he couldn't see her face. He would think she was unfit for duty.

"Five more seconds," Elena signaled as she ran into the nearest office. She found two fleece blankets and a rolled-up rubber mat in what appeared to be a yoga room, wondered what kind of business provided places to stretch and relax during the day, and brought them back to Alissa. She spread the mat on the floor and her sister curled up on it with the baby snuggled against her. Elena tucked the blankets around them. Alissa had been in labor on her own for more than twelve hours. She'd be exhausted. Elena gave them one last longing look and left. Mother and baby were busy with each other and didn't notice her departure.

She and John cleared the rest of their section of the floor and went down the stairwell to the next level. On the nineteenth floor, as they expected, they found more terrorists. John snapped the neck of the first man in a bomb vest they came to at the stairwell door. Elena got the next one with a shot to the back of the head from ten feet away, her silencer emitting a brief *whift*. Over their communication devices they heard teammates encountering combatants elsewhere on the floor.

They disabled bomb vests and moved on until they came around a corner and walked into a large open area with two-hundred hostages lying on the floor with their hands over their heads. Men in balaclavas and vests got off two shots, killing the women closest to them before John shot the hostage-takers square in the head from twenty feet away. He held up four fingers. Under her mask, Elena smiled grimly, and scanned the space for more monsters.

People dragged themselves to their feet weeping, hugging each other, reaching for cell phones. Elena held up her hand. They turned to her, some holding their hands over their mouths, mid-sob.

"No calls, no postings, please," she told the civilians in a stern whisper. "The terrorists are holding more people on floors below this one. We need to free them also."

A woman, huddled behind a burly co-worker, whimpered. "Be calm," Elena said. "We're working to get you to safety." She didn't want to promise what she wasn't sure she could deliver. "We need your cooperation."

She heard a scuffle down the corridor beyond the reception area. The hostages dropped to the floor. John and Elena braced themselves and aimed their guns in the direction of the sound. Gun shots rang out. Two members of her team strode into the area. All eyes on them, the

police commandos gave two thumbs up. "Seven of fifteen," John said.

*Why did the terrorists let the hostages keep their
phones?* Elena realized with a jolt that they intended their
victims to hop on social media and spread the word about
their exploits in a viral contagion that infected everyone—a pandemic of fear. They weren't dummies, whoever they were. *There had to be more terrorists in this
building.* There was no way to corral all these hostages
with only two attackers on each floor, no matter how bru-
tal they were.

She was sure the terrorists had people on the inside,
people who already worked for these businesses in some
capacity. Maybe they were accountants or lawyers or
business owners. Maybe they were American citizens.
Elena thought of how those people must have felt, coming to work every day simmering with hatred, thinking
about how they were going to kill their colleagues. It
gave her the creeps. She shook off the thought. *Stay focused.*

Elena gathered the civilians in two lines in the stairwell closest to the room they'd been held in. Her plan
was to use the concrete and steel stairwells specifically
designed to resist fire and bomb blasts to safely stash civilians while they waited for the all-clear. It was a risk.
The stairwells might be rigged with explosives, but their
quick assessment showed no bombs in plain sight attached to either steps or girders.

Elena looked over at John and he nodded. Using a
kind of divining rod technique to figure out who the natural leaders were who would calm others, know how to
hold a position, and be able to muster the group when it
was time to go, she pointed to a man and a woman and
said, "You, and you." She signaled for them to stand near
her. "You are the team captains." This was an iffy propo-

sition, but they couldn't leave any of their team members to babysit the hostages.

John pulled an extra communication device from his pack, quickly teaching them how to use it and to stay alert. "Stay off comms," John said. "You'll hear us tell you when you're good to go."

"You got it," the woman said. The man nodded. He turned and faced his colleagues, signaled with his hands for everyone to sit, and they did. Elena counted this as this day's second hopeful event.

According to intel, four more floors of terrified hostages and nine more floors with terrorists strapped into bomb vests were yet to be cleared. More lunatics with guns pointed at innocents. Fury flashed through Elena. The image of Alissa's baby fixing her with those huge blue eyes floated up. They couldn't get this done quickly enough.

With the hours the terrorists had before the squad infiltrated the building, every floor might be rigged to explode, detonated by someone who wasn't even there, by someone who would rejoice when the bomb went off. Another image of Alissa on the bathroom floor with the baby rose in Elena's mind.

She needed to get back to her sister. She needed to get her out of there. Feeling like a kindergarten teacher, she instructed the civilians again to wait for an all-clear signal before they went down the stairs.

"Move out," Elena signaled.

All eight members of the squad ran down another floor using the four separate stairwells in the corners of the building. It was too soon to congratulate themselves. They would wait until the day was over and then tote up the score.

ം‍ടി‍ം

Two more hours passed before Elena's squad cleared the skyscraper. Way too long, in Elena's estimation. Twenty terrorists and one-hundred civilians were dead. You couldn't call that a victory, but she decided it would have to do. They had the building back.

Half a floor had been decimated by the blast from a bomb vest an assailant managed to set off before they got to him. Police had no idea how many of the terrorists had pulled off their black garb and blended with hostages as they fled the building. SWAT entered the building with enough personnel to sweep through the cracks and crevices the squad hadn't covered. Shouts echoed in corridors all over the building.

The enemy's whole operation didn't make sense to Elena. They had enough people with bombs deployed throughout the building to send all the hostages they had gathered to their deaths. *Why hadn't they?*

As quickly as possible after they were sure they had secured the building, bomb squad teams, dogs, and robots swarmed through every floor, sniffing out bomb components, defusing bomb vests, searching ceilings, closets, stairwells, and floors for bombs set to detonate by timer or at will by someone with a cell phone and the right code. The idea that when employees returned an undiscovered bomb might explode terrified everyone.

All together including emergency medical technicians, five hundred city personnel were deployed to the site. In the large scheme of things, that seemed efficient, but something about the deployment of so many resources to one location worried Elena.

Elena called in to headquarters to report. Chief Ruggiero told her about attacks all over the city. "It's like Mumbai," she said, and Elena recalled it took four days and an army to quell the terrorist assault on that Indian city. Elena didn't want to know anymore.

The governor had issued a system-wide shut down of mass transit. Tunnels and bridges were closed to vehicular traffic. All air traffic except official police helicopters had been stopped. She didn't want to think about poisonous gas, anthrax, or some other biological threat.

Ruggiero told her a bomb blast at the Grand Hyatt Hotel adjacent to Grand Central Terminal pushed the civilian body count up two hundred more. Elena's heart contracted. She put her hand on her stomach to quell queasiness. She swallowed and asked the chief, "Where do you want us?"

"You'll be assigned to clear a specific section of the subway system. Hold your position for details. I'll get back to you."

Civilians evacuated the skyscraper in as orderly a fashion as could be expected. They helped each other, people teaming up to support someone who clearly couldn't make twenty yards on his own. Out in the plaza, many broke down, sitting on the pavement weeping, or walking dazed away from the building. Some ran, their arms waving, their mouths open as if to scream but no sound emerged.

They had survived. It amazed them. Freed, terror took hold of their bones and made some too weak to walk. Police on the ground worked to keep everyone moving away from the building, just in case it blew. A blink away was the memory of the twin towers collapsing. Emergency medical staff loaded people about to stroke, too shocked to walk, or ambushed by hysterical tears into ambulances and drove off, sirens blaring.

Elena issued orders to the squad about their next target as soon as she got them. She sent them on and said she'd catch up. She put Sergeant Mary Cantor in charge. Cantor smiled grimly at the honor and the team took off.

Amid all the mop-up turmoil, Elena kept one objective in mind—to get her sister to the hospital. As soon as her squad left, she nabbed two emergency medical techs on their way in and rode the elevator back up to retrieve her sister, her heart in her mouth. If anything had happened to her sister...

But Alissa was fine, asleep in the same position Elena had left her in, on the floor of the women's room, cradling her baby close to her body. Elena needed to make sure she stayed fine.

"Alissa, honey, wake up now. We've got to move you. Do you think you can walk?"

Alissa opened her eyes, checked first that her child was breathing, and said, "Yes, I think so. I hope so."

Elena helped her sit up, took the baby from her, and with her other arm, supported her sister as she stood. The EMT made a quick assessment: Alissa was shaky but stable. Elena wrapped a blanket around her sister, folding the baby into it.

Gripping the blanket in one hand, her child clasped in the crook of her other arm, Alissa took a few trial steps. "I can do it." Alissa was using her determined voice, Elena noticed, the steely sound that emerged when she was attempting to do something that was hard for her. *Well, she'll need that determination. The day isn't over.*

"Let's use the carry chair, anyway," Elena insisted. The EMTs loaded Alissa and the baby in the chair and picked it up as if they weighed nothing. "We're going down in the elevator. We'll take a police cruiser to the hospital and let these good folks get back to taking care of other people. You should be okay from there. I'll call Dad to come and be with you."

Alissa nodded, leaning her head down to kiss her child on the forehead. They moved slowly across the corridor and went down in the elevator. In the chaos of the lobby on the first floor, Elena spotted John waiting for her.

He ran over. "I've got a vehicle." He looked over at Alissa and the baby, and then at Elena. "I'll drive," he said in a way that cut off all discussion on the subject. He lifted Alissa and the baby out of the chair and trotted to the vehicle he'd commandeered.

Elena was relieved. It would be a break for her. "The nearest," she yelled, running after him.

"Yeah, got it."

John buckled Alissa and the baby into the back seat. Elena climbed in next to her sister and put her arm around her. She couldn't take her eyes off the baby. She didn't ask where John had acquired the four-wheel drive vehicle. If it was near the building, it must have been cleared by security when its owner arrived. It gave her a moment's shaky pause that maybe its owner had been killed, but, frankly, right now she didn't care.

She didn't care if John drove on sidewalks or through the middle of a park. Her only concern was getting her sister to a doctor and a clean bed. *God knows what kind of bacteria was on the floor of that bathroom.* She closed her eyes, blocked out everything else, and listened to the sound of the baby breathing. Other than the ocean, that sound might be the most wonderful she'd ever heard.

Seemingly within minutes, John screeched the vehicle to a stop and ran around to open the back door. Elena jumped out to help her sister inside the hospital. She talked her way through reception, explaining that she'd delivered the baby under the greatest duress. Elena saw the nursing staff take note of her combat police uniform, the badge on her shoulder. She pressed her advantage. "My sister's been in the terrorist attack on One World

Trade Center. She gave birth in a public bathroom in the middle of it."

An aide rolled a wheelchair toward Alissa. "Here, Mama," the woman said, "looks like you need a seat."

Alissa sat down in it, wincing.

The aide patted Alissa's arm and cooed to the baby.

After what seemed to be a century, a doctor examined Alissa. She was sutured, bathed, given a clean hospital gown, and hooked to an IV of antibiotics. The baby was cleaned, seen by a pediatrician, tested, diapered, swaddled, and returned to her mother's arms wearing a small white cap on her head.

It was the cap that got to Elena, that small comforting touch. She waited for Alissa to be taken to a room, even though she knew her absence from her squad was tantamount to desertion. Frankly, she didn't care if the chief fired her. It was a crazy day. All the rules had been thrown up in the air like a pack of cards. She would follow the ones that landed on her forehead, but she had to know her sister and niece were okay before she moved on.

She had embroiled John in this missing-in-action jaunt also, although he seemed to come willingly. She looked over at him, standing at ease, but with his weapons handy, at the entrance to the emergency room. He was a good partner, she thought, a man of few words and the right actions. She had always trusted his competence under fire and enjoyed his company when they weren't, but it took this personal act of support for her to realize that she loved him, not in that breathless can't-keep-their-hands-off-each-other way they'd experienced when they were both grunts in a strange land together, but in some quiet, sure way as steady as the pulse of her blood. *If only there were more words to capture the nuances of love.*

"Mother and baby are fine," a nurse said, interrupting Elena's thoughts. "We're moving them up to the tenth floor. The baby will room in with her mother. Is there a partner we should notify?"

"Oh, God, I completely forgot about Carl," Elena said. "Yes. Carl Daniels. I didn't even call him." She thumbed through the contacts on her cell phone and found Carl's number. She read out the number to the nurse but while she was at it, she asked to use the landline at the nurse's station.

When Carl answered, she said, "You're a Daddy." She heard the sharp intake of his breath.

"Where, where are you?" Carl's voice was ground glass. His wife had been missing for nearly twenty-four hours.

"New York University hospital, the building off First Avenue near the East River. She'll be on the tenth floor. I've got to move on."

"How is she?"

Elena heard the worry in his voice. "They're fine. Alissa's calling the baby Hannah."

Carl exhaled into a sob. "I'm on my way." He clicked off the call.

Elena's next call was to her father. She left off the usual preamble. "She's okay, Dad. You're a grandpa. We're at NYU hospital downtown. You should come here. Alissa and Hannah might need you."

Aden Labat didn't need any more information than that. His daughters were his whole life. A granddaughter named after his wife was more joy than he deserved. "Leaving now. Might take me a couple of hours, though. Tell her I'm coming."

Elena told John she was going to make sure her sister and niece were okay. He saluted—a joke between them that made her smile. She rode the elevator up to the tenth floor, found the correct wing, walked into the room, looked at her sister's beautiful face, and smiled. "Hard to believe this happened today."

Alissa reached her hand out for Elena. She hadn't mentioned having pain, but she wouldn't. She was as strong in her own way as Elena was. The loss of their mother when they were young had made them strong together.

Elena held her sister's hand for a few seconds, told her that Carl and their father would be coming, stroked Hannah's cheek with her finger, and wrenched herself away. She waved from the door and started to walk out of the room.

Alissa called out to her, "Get them, Elena. Get every single one of them," in that shaking, determined voice Elena knew so well.

Elena nodded, her heart quaking. She blew her sister a kiss and left the room.

Chapter 8

HANA

Hana squatted outside the cave, ten paces from the entrance, her skirts gathered around her knees, and hoped Danel wouldn't come out until she was done. She had awakened before dusk specifically for this purpose. She wished for privacy, but her body insisted on having its way and she was afraid to wander far from the cave. In the dying light she could see a thin, shimmering golden line on the horizon as the sun went down. That was the direction of Sidon.

Danel's plan was to reach Sidon in early morning. That meant they would be walking all night. She thought of the descent from the mountain Danel described to her and her stomach clenched. They had eaten most of the food Osnot packed for them. Some water was left. She should have felt relieved that she could see her destination in the distance, but she didn't. She shut her eyes.

"When you're afraid, my sweet one," her mother had said, "close your eyes and we will be right by your side. We are always there with you, no matter what strange places you travel to, no matter how different the people seem. We will always love you."

Somehow, these comforting words did not work to ease her worry. When Hana opened her eyes and looked around, there was only Danel with his threatening eyebrows glowering at her.

"Are you done yet?" he shouted at her from the cave opening, turning his back to her.

She blushed, shook out her tunic, and walked over to him. "You don't need to be mean."

Danel laughed. "This is me being kind. Osnot warned me about you but I don't see what's so special. So your eyes are the color of water. What does that signify? All this fuss for a girl. There are more girls than boys in Sidon. I can have my pick any day. Your breasts are hardly bigger than sour apples." He swaggered away, gathered the food bag and water pouch, and started off, leaving Hana speechless, standing in the shadow of the cave.

They walked through the night, the sky above them a path of stars, and arrived at the escarpment as the sun sent its first rays over the edge of the earth. In the gray light, Danel showed her how to sit on the edge of the land—a red lip jutting out high above the grassy plain below. He instructed her to turn, grip the rope, and find her footing on rocks that stuck out sideways from the earth.

"Take off your sandals. They won't help you here. Always find your footing first," he said. "Then lower your hands one by one and search with your foot for the next flat rock that sticks out from the wall." He demonstrated the technique and then pulled himself back up over the ledge.

Hana looked down to the plain below them. The mountain face was the height of ten cities stacked one on top of another. *How did the earth thrust itself up into the air this way?* Her heart squeezed itself into a tight ball.

Her breath came quickly. No one had told her she had to be strong and agile to undertake this mission. What else hadn't they told her? As she removed her sandals, she looked to see where Danel had attached the rope that would help her make the descent. It was tied around a huge boulder and secured with a knot. Somehow, the size of the boulder didn't make her feel safe. The rope could slip. But there was no going back. Her only choice was to go down the mountain. *No point in weeping,* she told herself, although unshed tears flooded her eyes and made them sting.

She looked over at Danel, her heart in a knot. "I understand."

Danel tied a rope around her waist, wrapped it again under her arms, and wound the other end of it around his own body, tying another knot. He glanced at her and shrugged. "Just in case you lose your footing or let go of the rope." He stood a few feet back from the edge in a wide stance and gripped the rope he had wrapped around her with both hands. A pool of rope puddled on the ground in front of him.

He called out to her to start. "Go on. You can do it."

Hana took several deep breaths, imagined her mother at her side, sat down on the edge of the earth, took hold of the rope, and, with a sharp thrust, turned her body toward the rock wall. It took all her courage to get that far. For many heartbeats her feet flailed, not finding anything but air beneath them, and then her toes touched rock and her feet gained purchase. She stood there clinging to the rope for what seemed like an entire cycle of the sun. Sucking in courage from the air around her, she lowered her hands to get another grip and inched her feet lower along the mountain face.

"That's the way!" Danel called out. "Keep going."

Sweat rolled down her forehead stinging her eyes. She closed them. She didn't need to see what she was doing. It was all done by feeling the strands of the rope beneath her palms, the rocks under her toes. Within a few handholds, her palms burned from the rope's twisted fibers. She moved down the mountain, pausing for deep breaths to quell her panic that at any moment her hands would slip, her feet would slip, and she would go tumbling through the air until she crashed on the ground below. Her hands, already tired from gripping the food and water bags during the previous day, felt weak and incapable of holding on. She gripped the rope tighter and crept down the wall.

"You are there!" Danel shouted down to her. "You can open your eyes. You made it. You're a brave girl."

She stood clinging to the rope, her feet on the ground but her body still feeling the precariousness of only air beneath her. Danel descended so quickly he seemed to slide down, jumping free above her to land on his feet on the ground beside her. One by one, he peeled her fingers from the rope and untied the knot at her waist. She felt his warm breath on her cheek. She opened her eyes and looked at him. He smiled.

For a blink, Hana had the urge to slap him for putting her through this ordeal, and then she was suddenly elated at having survived it. Blood beat hard in her temples and her breath came fast. She looked around at the wide grassy plain ahead of her. Birds, she heard birds. Grasses swished together. She looked up at the mountain face she had descended, higher than she had a number for. Instead of slapping him, she threw her arms around Danel's neck and kissed his cheek. When her lips met his skin, a strange sensation in her stomach made her heart stutter for a few breaths.

"Thank you, oh, thank you for getting me safely here." Her voice was husky with a combination of unshed tears and glee.

Danel shook off her hug. "Don't thank me yet. We've got the entire plain to cross and the city wall to conquer. Thank me when we're inside the city." He shook his shoulders again as if to banish the feel of her arms, rolled up the rope that had connected them, slung it over his shoulder, and stalked off in the direction of Sidon.

She walked a few feet behind him for a while without saying anything. When she couldn't stand her own curiosity another second, she blurted out, "How old are you, Danel?"

"I've been on the earth for fourteen reapings," he said, "and keep your voice down so they don't hear you."

"So who doesn't hear me? There's no one around for as far as I can see."

"Ghosts live in the plains around the city, those who had a horrid disease and were taken outside the walls to die so that breath from their bodies wouldn't infect others. They live beneath the ground and sometimes come out at night if they're bothered by someone, particularly girls who talk too much. Watch out for their bones. Don't step on them."

"Oh, that's ridiculous," Hana said. "The spirits of the dead have been gathered into the universe. Everyone knows that." Briefly, she felt the breath of the dead whisper around her ears and neck. She shivered. *What if Danel was right?*

Looking back at her over his shoulder, Danel whispered, "Explain, then, how people traveling alone to Sidon die outside its gates with no wounds on their bodies."

"Perhaps their hearts gave out from grief."

Hana's voice was so quiet that Danel stopped walking, turned and looked at her. "Oh." He lowered his gaze.
"I'm sorry. Walk closer but be quiet. Voices carry a far
distance here and we don't want to alert the guards or
anyone else who might be lurking in the tall grass. It will
be hard enough to get you into the city."

She scurried to keep up with him. "Why is that?"

"You must be a citizen with a mark on your arm to
come into Sidon and walk around freely." He held out his
arm and showed her two lines crossed by another etched
in blue on the inside of his right arm. "Strangers are sent
first to a place you won't like, a dank hole where rough
men inspect you for disease and concealed weapons in
case you mean to harm the king."

Hana thought of the dagger concealed in the pouch
in her girdle. No one must find it. Although she couldn't
imagine ever using it, it was a gift from her father she
didn't want to surrender to a stranger. She sighed. No
matter how close they were to their destination she was
still in danger.

"Not that you have a disease or a weapon, but Osnot
said to get you inside the city without anyone seeing you,
and that's what I intend to do. Once we're inside, I'll take
you to my father Batnoam's house where Ashirat, his
second wife, lives. Then you'll be their problem."

Hana changed the subject. "Is Osnot your grandmother?"

"She is my mother's grandmother," Danel said. "She
has been on the earth forever. When she dies, my mother
says that one of truth's handmaidens will return to sit by
the side of the wise lord."

Hana nodded and smiled. She could imagine Osnot
would be happy to tell the wise lord what she thought
about everything she had seen on earth.

They walked along companionably through the high grass, the soft ground easier on their feet and knees than the terrain they traversed before.

Hana, grateful for the sweet smell, trailed her hands over the fronds and watched white butterflies fly up as they walked.

Overhead, flocks of birds swarmed in all directions, chittering and screeching as if the humans below had upset their peace.

In the early light, she could see the walls of Sidon growing higher as they walked closer. In the far distance, she heard a sound she had never heard before, a pounding and swishing as if a great broom were beating and sweeping the earth like a rug.

"What is that sound?" she asked.

"The sea," Danel said. "In the city the sound will be obscured by all the noise but out here we can hear it even before we can see it."

"The what? What is the sea?"

"You've never seen the sea?"

"No. I have no idea what you're talking about." Hana felt her impatience with him growing. Why did Danel assume that what he knew was known by everyone?

In the growing light, Danel smiled at her. "The sea is a body of water bigger than any city, bigger than any land. It goes on and on. During storms, it swells up into walls that crash on the beach, and then heaves itself back out, like your body filling with air and expelling it. When it's calm, it lays on the earth like a shining blanket and whispers. It is a wonder, teeming with life. Men go out on it in boats to foreign lands and bring back things no one has seen before. The merchant traders who sail far away say they have seen fish in the sea that are the size of ten dwellings."

Hana could barely believe what he was saying. "Have you ever been on the sea?" She wondered if Danel was simply a really good storyteller.

"Not in a boat, but I've swum in the waves near the beach and felt the sea's power, its desire to pull me out so that I am one with it." He looked over at her. "It's glorious," he said in a low voice, as if he were sharing his deepest secret with her. "And terrifying."

Hana was quiet for a while trying to imagine a body of water bigger than the river, bigger than a lake, bigger than any land. She couldn't. She would have to wait to see it. "Will I see the sea soon?"

"For now, we have to figure out how to get you into the city. I'm to take you to my father's home and from there someone else will take you to see the queen."

"The queen? I thought I was supposed to meet someone called the matron."

He looked at her sideways and made a face of complete disbelief. "A girl who doesn't know about the sea or how important a queen is. Unbelievable. I can't imagine what they want with you."

Hana looked away from him. "Just tell me," she mumbled.

"You are going to see Queen Peri, the wife of the king, the most beautiful and dangerous woman in the world. And don't tell me you don't know what a king is."

Hana shook her head. "I know there is a king. My father made a crown for him. But why is he so important?"

He looked over at her, drew in a long breath and sighed. "The king is the top man, the chief of all the tribes, the one who gives the orders and does no one's bidding but the god's. The god Baal made him king and it is Baal from whom the king's power comes. The king's name is Zimrida. He owns everything—all the land, goods, livestock, crops, all that is made, all the people in his realm. We little people have what we have only by his beneficence to us."

Hana cocked her head and looked at Danel sideways. She knew in advance he wouldn't like what she was about to say. "You don't worship the wise lord, the one called El who we cannot see and whose true name we cannot speak because to do so would strike us dead?"

Danel stepped back and gave her one of his glowering looks.

She persisted even though she could see he was upset by her words. "You know, the wise lord who made the sky above us and the earth below, the winds and the water, and all the animals including us, the one whose companion, the Shekinah, brings light and love into our lives."

Danel stopped walking and turned to her, as if to emphasize the importance of what he was going to say. He took her by the shoulders. "Listen to me. Don't talk about the wise lord or this Shekinah. Baal is our god now, whatever the people of your clan, or Osnot, say. He made Zimrida king. And that's that. Someone like you, people who think like you, can't change that just because you say so." He glared at Hana as if to emphasize her diminutive powers. "It's dangerous to say what you're saying out loud."

He strode away from her again and Hana ran to catch up to him. A swarm of birds cast long shadows across the grass as she ran. She looked up quickly and saw their wide wingspan and the early sunlight glinting off their beaks. It was clear to her now. She had entered a different world when she descended the mountain. Even the birds were different here. Somehow, she had thought that everywhere in the world would be the same as her village was, everyone would look as her people looked, speak as they did, believe as they did. She was wrong.

"Recently," Danel continued as she drew closer to him, "King Zimrida declared that his people are free to do as they choose. He said Baal told him the people must have free will, but the king still demands that we pay him tithes."

"Tithes?"

"Never mind that." Danel shook his head and continued the lesson. "From his free people he chooses certain strong men to serve as his guards because there is evil in the world and kings of other cities may want to kill him and take over his kingdom. He also chooses certain beautiful and talented women…" He stopped and looked at her sideways for the flick of an eyelid, then continued, "to serve him in his bed and give him children."

"What are you saying?"

Danel waved his hand as if to brush off her question. "He employs artists to create beauty around him, healers to take care of him when he is sick, scribes and counters to keep track of all he possesses, and priests to tell him what Baal wants."

"Baal does not speak to him directly as the wise lord speaks to Osnot?"

Danel again waved his hand in the air. Hana thought the gesture must be a kind of magic practiced in Sidon, wiping away the sound of spoken words as if they had never been said.

"The people can do as we please," Danel continued, "well, except for killing each other. Zimrida puts most of his wealth into building big boats to go out on the sea and trade with people from other lands. The kings of Tyre and Byblos also have many boats, trading goods all across the known world. The future is out there, on the sea, bringing our purple cloth, glass, and strong cedar timber to other lands."

Danel paused, his eyes seeming to follow his mind, looking out in the direction of the sea for a while, and then he began walking again and resumed his instruction.

"The queen is the king's first wife. She is the one who birthed the next king, the prince. That makes her very powerful. She can do anything she wants, including kill whomever she pleases, with no punishment." He looked at Hana from under his eyebrows as if to underscore those last words. "She has already demonstrated her willingness to kill concubines who displease her. Everyone is afraid of her."

Hana nodded as if she understood but she didn't. *How could one man own everything?* In her own village, no one owned anything. Growing food, fishing, building huts, weaving baskets, making pots, all of that was done by people who were best at it. Harvesting flax to make cloth, finding herbs for healing, those gifts were shared with the clan. There were rarely squabbles about anything, much less killing each other. Hana's mother explained that all children belonged to the clan and all shared their gifts with everyone.

That was why the elders could tell her that she had to go on this journey even though her own parents had misgivings, even though she didn't want to leave her home. "It is for the good of all," her mother said. Hana had brushed away the tear on her mother's cheek with her hand and told her she understood. But she hadn't. She had simply decided to be brave because that was easier for her mother to bear. Choosing to be brave had been a mistake. She should have made them tell her what was going to happen until she truly understood. She should have been timid and stayed at home or run away when they could no longer see her on the mountain. But where would she have gone alone, in a world completely unknown to her?

"What is a concubine and why does the queen want to see me?"

Worry flashed across Danel's face. "A concubine…" he paused and looked into the sky for the words, "is a woman the king mates with but does not make his wife. No other man can ever marry her." He looked into Hana's eyes as if begging her to understand him. "As for the queen, I'm told you have something she wants. That's all I know."

He looked around them, watching something in the far distance. Hana's eyes followed his. Something shimmered with heat as sheaves of grass parted, moving swiftly toward them but still too far away to see clearly.

The elders had kept secrets from her that other people knew. They must have kept secrets from Danel as well. Now that she knew more, she wondered how the elders in her village knew about Sidon and the queen or that there was someone named Danel who would guide her to the city. Ignorance was bitter in her mouth. The elders and her parents had kept the most important information from her. Was that because if they'd told her of the danger, of what was in store for her, she wouldn't have gone traipsing up the mountain as if she were going on a picnic? She knew nothing. *Maybe they knew nothing. That's why they couldn't tell her.*

Her stomach heaved. "Excuse me, I have to…" Hana ran away from Danel and dropped to her knees in the tall grass.

Danel waved his arm, impatient with her frailty and turned his back to give her additional privacy.

She heard a swooshing sound as if a sudden, strong wind blew through the grass. And then the ground shook with the sound of many heavy feet—too heavy to be people or any animal she knew—pounding rhythmically over the ground.

Danel yelled, "Stay down, stay down." The pounding was all around her and then receded into the distance until there was no sound but the birds reeling above her, screeching.

She waited, hidden in the tall grass, for as long as she could squat in one position. She heard nothing but the distant sea. A green butterfly danced over her head and flew off. She stood slowly and looked around.

Turning in circles, she called his name, "Danel! Danel! Where are you?"

There was no answer. A wide track of matted grass ran across the plain as far as she could see. Her one friend in this new land was gone and she was alone. Nearby, high city walls glimmered white in the morning sunlight. She walked toward them.

Chapter 9

ELENA

Waiting by the tenth-floor elevators outside the maternity ward, Elena realized something was wrong. No one was behind the nurse's desk as she walked past it. She looked around more carefully. No one was in the corridors. The nurses who had efficiently managed Alissa and Hannah were gone. *How long had she been in the room with Alissa?* It couldn't have been ten minutes. She pushed open the set of swinging doors that led to the labor and delivery area. No one. It was too quiet. She walked back into the maternity ward and checked each of the rooms. The new mothers seemed undisturbed. Only the staff was missing. They couldn't all have gone to lunch at the same time.

She touched her communication device and said, "John?"

"Six of them, same set up, explosive vests. They came in blasting. Ten civilians dead down here. I got two of the bad guys. Three got up into elevators. One ran for cover before I could tap him. Call for backup. I'm going silent."

His voice was tense. There must still be a gunman holding hostages down there. Elena did as John asked.

"On the way," the dispatcher promised.

Six gunmen might have been the advance team with more to come. There must have been an incursion elsewhere in the building. At least one gunman had made it up to the tenth floor. She needed to take cover and assess the situation, but there wasn't any time for an assessment. She had to act. She had to clear the floor, make sure everyone was safe.

Elena went room by room, moving close to the wall, constantly checking her perimeter, aware that at any moment she could be ambushed or attacked from behind. *And women in labor. Oh, God, I can't think about that.* The patients appeared to be undisturbed. It was staff and visitors who had been scooped up and silently herded somewhere else. She imagined a masked man with an automatic weapon standing in the corridor, signaling to the nurses to be quiet and move through the door. It bothered her that it must have happened in the brief time she was talking to her sister. The terrorists were running the same kind of scheme as in the skyscraper: take hostages, make demands, and funnel police attention to the new disturbance.

She found no one with a gun or bomb vest on the tenth floor. There were also no doctors, nurses, aides, custodians, or visitors.

She opened a stairwell exit door and scoped the area. Quiet. She descended, keeping her back to the wall, her weapon ready. At the bottom of the stairs, she walked out into the ninth-floor corridor. Same eerie quiet, no nurses at the station, patients all in their beds. As she stood at the doorway of a patient's room, the man lying in the bed caught her eye. He looked at the bathroom door and then back at her. He looked terrified. *Someone's in the bathroom.* She couldn't risk the patient getting shot or being shot herself. She had to breach the door. She wouldn't have time for a careful analysis of whether the person in the bathroom was friend or foe.

In four long strides, Elena made the door, yanked it open, and shot almost without looking. The terrorist, mid-piss, dropped to the floor, smacking the back of his head on the sink. She seized the gunman's weapon, de-fused his vest, and moved on. The patient in the bed gave her a thumbs up.

On the next floor down, all personnel were missing. Where were they all? She tried to think through what was happening. Nobody wanted to die. Once they unfroze from their initial fright, unarmed civilians would walk in the direction you pointed if you pointed with a big gun. Able-bodied people might try to run away. Some would try to hide. Crazy, courageous folks would fight. They stood the highest risk of being killed.

But where were the terrorists holding the hospital staff? The largest space would be the cafeteria or an audi-torium. She cleared the floor and went down another stairwell. By the time she got to the ground floor, she had reloaded. She had taken out a total of four gunmen, shooting them in the back, the head, groin, whatever would take them down the fastest without triggering the bomb vest, and then finishing with a kill shot in the head.

There were obviously more attackers than John had counted at the main entrance. She didn't have time for questions. She didn't want them to get off any rounds that might spray patients. *These assholes had deliberately selected locations where defense was hampered by pa-tients.* Her mind on automatic, she thought of the decades of London bombings, British police rounding up IRA fighters, tanks in the streets in Ireland. She thought of Israel and seventy years of the constant threat of violence in cafes, villages, school busses. *Is that what was coming to America? Not on my watch.*

She heard murmuring ahead of her, the kind of sound that indicates a crowd of people trying to be silent. People were noisy animals, coughing, sniffing, whimpering, incapable of quiet. She paused in the corridor, her back against the wall, and listened. Her guess had been right.

Flattened against the wall, she turned her head to peer through the glass wall on which was etched the word CAFETERIA and saw hundreds of people in white coats, blue scrubs, pastel scrubs, guard uniforms, jeans and t-shirts, and office clothing lying on the floor, their hands interlaced on top of their heads. A few were weeping. A man in a yarmulke nearest the door seemed to be praying. Blocking the two exits from the cafeteria were heavily armed men in balaclavas and bomb vests. Another attacker, his head covering rolled up to his forehead, was helping himself to food from one of the restaurant kiosks.

Given the four she had killed, the two John dispatched, and the three in this room, Elena realized a second group of terrorists must have infiltrated the hospital at ground level, maybe through the delivery entrance. That meant there were more of them somewhere else. There were only two reasons to take a hospital: you thought you might need medical attention for your team, or you really wanted everyone on the planet to hate you. *Maybe both.*

In Iraq, insurgents had thought nothing of killing patients in their cots when they took cover in a hospital. In her first deployment in 2004, the callousness toward life struck her as odd. Now, tyrannical leaders trained beardless boys to shoot unarmed people in the head in an amphitheater of cheering spectators. The Syrian government bombed its own hospitals.

Disregard for human life was one of the bad guys'

biggest assets. But taking a hospital made no sense for this group of murderers. Even if they expected casualties in their own ranks, they wouldn't be able to set up a triage hospital for them. Something else, something bigger than seizing this hospital or taking down the skyscraper was in play. Storming the hospital was like moving a piece on a chess board. What then was the equivalent of taking the city's queen? She had to let the Chief know her suspicion.

Before she did that, she had to figure out where the rest of these monsters were. She'd have to clear this floor before she took out the guys in the cafeteria, where there was the greatest risk of civilian injuries. It would be too easy for the gunmen to explode themselves before she got a shot off. She looked around and went down the corridor in the other direction. She'd check radiology and the subbasement and come back through the kitchen behind the cafeteria.

Her communication device vibrated on her shoulder. She pressed it. "Labat."

"Cavalry are here." John's voice sounded weak. "Where are you?"

"Cafeteria. Couple hundred civilians here held by three gunmen."

"Stay there. Take cover. We're on our way."

Elena took a step back, looking for a place to hole up. She noticed a custodian's closet with a small window. She walked toward it and opened the door.

The hard steel bore of a gun muzzle pressed against the back of her neck where spinal cord met brain stem. "Clever female," said a man's voice. "Just not smart enough."

Time expanded. She heard the trigger being drawn back. In one swift motion, she ducked and pushed back against the assailant, making him stagger. The gun fired;

the bullet hit the closet ceiling. The gunman chambered another bullet. Elena jumped, clipped his legs, taking him down on his back. She fell on him with her knee against his windpipe and bore down. His arm dropped. His second bullet hit the wall.

As much as she wanted to ask this guy why his gang of thugs was doing this, she wanted him dead more. Holding him down with both legs, she shot him in the head. His buddies would have heard the scuffle at least, if not his shots. They would be here in seconds. She pulled his body into the closet and closed the metal door, squatting against it, hopefully out of sight. They'd have to push the door open to shoot her. She'd have the drop on them.

Elena heard the terrorists talking to each other in the corridor. She couldn't make out the language, but it wasn't Arabic. She'd picked up Arabic and a little Pashto on her three tours of duty in Iraq and Afghanistan. Although officially an Army medic, she also drove transport, alternated as Stryker gunner in a pinch, and always protected her buddy's back. Who "we" were, and who "they" were was always abundantly clear. Elena was momentarily shaken by the idea that she didn't know who her enemy was. She righted herself. *Knock it off. The enemy is always the same: it's the guy trying to kill you.* She shouldn't be fooled by location, language, or method.

She could hear footsteps. They were clearing the floor door by door. They would find her. She thought about Alissa and the baby, about holding Hannah's tiny, gooey body in her hands. She saw the infant's amazing eyes open and steeled herself. *I'm not going to die today.* She had to be in Hannah's life. Then she heard someone lay down enough fire to kill fifty people. She sucked in her breath. *Please, not the hostages.*

In the next moment, she heard John's voice yell over her communications device, "Clear, all clear."

She opened the closet door an inch, still in a squat, and peered out, gun muzzle first. Three more terrorists littered the floor. There was John, his shoulder bloody, grinning at her from ear to ear.

"Damn, you're good, girl," he said.

Elena stood from her crouch, strode to John, and punched him on the unwounded shoulder. "Not so bad yourself."

෴

"Dad," Elena yelled into her phone. "Dad, are you close?"

Aden gulped air. "I'm running the last few miles."

Elena imagined him bent over, hands on knees. "What's it like out there?"

"Traffic's at a complete standstill. People are in shock."

"Dad, get hold of Carl. He's on his way over too. When you get here, I think you need to take Alissa and the baby somewhere else."

Elena stood near the helipad on top of the hospital. She, John—patched up and ready to go again—and two other officers were joining the team deployed to midtown to get control of the subways.

She looked out over the lower end of the city, at the bridges spanning the river between the Manhattan and Brooklyn boroughs. Thousands of people were walking across the bridges. She'd bet it was the same on all the other bridges as well. *Like a photograph of the apocalypse,* she thought and then blinked the thought away.

Damn these guys, she wasn't going to think like this. She just had to keep her mind on her job. *Keep track of the right stuff, forget the rest.* They had cleared two targets. Before calling her father, she'd tuned into the squawk on her radio and learned more about the hotel bombing. All personnel not directed to the subway system were being sent to the hotel. The fighting was hot. She still had the uncomfortable feeling that they were missing something. The terrorists were always going to be ahead of them; they knew what they had planned. Surely the FAA had shut down airline traffic into and out of the city.

"Like where?" her father asked, interrupting her thoughts.

"Like out of New York City, off the island. Chalk it up to intuition or a case of nerves. I don't know how you do it. Alissa can't walk far, even if she thinks she can. She might hemorrhage. And, Dad, don't take any bridges. They're wall to wall people."

"I have an idea," Aden said. "Don't worry about it. Go save the world, sweetheart. I'll see you when it's over."

Elena chuckled at their old joke, amazed that her father could make her laugh today. "Thanks, Dad. Love you." She clicked off and turned to John.

Before they could say anything, the helicopter loomed above them, sweeping away all sounds beyond its roaring. They climbed aboard and took off. Looking down, they could see streets filled with people moving in all directions like blood flowing backwards in arteries and veins. So many people were jammed together at key intersections that all movement stopped, the city's circulatory system blocked by a huge clot. *The city is having a heart attack.* Huge screens on Forty-Second Street projected an image of the President mouthing platitudes. No one was listening.

Elena was struck by the idea that it would take very little, maybe only this action today, to transform the country she loved into a military dictatorship that ruled a shackled people whose every thought was monitored and whose every free action was checked in the name of security. Maybe that's what the terrorists were trying to accomplish: To make us like them. She shuddered.

"Hey, we're okay, Labat. We lived," John said into his mouthpiece.

Elena nodded. Maybe simply staying alive wasn't the gold standard anymore. But she didn't say that out loud.

Chapter 10

HANA

Hana emerged from the high grass onto sandy ground littered with small rocks. It was just after dawn. Pearly light glinted off the high, white stone walls looming up in front of her like a mountain rising up on the other side of the lake. From where she stood, she could see two arched openings in the wall. Ruts in the ground led up to heavy wooden gates.

Danel was right. The city was much larger than her village. If only he were here to guide her. In a flash, she remembered the pounding feet, the whooshing sound, and then the empty plain stretching ahead of her without him.

Hana dragged her mind back to examining what was in front of her. She couldn't give in to fear and loneliness. Many people and animals must have gone in and out of the city through these openings for the ruts to have gotten that deep. She walked closer until she could touch the wall. Her fingers traveled over the rough surface as she walked. Each white stone seemed to be the width of five people and higher than her arm could stretch above her head. The wall was the height of ten men. She had never seen anything made of stone in this way. The effort of making it took her breath away.

The stones had been cut many times and placed one on top of the other without mud between them. *Men made these stones into this shape.* She wondered how long it had taken, how many men worked on the wall and what tools they used. A ring of small wood dwellings with thatched roofs huddled near the city gate closest to her but no people were moving about the area.

Perhaps it was too early in the morning or these people stayed asleep much longer than those in her village. Only she, a few goats, and white birds with wings constantly in motion appeared to be out. Leaning against one dwelling wall were two large wooden circles with smaller, centered holes. The wooden circles were larger than but not as thick as threshing stones. She had no idea what their use could be. What a strange world she had found simply by crossing the wasteland and climbing down a mountain.

She remembered Danel's warning about being seen or stopped by guards and looked over her shoulder. With a sigh of relief, she realized there was no sign of guards. Hana had no intention of being taken and searched for weapons or illness by strangers. She put her hand over the dagger her father had given her. It was safe in its pouch. Her other hand she placed on her midriff where the blue feather meant to identify her nestled against her skin under her clothes. No one but the woman her mother called the matron was to see the feather. Then she worried that the brilliant blue scarf wound around her head would draw attention. She unwound the scarf and wrapped it around her waist. She undid the leather ties on her hair and wrapped the bindings around her wrists. *My hair is long enough to be a veil. I can hide my face if I look down at my feet.*

She looked up to assess the wall and figure out how to enter the city. Stepping back fifty paces, she regarded the wall again. It was too high to climb and with the stones sunk into the earth at the bottom, she couldn't crawl under it. Perhaps when there were many people going in and out of the gates, she could walk along behind a family as if she were part of their party. She would have to ask their permission first and she had no idea who to trust. *Do they even speak my language?* She wished again that Danel was still with her. His departure was inexplicable. He left no trace, as if he'd been lifted up off the ground and whisked away. A wide path of flattened grass as far as she could see across the plain was all that remained as a sign that he had been there with her. An ache galloped across her chest.

She could hear the sea continually whooshing against the shore like the blood through her body. She longed to see it, if only because Danel said he loved it. This might be her only opportunity. On a whim, she decided to find her way to the shore. Entering the city could wait. She had no idea how large the city was, how far she would have to walk to get to its end. From a distance, when she and Danel first spotted it, the city hadn't seemed that big, perhaps the size of four small villages, but now that she was upon it, she could see she'd been wrong. Sidon was vast. Nevertheless, she was determined to go around the city and find the source of the sound that beguiled her. She couldn't wait any longer. As the sun rose higher, people would begin to walk out of their dwellings and into the city.

She watched the birds and decided to go to her left, away from what appeared to be the larger main gate. She found a sand path encircling the walls. Other people had obviously had the same idea she did. It must lead to somewhere. She stepped onto the path and began to walk, thinking of the many steps she had taken away from her home and how she now had no guide. With each footfall, she was farther from her home and everything she knew.

If only Danel were with her, she wouldn't feel so alone. She had gotten used to his rudeness and missed his company. Hana didn't want to think that he might have been lifted off the ground by a huge bird that had carried him up into the air, back to the mountain, and dropped him against the rocks, leaving him broken and helpless. She turned her face away from the thought and looked ahead at the trees surrounding the city—lemon and olive trees, eucalyptus, all familiar to her. She inhaled their tangy perfume and caught the smell of something else she had never experienced. The farther she walked, the stronger the other smell became.

Before the pink rays of the sun had dispersed into the blue sky, she had found its source. There in front of her stretched endless, moving blue water, the most incredible clear water, the varied blues of it surging toward her and pulling away, far into the distance, far out past the horizon where she couldn't see. Sun glinted off it. Clouds were reflected in it. That tangy smell came from here. That sound like a lullaby, *shuuush, shuush*, this was the source. More birds with white wings swooped around her, screeching. She wanted to walk into the water, but fear held her back. She had no idea how deep it was. She wanted to weep with the beauty of it. Hana sank to her knees and watched until her breath quieted and her heart beat at a normal pace.

Large wooden structures floated on the water like leaves that had fallen onto the surface of the river. They looked like upside-down huts, the curved wood plank walls meeting the water and the top open to the air. Long poles rose up from the center toward the sky and were crossed by other poles. Ropes were attached to the poles.

Hana considered the possibility that these floating up-side-down huts might be like the rafts her people used to go downstream on the river but with sides. *But surely, they are too heavy to float. How would a man pick one up and carry it across a waterfall? If a man went out onto the sea in this craft, how would he get back? How deep was the sea?*

She watched two men walk toward one of these structures and push it off the shore into the water where it floated. They clambered up a rope and over the side into it. When they stood inside the wooden structure, she couldn't see their legs. She had underestimated its size. Now that two men were in it, she could see that six or more could comfortably fit in it. A third man threw supplies into a large net which the other men pulled up over the side and then he climbed in.

As she watched, one of the men picked up a long pole and pushed the wooden float farther away from the shore, deeper into the water. She stared. *Now they will sink and drown.* Two of the men worked the ropes and then a large red and white striped piece of rough cloth unfurled. Wind puffed out the cloth, and the craft moved out, farther and farther from shore. Hana put her hand over her mouth and waited for the craft to tip over and the men to fall into the water. Hoping they knew how to swim, she watched until the men and their strange raft were only a speck on the horizon.

"It's a boat, young lady," said a man's voice behind her.

Hana jumped. She leaped up and turned. The man beside her wore a head covering made of a material she didn't recognize, thicker and flattened out, fitting close to his head. She looked at him, trying to determine whether she should run. But where would she run to? Although his face was creased, he seemed young enough to catch her if she ran. He wore a simple linen cloth wrapped around his waist that hung to his knees and a folded cloak wound over his shoulder and chest. His feet were bare. The veins in his hands and arms stood out as if he did heavy work much of the time. He had a long beard, the center of which was a stripe of gray. His skin, unlike Danel's bronze color, was a tanned version of hers, as if he spent his time in the sun. Just above his wrist, tattooed into his skin, was the mark her mother made her memorize: the C'hai, the symbol for life. This man, according to her mother's teaching, should be someone she could trust.

"A boat?" she said, not knowing what else to say. Danel had spoken of boats. She'd had no idea what he was talking about. This is what Danel wanted to do. He wanted to go out on the sea in one of those boats. It seemed like a very dangerous way to live.

"It's made from boards of our abundant cedar trees and floats on the water. Those are fishermen, like I am. They go out onto the sea, catch fish, and bring them back to market. They'll be back before the housewives get to the fish stalls."

Hana shook her head in mild disbelief. "I've never seen the sea or a boat. I'm, I'm…"

"Speechless," the man finished her sentence for her. He grinned and peered into her face with his warm brown eyes. "We're even. I've never seen a person with eyes the color of the sea. You aren't from here."

"No. I was sent here." She stopped herself. *Can I really trust this man? Was my mother right? He does bear the sign.* Her lips trembled. "I need to find a way into the city, to the house of Batnoam, father of Danel," she blurted. "But I can't go in through the gate." She looked around her and out to sea, as if to summon help, and then back at him. "The mark on your wrist, what does it mean?"

"This mark?" He held out his wrist for her inspection. "It means I believe the wise lord breathes life into all things. Do you know the wise lord?"

Hana nodded. "My mother spoke of the wise lord, as did Osnot." She had to trust someone. She gathered her courage. "Can you help me?"

The man stroked his beard and looked out to sea also. It seemed to Hana that they stood there for all time while he pondered. Finally, he said, "I can help you, but it may be dangerous. Are you prepared to deal with danger?"

Hana looked up at him and laughed. "How do you think I got here?"

"When you laugh, your eyes flash like sun off the water." The man sighed as if someone invisible had spoken to him of home. "Well then, we will walk a little farther on. Close to where this beach forms a spit out into the sea and the large boats are moored, there's a narrow crack in the city wall from the last earthquake. I've used it myself, so I know that you will fit through it. It takes us into the city behind the marketplace. It's noisy and dirty there, with many unsavory people—thieves, performers, pick pockets, failed priests—who hang around looking for handouts of food and drink..." He paused and squinted at her. "And young girls to spirit away. Of course, there are also many dogs and rats."

Hana scrutinized his face. His eyes were twinkling. *Is he testing me?*

"You must cover your hair and face and keep your eyes down so that you don't attract attention. Follow behind me as if you are my daughter. Don't say anything to anyone, don't look around, and don't lose sight of me. Do you understand?"

"Yes." Hana wrapped her scarf around her head and pulled the fabric down over her eyes. "How's this?" she asked.

The man frowned. "It seems you are incapable of being invisible." He took his own plain cloak and put it over her head. It reeked of his sweat and fell to her ankles. "Hold it closed in front just below your chin," he ordered. "Look down at your feet." He stood back to look at the effect. "Yes, that's better. You look like any nondescript girl now."

He walked off toward the wall and Hana followed fast on his heels, half holding her breath and terrified she would lose sight of him. "Wait, wait." She reached out her hand and touched his arm. "What's your name in case I lose you?"

"I am Abirami," the man said. "And I won't lose *you*. You're worth something and I would like to find out what. What is your name?"

"I am Hana of Andulat."

❧❧❧

The break in the wall was jagged but wide enough for Hana to slide through sideways. She looked above her, worried for a moment that one of the large stones would fall on her head. She took one last look at the sea and then turned her face towards Abirami, who was already midway through the gap in the wall and moving forward. It was dark for just a few breaths as she shimmied between the stones, and then light, color, and movement assaulted her eyes.

The marketplace buzzed with merchants dressed in many different garments, calling out to shoppers about their wares. Purple, red, and blue awnings above the stalls flapped in the breeze. Metal clanging against metal reminded her of the sounds her father made at his forge. She heard music—pipes and some kind of stringed instrument accompanied by the bleating of sheep and goats. Birds trilled and chattered.

Blood oozed across the sandy ground. Violating Abirami's warning, she looked up and saw the butcher hanging half a sheep from a hook in his stall. He stared back at her, his body completely still as if he were sizing up what knife he would use to carve her into edible pieces. She shuddered.

Abirami walked back to her and gripped her arm. "Come with me, daughter. I told you not to stop and look at anything."

They walked on through the market. Hana stole glances at tables loaded with fish larger than any she had ever seen, one fish large enough to feed an entire village. *It must have come from the sea.* She saw yellow, orange, and red birds in cages. A man held a long tube up to his mouth and at the other end of the tube a glowing green ball became larger and larger. She gaped.

Abirami squeezed her arm and pulled her along. "Let's find Batnoam first and then you can come back properly chaperoned and gawk at glass blowers." Under his breath he muttered loud enough for Hana to hear, "I hope this girl is not more trouble than she's worth."

They walked out of the marketplace and into a central plaza paved with stones laid in circles, each larger circle flowing out from the one before. Hana had never seen a space like this one. She turned in circles to take it in. Abirami stopped to talk to a man. He gestured toward Hana and spoke with great emotion, his hands fluttering in the air. They spoke a dialect she didn't understand. Breaking Abirami's rule about raising her face yet again, she tried to absorb the sight of everything around her.

Surrounding the plaza were houses made of the same stone as the wall. Heavy wooden doors set in archways the height of two men stood open into courtyards, revealing small paved terraces with trees and fountains in the center. Houses had openings in their stone walls higher than the height of the door. Boxes of red flowers hung from these openings. Above those openings, the roofs were flat. The houses must have ladders inside going up to another landing, Hana reasoned. *How many people live inside a large structure like that?* She glimpsed date and olive trees in the courtyards and marveled that city people had only to walk out of their homes to find food.

She started to walk closer to one of the open doors to peer inside the courtyard. Abirami took her arm again and led her down a narrow alley between two sets of houses. "It's just a few houses from here," he said. "Please stop looking around. People are starting to notice you. It may seem like no one would notice you in such a big city with so many people, but here everyone gossips."

Hana looked down at her feet. She was tired, thirsty, hungry, and starting to feel like a captive. She had asked for help but perhaps it was time to go off on her own. Abirami seemed to know no more about how to find Batnoam's house than she did. She looked behind her and saw a man striding toward them.

He was wearing fine linen and a purple sash. Tall and slender, his skin was the same bronze color as Danel's. He was younger than Abirami and wore a pointed, purple head covering. A narrow beard jutted out from his chin but otherwise his face was clean shaven.

He walked up to Abirami and put a hand on the man's shoulder. "Old man, I thank you for finding my aunt's granddaughter and bringing her to me. It's now time to relinquish her to my care."

"How do I know who you are?" Abirami clenched his fists on his hips and tilted his head back to glare at the taller man. "What proof do you have that this girl belongs to your family? For all you know, she is my daughter."

"I have the proof she carries with her." The man turned to Hana. "Show him the proof that you come from Andulat, girl."

Hana had no idea who this man was or whether to produce the feather hidden under her clothes. Her mother had said to show it only to the matron, whoever that was. She put her hand on the dagger in its pouch, but she knew she couldn't stab anyone with it. Even if she did, where would she run? She knew no one in this huge city. *If only Danel hadn't disappeared. This would be easier if he were here with her. Danel. Of course.*

"What is the name of your son?" She looked straight at the man. "And what is your name?"

The man looked at her closely, staring into her eyes as if transfixed. "My son, you clever girl, is Danel, and I am Danel's father, Batnoam, for whom you are looking. But where is my son? Why isn't he with you? Why did I have to hear you had entered the city from the man who dances in the market who heard if from the juggler who heard it from the butcher?"

Hana wanted to smile at him but couldn't. She felt instant sorrow that Danel wasn't standing there in front of his father. She imagined her own father longing for her, imagining the worst had happened. "He disappeared on the plain," she said, her voice barely a whisper. "We were walking and then suddenly he was gone."

"Gone?" The man looked at her as if he could tell whether she was making up a story or telling the truth by looking at her face. "What did you see before he disappeared?"

"I saw nothing. I'm sorry. I heard the pounding of feet on the ground, heavier feet than people running, many feet, and a whooshing sound. Do you know what that was?" Hana said.

"I'm afraid I do," the man said. "My son has been kidnapped by the horse people. They often waylay people in the plain. Their horses move faster than any man can run. That is why we rarely travel that way. How is it that they didn't get you also?"

Hana blushed. She looked down at the ground. "I was on my knees in the tall grass. I guess the horse people didn't see me. Danel yelled for me to stay down and I did."

Batnoam looked sad and angry at the same time. Hana didn't know what to say to him. If she missed Danel, how much worse did his father feel?

"Come along with me to our house. You must be exhausted." He turned to Abirami. "You too, old man. You look like you could use a drink and a meal, and I will reward you handsomely for bringing the girl to us and for your future silence."

Abirami smiled, his face breaking into creases. "That's exactly what I hoped you'd say."

A few hundred paces more, off another square, Batnoam turned into a walled courtyard in which three young boys played. They jumped up from their game and ran to him, hugging his legs and chattering at the same time. He staggered, laughed, and called for his wife. Ashirat came out of the house, saw Hana, walked up to her, and pulled Abirami's heavy cloak off her head, waving away the smell of the old man with both hands. She unwound Hana's scarf and kissed the girl on both cheeks.

She turned Hana to face Batnoam. "This is why she was sent to us," she said. "We will be in great favor with the king very soon."

Hana, mystified by Ashirat's comment, nonetheless drank several cups of the cool water she was offered, ate sparingly from the plates Ashirat put out for the mid-day meal, and caught herself dozing against the pillows without intending to sleep.

"Come with me." Ashirat pulled Hana up by the hand and led her to a bed in a room that opened off the first one they entered. Hana marveled at the number of rooms in the house. It was cool and dusky in the chamber, shielded from the sun.

Ashirat patted Hana's shoulder. "Rest here, child. After you have slept for a while, I will take you to the baths so that you can be clean for your introduction to the matron."

"What are the baths?"

Ashirat looked at Hana oddly. "Have you never taken a bath? At home, do you immerse yourself in water?"

"Oh." Hana giggled, glad that this new thing called a bath was simply washing herself. "Yes, of course. I didn't know this word, bath. Is there a river or lake nearby? Do I wash in the sea?"

"No," Ashirat said. It was now her turn to laugh. "We have a women's bath house with a man-made pond where the floors are covered with colored tiles in beautiful designs. The water is warmed by a fire and you can use perfumed oils. I will wash your hair. I'm sure there are others who would like to help you as well."

"I know how to wash myself," Hana retorted. She didn't like the idea of strangers helping her to wash. She wasn't a child.

"Don't worry about this, my dear." Ashirat smiled. "Sleep now. Then we'll eat something and celebrate your being here. You can tell me about your trip. After your bath, we'll go to see the matron at the queen's house."

"I'm sorry about Danel."

Ashirat turned her face away from Hana's gaze. "Yes. I am too." She walked out of the room.

Hana unwound her scarf and placed it on the bed. She took off her girdle and the pouch that held the knife, dropped her tunic to the floor, and lay down. The softness of the bed soothed her skin and muscles. She was asleep before she could think about anything else. In her dreams, she saw herself standing at the prow of a boat floating on a dark sea. Danel stood by her side. A full moon floated above them, its reflection following behind the boat, folding and unfolding in the black water.

Chapter 11

ELENA

The helicopter hovered over the red target painted on the rooftop, waiting for the wind to die down long enough to drop off Elena and John. Their orders, along with five hundred other tactical officers, were to take back the city's subway system.

All trains had been stopped. As many civilians as possible had escaped from the subway stations. Reports came in of people trampled on the platforms and exit stairs in a stampede of terrified riders. Hospital emergency resources were stretched to the limit. People were trapped in subway cars, perhaps killed.

"What's the death toll going to be today?" Elena asked.

John scoped their landing, watching for the opportunity to leap out. "Don't think about it."

"What? Oh." Elena hadn't realized she'd asked the question out loud. Statistics rolled up in her head without her bidding. She couldn't stop her mind from counting the possible dead. "Nearly two hundred died in the Mumbai attack."

"I know," John said. "Breivik, by himself, killed seventy-seven in Norway."

"McVeigh killed one hundred sixty-eight in the 1995 Oklahoma City bombing."

John shook his head. "This arithmetic isn't going to help you cope." He knew once Elena started thinking, there was no stopping her. "Thinking can kill you."

She almost smiled. "One-hundred-ninety-one people died in the Madrid train bombings. Eighteen hundred were injured. It's too easy to kill people."

"Whatever the number, it's never good. Focus on doing something about it."

Elena knew John's coaching was right, but one death was all it took to make her day go bad. That woman lying on the floor at the Trade Center early this morning was enough to make this a bad day. Her mind had tagged two-hundred civilians lost in the trade center building, four in the hospital. There would be more. She couldn't stop her brain from rolling out the numbers.

The helicopter's rails touched down and John and Elena unbuckled their safety harnesses, threw off the headsets, jumped out onto a roof-top pad in mid-town, and sprinted toward the door to the stairs. Elena waved to the pilot to signal they were clear, and the copter lifted off.

"C'mon," John said, shaking her out of her mind. He gripped her arm and pulled her to the stairs. "Places to go, people to kill."

Elena looked at him. As long as she'd known him, she still had trouble with the idea that he could joke at the oddest times about the oddest subjects. She grinned without wanting to from the sheer ridiculousness of his comment.

On the street, they climbed into another four-wheel-drive vehicle he commandeered—"Police business, thanks, buddy," she heard him say—and sped north, hoping to get to the rest of their squad in time to do something besides congratulate them on a spectacular success.

Elena watched pedestrians wandering around the city like lost children. "Do you think it's too easy?"

Some people gathered in small groups. Strangers consoled each other. Some walked weeping down the street without caring if a car hit them. Some stood like statues on the sidewalk trying to get a call to go through on their cell phones. Then they walked a few feet and tried again, over and over, like a word trying to break through a stutter. Those determined lines of people striding at full speed to their next important destination were gone, decimated by fear and indecision like bees that had lost the scent of their home hive.

John gave her a quick look. "Too easy? What are you talking about?"

"I mean, we took the terrorists out at the Trade Center, at the hospital, and likely as not we'll rout them from the subway system either by killing them, or when they kill themselves by blowing up a station. What are they gaining from all this effort?"

John looked over at her and then back at the sidewalk on which he was now driving at fifty miles an hour. "What do they ever gain? Terror. Panic. Disruption. That's their game. They're forcing us to play it. That's enough of a win for them. What're you thinking?"

"I'm thinking that all this is some kind of elaborate smoke screen, that there's something else in play that we don't see." She stopped describing her thought process to yell, "Pole, pole!"

"I see it." John swerved twice and avoided both the pole and the people jumping up from a small outdoor café table to get out of his way.

"Anyway," Elena continued, "they took the Trade Center, the hospital, the subway system, the hotel, scared the bejesus out of everyone, for what? What do they get? They know we're not going to give in to their demands. They know they're not going to live through it. Or get the money they demanded. Or land in a posh desert resort with gorgeous virgins serving them cool drinks. They're not going to wind up in some comfortable prison with a private room and get their college education and an X-box for free."

John kept his eyes on the many obstacles in the way of his vehicle. "They don't have the same values we do, Elena. Besides, this kind of thinking is for the big guys, the ones who wear suits and make the big bucks. We're just the muscle." But his voice was quiet as if he was considering what she'd said.

Elena looked over at him. "Just because we're the muscle doesn't mean we can't think." In a flash, she remembered her father saying, "Tell a boy to run a hundred yards and yell 'Go!' and he's off like a shot. Tell a girl the same thing and she cocks her head to one side and says, 'Why should I do that?'"

She glanced at John gripping the wheel and looked out of the window again. *What had her father said? When someone is driving like a maniac, it's easier to look out the side window.* They were headed for the station at Rockefeller Center. They were to clear the station, the train cars, make sure all civilians were freed, then follow the tunnel in both directions to the next train and the next.

Everyone on the force knew this was a suicide mission. Hundreds of miles of track with trains possibly rigged with explosives, hell, even the tracks could be rigged. And the terrorists themselves were likely wearing explosive vests. The moment her team stood on the platform, there was less than a fifty percent chance they would see daylight again. *Terrorists won simply because they embraced death.* That was her refrain today.

"Not today, you bastards."

"What?" John shot a glance at her as he pulled up in the Rockefeller Center courtyard. He put the keys under the mat, and they ran to the subway entrance.

"You doing a new kind of ride share deal here?" Elena said, her voice rising just a little bit.

John clasped her shoulder with his large hand. "Get a grip, Labat. It's a strange day. Maybe the guy who owns the Jeep will find it and take it home. I told him where we were going. Let's go."

They ran down the long flight of grubby cement steps into the murkiness of the platform below. No matter how the city tried to say the subways were safe, Elena always had a few moments of hesitation, a feeling she was descending into hell. Today that vague misgiving turned out to be true.

Their squad had already retaken the platform and cleared the train stopped in this station. Train doors stood open. Ten civilians caught in bullet spray lay dead on the platform in various crumbled positions. *Two-hundred-fourteen.* Three men in balaclavas and bomb vests were dead, sprawled on the platform, masks pulled back over their heads revealing their faces. Elena shined her flashlight on them and took a long look. These three were as blond as Scandinavians and as blue eyed as she was.

This was the new terrorist, then, a world-wide army of angry white people who learned their tactics from the Chechens and could blend into the population of any Western country. The Beslan school siege—385 hostages died—flashed in her mind. She didn't have time to think through this terrifying idea. She needed her father to bounce her thoughts off. Her mind hooked out toward her sister, the image of the new-born infant in Alissa's arms.

She hoped her father had reached them. John grunted something at her, and Elena came back to the present with a thud, the gritty platform under her feet.

She turned away from the dead terrorists and looked around. *More bodies.* Two were from her squad. She and John missed the firefight, a fact she was secretly glad about at the same time that she felt grief and fury. They walked through the train. More dead, Elena noted, transit personnel by the uniform.

At the last car, they jumped down onto the track and started walking south, guns out, flashlights on. John signaled her to stop and be quiet. They turned off their lights and stepped backward toward the wall. Running footsteps came toward them—more than one person. It was impossible to know if they were friend or foe. They squatted and took aim. Whoever was running through the darkness at them would be in their sights in moments.

☙❧

"Labat, it's us. Cantor, Fuller. Don't shoot."

Elena heard the IDs loud and clear. She drew her finger back from the trigger but didn't lower her weapon. Turning on her flashlight, as did John, she watched two officers from her squad limp into view.

"We're what's left of the squad." Sergeant Mary Cantor gasped, attempting to keep her voice neutral, but she faltered, turned her face away, and stopped talking until she regained her composure. "One of those monsters blew himself up in the tunnel." Cantor paused for a few seconds. "Took out two of his own people to get four of ours. Damaged the tunnel. No trains will get through there until it's cleared out and the tracks are repaired. Our guys...our guys are splattered everywhere." She put her hands on her knees, leaning over to catch her breath and stifle a sob.

"Let's get out of this damn tunnel."

"Are you injured?" John asked.

"Not a scratch," Corporal Ralph Fuller said, his voice rueful. "We were half a mile back from them when the bomb went off. We cleared the other side of the track for two miles up first and were headed back in their direction."

Fuller cleared his throat. "We saw the blast and felt the tail end of the shock wave. Part of the tunnel ceiling caved in." He shook his entire body as if he could shake off what he had seen. "We searched through the debris. No survivors." He paused again, swallowing hard. "I'm done in. Sorry. I'd like to get up to daylight and find out what all's going on out there."

For a full two seconds, Elena scrutinized Cantor and Fuller. The whole team was in top notch physical shape. They wouldn't have been in the Fifth Squad if they weren't. If what was happening was too much for Fuller, then it was too much for anyone.

"My thinking?' Cantor offered.

Elena nodded, indicating it was okay to speak freely.

"We should let the bastards keep the subways and blast the whole thing to dust with them in it. Start over."

"Got it," Elena said. She needed to make the call. They would go back in if she asked them. This dark tunnel was a metaphor for everything that had gone wrong today. They couldn't see where they were going or what they had to deal with when they got there. It was futile to grope around in the dark for the enemy. They had been sucked into a bad situation. She had lost half her squad in that dark hole. *Had the terrorists deliberately manipulated the police to get them off the surface streets?* She went back to her idea that all of this was a smokescreen for something else, something bigger, worse, more terrifying.

"We're out of here," she said, turning and leading the way back toward the platform, the steps, the exit and fresh air. "I'm calling the Chief. We need all subway entrances and exits guarded and a much larger team with heavier artillery sent in."

"What about the hostages?" John asked.

Elena turned to Cantor. "Did you see any civilians in the train as you approached?"

"No sign of life," Cantor said.

"We're going to lose more civilians, I think." Elena's voice, low and brusque with sorrow, was enough information for her partner.

John turned toward the direction that would take them up into the air. "Outta here," he said, vaulting up onto the platform and sprinting up the exit stairs. The others followed with no hesitation.

Back on the surface street where she could see in all directions, Elena called her Chief. Standing in sunlight, she reported casualties and their mission outcome. She listened to Ruggierio ream her out from the safety of the bullet-proof, fireproof bunker where she was lodged for the duration, and said "Yes ma'am" when it seemed appropriate. She waited for her to be done talking. Elena understood her frustration.

Everyone was on their last straw. Across the city, other teams had run into the same brick wall. The commissioner had called up all 36,000 active duty officers, pulled in more than four-thousand auxiliary officers, and tasked five thousand school safety officers with crowd control at pressure points. It wasn't enough to deal with this mess. Every counterterrorism inspector, every foot soldier was in play. Everyone was on edge. Enforce the law, preserve peace, reduce fear, maintain order—none of those goals envisioned fighting an army of trained assailants. They needed far more firepower than they had brought to this party—and better tactics. They weren't fighting one-off criminal activity. They were fighting an asymmetrical war with a ruthless, world-wide gang that didn't play by their rules.

"Permission to speak frankly, ma'am?"

The Chief gave it. In her imagination, Elena saw her square her shoulders in readiness for a raft of shit. "Ma'am, I think all of these individual attacks are a smoke screen for the big takedown, the one that kills civilians right off, right in front of everyone on television. I think we're not seeing the big picture because we're distracted by each episode. Get up in a helicopter, ma'am. You'll see hundreds of thousands of people on or walking toward the bridges. They're walking over to Brooklyn and New Jersey, out of the city. Thousands of them, completely unprotected by us, or by anyone. They're a perfect target. If the bastards succeed, they'll cut Manhattan off from the rest of the city and the country. It'll be worse than New Orleans after Katrina. Manhattan will become a massive refugee camp. It'll be total chaos."

"Shit," Chief Ruggierio said. "Of course."

Elena heard her talking to someone about getting a helicopter and telling someone else to get a line to the commissioner. To Elena, the chief said, "Get what's left of your squad to the helicopter pad by City Hall. I'll send you reinforcements. Your assignment is the Brooklyn Bridge. Find whatever's there that can harm people—bombs, lunatics, whatever. I'll get teams to the other bridges and tunnels. I'll redirect the bomb squads. Let me know what you find the second you find it."

Elena had nearly disconnected when she heard, "Good job, Lieutenant Labat. Ruggierio out."

That small acknowledgement gave her a new, very necessary jolt of energy to go on. She mustered her small band of stalwart officers, told them their next assignment, and moved out. "You should've kept that vehicle, John."

"Don't worry about it. I've got my eye on a solution."

John ran to a police van idling at the intersection, talked to the driver, and signaled them over. They had a ride with all the bells and whistles. It would still take twenty minutes to go four and a half miles on streets packed with pedestrians wandering in all directions

Chapter 12

HANA

Ashirat woke Hana gently, placing a soft hand on her shoulder, brushing Hana's hair back from her face. For a moment, Hana thought she was home and looked up, eager for a hug from her mother. Then she thought perhaps Danel had returned and was waking her. She opened her eyes. Disappointment hollowed out her bones.

Ashirat stood back from the bed and surveyed the girl. "Do you bleed?" she said.

"Bleed? No. I'm not injured."

"No, I don't mean from an injury. Do you bleed when the moon is full, when all of Ashtart's daughters bleed?"

Hana shook her head. Her mother had told her that when she was ready to bear children she would bleed. It hadn't happened yet. When it did, there would be a ceremony to mark her entrance into womanhood and soon after that, her father would choose a husband for her from another clan.

"Hmmm." Ashirat breathed deeply. "Stand up. Let me see you."

Hana stood up from the bed. Her hair hung to her waist. Ashirat swept the girl's hair up off her shoulders and gently turned her around in a circle. She touched Hana's back, under her shoulder blade. "What is this mark on your back?'

"It's the blue bird of Andulat. I was born with it. Together with the feather I've brought with me, it's supposed to prove my origin."

She dropped Hana's hair. "Let me see the feather."

Hana looked through her clothing, panicked for a moment that she'd lost the blue feather. She pawed through the folds of her tunic and finally found the feather under her scarf. *I should be more careful.* She held it out for Ashirat to see but would not relinquish it. "I must give it only to the matron, my mother said."

Ashirat lifted one shoulder and turned her head as if to say she didn't care. "Get dressed. We'll have some food and then we'll go to the baths and get the grime of the journey off your skin and out of your hair. When we're done, you will glow. Perhaps we'll get you a new tunic of better cloth. At the very least, I will have these cleaned." She smiled at Hana and turned away.

Hana looked up to see Batnoam staring at her from the doorway. She quickly pulled up her tunic. There was something in his eyes, as if he had not eaten in days, when he looked at her. The look frightened her. She looked at Ashirat, who walked up to her husband and brushed her body against his as she passed him. He turned and followed her. She heard Ashirat laugh. Hana felt uncomfortable, not knowing the customs here. Had she done something that was funny?

Wrapping the scarf around her shoulders, she noticed a lump in the hem. She examined the cloth and saw something tied inside it. Hana unknotted the end of the scarf and found a tiny scroll. She flattened the small sheet of papyrus to examine it, expecting a drawing of something that would remind her of home, but the marks, which looked like bits of straw from the threshing floor arranged in odd ways, meant nothing to her. She couldn't decipher the meaning no matter which way she turned the papyrus. *Did my mother put this message in my scarf?*

Was this the message she was supposed to deliver to the queen? It must be important, or it wouldn't have been tied up in this way. She must find a way to keep it safe, she thought. If Ashirat was going to clean her clothes, she had to find another place to put the feather and this scroll. Then she remembered the dagger pouch her father gave her. It was the perfect place. She opened the pouch, placed the feather and scroll inside, tied the leather cords around her neck, and tucked the pouch inside her tunic.

Proud of herself for solving this problem, she walked into the front room to join the family for the morning meal, hoping that she would see Danel sitting there on the floor with them. But there were only Ashirat, Batnoam, and their other sons. No one said anything about Danel.

෴

"Oh, look at this wonder Ashirat has brought us today," exclaimed a woman with golden skin standing up to her waist in the bath. "We must be from the same tribe."

"I must get close enough to see if those lovely features stand up to scrutiny," said another whose ample breasts bobbed in the water.

One by one the women walked out of the bath and stood naked and dripping in a circle around Hana and Ashirat, removing the girl's clothing, examining every inch of her body, running her long curls through their fingers, massaging her skull.

"Look at these eyes! I've never seen eyes the color of the sky and sea."

"Yes! And this mark of a blue bird on her back, she is obviously sacred to the goddess."

"And those breasts, like ripe pomegranates."

"Did you notice her thighs?"

"She is destined for great things," Ashirat assured them, her own status among the women increased by Hana's beauty and her impending meeting with the queen. "She does not bleed yet," Ashirat told the women, as if Hana's personal history was a coin she could spend to buy herself a gift. Ashirat stepped out of her own tunic, leaving it on the floor, and walked toward the bath. An old woman scuttled across the floor and scooped up their clothing.

Ashirat stepped down into the pool, turned and held out her hand for Hana to join her. "Come now, girl, don't be embarrassed. We are all women here. No one will hurt you."

Hana stood naked on the edge of the pool, staring at the images on the chamber walls of birds, fish, and people. Even the floor of the bathhouse and sides of the pool of water itself were adorned by mosaics. Water gushed into the pool from a small waterfall near the wall. Women lounged everywhere, sitting on the edge of the pool, lying on their backs in the water, standing in groups talking. If everyone bathed together in still water, weren't they passing dirt from one to the other? She was accustomed to bathing in the river where the rushing water carried grime away from her body.

"Why don't you bathe in the sea?" Hana asked.

Ashirat laughed. "The salt in the sea will dry your skin. You don't want that. You want your skin to be soft."

Hana nodded but she didn't see why her skin needed to be soft. What she wanted more than anything else was to go home, to be back in her village with her parents and the ways of her own people. These people looked similar to her and spoke like her, although they all seemed to have a lisp and they used words she didn't know. But they were not like her at all.

She let herself be pulled into the water and submitted to Ashirat's ministrations, lying back in the water, closing her eyes, feeling her hair floating around her. The oils smelled good, both sweet and tart. At least the bath wasn't unpleasant. She wished again her mother had told her everything that would be required of her. Perhaps her mother hadn't known. Hana didn't want to think her mother knew what would befall her and failed to tell her because she didn't think Hana was brave enough. *I am brave enough. I can do anything.* That's what her father used to tell her.

When Hana was clean and dry, the old woman who washed clothes squatted next to her and pared her toenails with a sharpened stone. She looked up and whispered to Hana, "Be careful where you put your feet, dear one," before she was sent away.

Ashirat helped Hana put on her now clean tunic and scarf. Hana noticed she was the only one wearing a blue scarf. The other women wore purple, red, orange, some white with a bright yellow border but none wore blue. *Does the color signify which tribe they're from?* Their tunics were the same unbleached linen as hers, but the cloth seemed softer. Some of them wrapped strands of gold glittering with shining stones around their waists, necks, and arms. One woman had a neckpiece of luminous glass beads. What other strange customs would she see today in this city of more people than she had ever seen before? Hana picked up her pouch from the side of the pool where she'd placed it, tied the leather cords around her neck, and tucked the pouch under her tunic.

"What is in that ugly pouch you wear?" Ashirat put her hand on Hana's shoulder and reached for the pouch.

Hana pulled away. "I carry special tokens from my father and mother. They are only for the queen to see." In the short time she had spent with these people, she had learned that things for the queen were considered sacred and not to be touched by others.

Ashirat raised one shoulder and tilted her head, a frequent gesture that seemed to Hana to say, *oh well*. "Come along. I'll take you to the queen's house where you will meet the matron. You can show her your treasures and she'll decide what to do with you."

They walked out of the bathhouse into the city. Heat enveloped Hana. Without the cooling shelter of the forest she was accustomed to, the afternoon heat was oppressive. Fronds of date and fig trees peeked above courtyard walls swaying in the warm breeze. Crisp sunlight reflected off the buildings' white stones. Above the sounds of so many people going about their daily tasks, Hana could hear the sea sigh just beyond the city walls. She yearned to be standing near it, watching the movement of blue water.

Hana wondered how this cold woman, Ashirat, could be related to Osnot, who had seemed so wise and warm. "Are you Osnot's granddaughter?" she asked when she couldn't bear her own curiosity another second.

Ashirat laughed out loud. "Me? No. Thank the gods. She is my husband's first wife's grandmother. Such an embarrassment…"

"Oh, I thought Danel said she was his mother's grandmother. I must be confused." Hana looked down at her clean toes in her new sandals. She had stumbled on a secret in Danel's family. She could see instantly she had made a mistake.

Ashirat stopped walking and put her hands on Hana's shoulders in a gesture reminiscent of Danel's when he desperately wanted her to understand something he was saying. "Look, girl, I understand that you are a stranger and special to the king and queen, but you must not be disrespectful to people about whom you know nothing. You are ignorant of our ways. It's best if you *say* nothing."

Hana's cheeks and neck flushed. *Is it possible to be more miserable than I am at this moment?* Then she remembered that she had left her home, probably forever, walked across a wasteland, clambered down a steep mountain wall, lost her guide and only friend, and was left alone to enter a strange city on her own. That brought her to another question. Why wasn't Ashirat worried about Danel? He was missing. She had only known him a few days and she was anxious about him. Maybe Danel wasn't Ashirat's son. It was a surprising thought but that might explain her cold reaction.

Hana couldn't keep herself from blurting out her next question. "Is Danel your son?" Even as the words hung in the air, she could see she had now completely exasperated her chaperone.

"No. He is the son of Batnoam's first wife. I am the second wife. Now be quiet. This is the matron's palace."

Ashirat took her hand and led her past the large wooden door into a courtyard with paved walks, a central fountain, and stone benches. Stone pictures decorated the walls, the individual stones sparkling in the sunlight. Hana stared. A man holding a spear was standing on a wooden platform above a circle with short wood poles radiating out from a smaller circle, exactly like the wooden circle she had spotted outside the city. The man on the platform held ropes attached to a four-legged animal much larger than a goat or a sheep. The animal had a thick, arching neck and a long body. Its tail was held aloft, and long wavy hair flew back from between ears that stood up in points on the top of its head. Following behind the man were women carrying baskets on their heads. Their robes fell over their arms, their breasts exposed.

Ashirat pulled on Hana's hand, moving her to the center of the chamber. "Stop staring. It's a chariot pulled by a horse," she said. "Do you know nothing? The man is hunting, and the women are gathering food from the fields. It tells the story of the abundance we have here in Sidon." Ashirat then turned, spoke to a woman who had entered, and turned to Hana. "Get ready. The matron is coming."

Her words sounded like a warning. The matron must be formidable. The only thing her mother had said to her about the matron was, "Give the feather to the matron. It will prove you are from Andulat. They don't have our blue bird in their city. Do whatever she tells you to do."

Hana pulled the pouch from under her tunic, opened the top and extracted the blue feather. Blood pounded in her temples. Her throat constricted.

She smoothed the feather between her fingers, comforted somewhat by the softness of the down close to the hollow shaft at the bottom, and felt homesickness rise up over her head. Her stomach clenched into a fist. She held the feather in front of her like a weapon and watched a woman approach her.

❧❧❧

The matron was not as old as Osnot, but she was much older than Ashirat or Hana's mother. She was tall, thin, and wore her scarf over her shoulders only. Her tunic fell all the way to the ground. A long gold chain hung around her neck and was fastened together by a flower woven from the same filaments. Sun glinted off the chain as the matron walked toward them. Her hair was short and white. Even her eyebrows were white. Hana found this fascinating. She had never seen white eyebrows before.

Osnot, she recalled, had no eyebrows. The matron's skin was the color of one of her mother's fired clay pots. Hana looked up into the woman's dark brown eyes and waited.

"Ah, I see," the matron murmured, staring at Hana's face, "she is the image of the goddess, Ashtart, exactly as in the priest's dream." She turned to address Ashirat. "You have done well. You may go. Thank you for bringing her to us. I will let the queen know that you have performed your duty. It will go well for you. You and your husband will be rewarded."

Ashirat bent from the waist and smiled. Hana started to say, "Thank you," but Ashirat held up her hand to indicate she shouldn't speak and walked out of the courtyard without looking back.

"Now, what shall we do with you?" the matron said, more to herself than to Hana.

Hana held up the feather. "I was told I'm supposed to see the queen."

The matron brushed away the feather, and Hana's statement, using the same gesture Danel used. "You are clearly not from here, girl. Speak only when you are spoken to."

"But you did speak to me. You said ..."

The matron reached over and put her hand over Hana's mouth. Her hand was soft and smelled like a tangy herb.

"I was speaking to myself. Be quiet or I will have your mouth stitched shut."

Hana pressed her lips together and said nothing more. She didn't think that someone who smelled that good could do something harmful to someone else, but, as the matron, and Ashirat, had pointed out, she didn't know their ways. They entered the matron's abode and Hana found herself surrounded by more pictures on the walls and floor. In addition to the piles of furs around the small fountain, there were also low wooden stools where one could sit and admire the walls. Two rooms opened from this first one. She wondered where the cooking pit was located. The matron must prepare her food elsewhere, or someone else prepared it for her. Hana wanted to ask how many people lived in this huge place, but she held her tongue for fear the matron would keep her word.

"How did you come to have these blue eyes?" the matron asked. "Did someone perform magic on you?"

Hana tore her gaze away from the pictures on the walls. "May I speak?"

The matron nodded, her annoyance apparent in the way her lips turned down.

"I was born like this."

"Did your mother tell you how it happened? Was she ill during the time she carried you in her body?"

Hana loved telling this story. "My mother said that one afternoon as she napped, Andulat's blue bird flew over her and dropped a feather onto her round belly. The feather, she says, was a blessing. That's why my eyes are blue."

"Do you believe this nonsense?"

Hana lifted one shoulder and looked away, a gesture whose value she had learned from watching Ashirat. Was it safe to tell this woman she believed her mother? She remembered what Danel said about the beliefs of these people and decided it was not. "I like the story," she said instead.

The matron muttered to herself and turned away from Hana to confer with a small man wearing a tall red hat who had emerged from a darkened corridor off the chamber. The point of his hat was balanced by the point of his beard, jutting out several inches from his chin. He had entered from yet another doorway in the side of the building. The matron and the man whispered to each other in a language Hana didn't understand.

Turning back to Hana, the matron put her hand on the girl's shoulder. She led Hana through one of the doorways to another room. This one was similarly comfortable with many places to recline. She could still hear the pleasant burble of the fountain from the front room. The walls showed a picture of men on a boat. Hana was grateful to the fisherman, Abirami, for giving her the word. The boat was in the sea, as shown by the wavy lines of blue stones beneath it. At the front of the boat was the head of the creature she had seen pulling the chariot on the courtyard walls picture. It was a confusing image. *Were these people so monstrous that they cut off the heads of animals to mount at the front of their boats?*

"Show me the bird on your body," the matron ordered, breaking into Hana's reverie.

Hana lowered the top of her tunic. While the matron was examining her, she realized that she must look like the women in the mosaic with their breasts exposed to anyone's view.

"Wait here," the matron said. "Don't move." She gripped Hana's shoulders and shoved her down onto one of the stools. "I'm going to ask the queen what she wants to do with you. You are younger than we expected, too young to sacrifice your virginity to Ashtart. Your hips are too narrow yet for childbearing. Although," she looked away from Hana at something seen only on the inside of her head, "you might not be too young for the right marriage, one that would be propitious for the king's house and would call down blessings from the goddess."

Hana went back to examining the picture on the walls. High waves, she understood now, were depicted by curved lines of blue stones going up on an incline and then curving back in the other direction. A second curve in a lighter blue beneath the first and then smaller curves in white stones falling away from the big ones completed the waves. The two curves seemed perfect to her. That was exactly right, she thought. The maker had captured her own experience of what waves of water looked like. The longer she stared at the mosaic, mesmerized, the more she knew this was what she wanted to do with her life: to make images using stones.

In spite of the matron's warning, Hana stood up to walk over to the wall and touch the stones. The matron, still standing in the arched doorway watching Hana, cleared her throat, put a finger to her lips, and held her hand out as if she could touch Hana from that distance and make her sit. Hana sat. The matron stood like that for a few seconds and then swept out of the chamber.

How long does the matron think that particular bit of magic will last? Everyone seemed to have the power to control her. Was it possible that the matron had the right to make her mate with someone she didn't know, that her parents had not approved? She couldn't have that kind of authority, to ignore Hana's wishes and the wishes of her clan. Could she? The elders of her clan had given her over to these people of Sidon to do with what they want-

ed. Not for the first time since facing the steep drop off
the cliff, her stomach quaked with fear. She had no
choice now.

Without understanding what they were discussing,
Hana had once overheard her mother whispering to her
father about ritual sacrifices of girls' virginity. That's
what the matron was talking about. "Our tribe should not
abide such evil ceremonies any more than we engage in
the sacrificial murder of our children," Hana's mother
said. Her father agreed. She had never seen her clan conduct those practices.

Hana tossed her head to shake these thoughts away,
got up from the seat in spite of the matron's admonition,
and examined the wall. She touched the stones to see
how they were set to create the effect of the whole picture. Close to the wall, the larger picture disappeared into
the many small stones it took to create the image. Hana
stroked the stones with her fingertips and marveled at
how the maker knew what color stone to put where.
Standing close enough to the wall to place the stones,
how did he know what effect he was creating from a distance? This kind of work must take many seasons of
practice, she concluded.

Regardless of what the matron and the queen had in
mind, she had to learn how to make these magical pictures. In her absorption with the stones, she completely
forgot that she had disobeyed an order. It would not be
the last time she failed to comply with someone's commands.

Chapter 13

Alissa opened one eye and saw her father, Aden Labat, in the doorway of her hospital room. He must have been watching her sleep. The baby was asleep on her chest, skin to skin, their breathing almost synchronized. She inhaled the infant's smell and her body relaxed. She had done it. They were safe.

She watched her father's emotions play across his face. His eyes brimmed. "I've never seen anything as beautiful as this," he said, his voice a whisper. "Except your mother, when each of you girls was born." He smiled, remembering.

Alissa stared at him and smiled. "Oh, Dad, I thought for a moment I was dreaming. How did you get here? Where is Elena? What's happening out there?"

He walked over to the bed, stroked Alissa's cheek with the back of his hand, and pulled a strand of long, black hair off her forehead. "Running mostly." He smiled. "Can I hold her?" He reached out his arms. Alissa nodded.

Aden scooped up the baby in the way his wife had first instructed him thirty-three years before when Elena was born. "Wow. It all just comes back." He looked into the child's face. She opened her eyes and stared at him. "Hannah," he said, as if the baby's name was a prayer. "Hannah," as if her name was a magical incantation.

Alissa watched as delight, joy, the entire chemical cascade of instant bonding, whatever anyone wanted to call it, enveloped him. He seemed happy to be swept away by it.

Aden grinned at the baby. "Hello there. I've waited a long time to see you. I'm so glad you're here." He kissed the baby on both cheeks and forehead and looked up at Alissa. "She changes everything." His face glowed.

Alissa, wincing, altered her position in the bed. "Is Carl here?"

"He's on his way. Are you in pain?"

She grimaced. "I think they call it discomfort around here. They gave me Tylenol."

"Do you think you could walk, like more than ten feet? Elena said we should get off this island. The attack is still going on. Those bastards are everywhere. There's a rumor the Marines are coming. I hope it's true."

Alissa looked at her father holding her baby. She understood he would never do anything to harm either of them. "How about we steal a wheelchair?" she suggested, with the impish gleam in her eye that her father loved.

"I think that could be arranged."

Her husband, Carl, swept into the room as if he had a cape. He put his backpack down on a chair, rushed to the bed, and pulled Alissa into an embrace. Everything rustled in the dramatic breeze Carl made. Alissa knew, without her father having ever told her, that he hated Carl's entrances, and the haircut that made him look like Beavis on a bad day. But Alissa loved the man, and so her father made his peace with Carl's theatrical behavior and said nothing.

Carl kissed his wife and made the right noises about his darlings and how brave and beautiful, but he didn't go over to his father-in-law and take the baby. Alissa could see that this instant failure had been added to her father's long list of Carl's demerits.

The truth was, Aden thought no man would ever be good enough for his daughters. She and Elena had laughed over this small flaw in their father's character many times. Most suitors didn't survive his scrutiny. Aden Labat was not a man with whom one trifled. At six-foot-five and sixty years old, he walked with the sure ease of an athlete accustomed to running marathons. He was fast, lithe, and could tango like a lover on fire despite the deep wrinkles around his eyes. But none of that mattered now. What mattered is that her father would keep her child safe. And that was all that mattered.

"Take Hannah," Aden said, putting the baby in Carl's arms, adjusting his son-in-law's hand so that it supported the infant's head, and guiding him to the closest chair so he wouldn't drop the baby if he fainted from the responsibility. "I'm going to find a wheelchair that can go a few miles. We're going to get Alissa and the baby out of Manhattan."

"We'll need baby supplies, Dad," Alissa called out after him as he left the room.

"On it," he called back.

She heard Aden greet the duty nurse. "He'll get what we need," Alissa reassured her husband. "He always does." She remembered being gathered into her father's strong arms at her mother's funeral, the comfort of his scratchy suit jacket against her cheek. The clean smell of his neck, how he shepherded them through their everyday routines until they could breathe again.

Years later, when Elena was overseas in Iraq and Afghanistan, their father Skyped with her every day she wasn't out on a mission. He told Alissa he could tell from the blasted look on Elena's face what had been going on at her end of the connection. He explained that Elena was the one standing in the fire. If she wanted to tell him what happened, she would. Otherwise, his job was simply to listen.

He listened, he said, to help Elena sharpen her own understanding of what she saw and heard. And then he told her he loved her. Every time, without fail. He told her to be safe and come home. Those were instructions. He knew his daughter. That's what she needed to hear.

He didn't worry about her as much as he did Elena. Alissa didn't chafe at that fact. She was a corporate lawyer. What trouble could she get into? Except today. Today she was in big trouble, and here he was. She could read his face as easily as he read Elena's. He was worried about the future, immediate and distant. It was time for her to step up and help him with that.

Aden rolled a wheelchair and a hospital-branded tote bag back into the room. "The very nice Nurse Burns says this is everything you need." He held up a few of the items. "Infant diapers, wipes, Tylenol."

He looked at Alissa's face and grinned. "She said the baby is fine. Just let her nurse on demand. You might be a little weak. You have to stay hydrated and eat small meals several times a day. We have to watch you for hemorrhage and fever."

The nurse came into the room and removed Alissa's IV line. Aden thanked her. Carl, sitting on the edge of Alissa's bed, bent his head down and kissed his baby gently on the forehead. His face looked as if he had seen God. Alissa put her hand on her husband's cheek.

Aden waited until Alissa looked up. "All right, guys, let's get this show on the road." He glanced at his daughter in the hospital gown. "Lis, you should put on some clothes that are good for travel."

Alissa frowned. "Dad, my office clothes are wrecked. I had the nurse throw them out. I thought I'd have a day for Carl to bring me clothes."

Carl jumped up. "Oh, I did bring you clothes, and the baby pack you had sitting by the front door. I'm sorry it took so long to get here. I had to walk. Traffic is a grid-locked mess and the subway system is down."

He walked over to the visitor's chair, awkwardly un-zipped his backpack with one hand, the baby firmly lodged in the crook of his other arm as if he was already an old hand, and pulled out Alissa's clothes, including a new nursing bra with the tag still dangling from it, hold-ing each item up as he retrieved it from the bag and put it on the bed.

Alissa smiled. "You're a genius, sweetheart."

Carl grinned, basking in his wife's approval. He lift-ed and kissed each of his baby daughter's hands.

Alissa carefully moved her legs off the bed, wincing from time to time, stood up, gathered up her clothes and went into the bathroom. From the bathroom they heard her say, "Oh, God, peeing for the first time without my belly on my knees. Priceless."

Aden and Carl stared at each other, ready to square off into their usual opposing stances and then realized there could be only one leader for this expedition. They were both smart enough to know there wasn't time to struggle about it. The whole point was to protect Alissa and the baby.

"We're going to get off this island," Aden said. "There's no knowing how long this attack will go on or what's next on the bastards' agenda. We need to get her somewhere that it's not happening, and then drive up to my house in the Catskills where Elena can find us later."

His voice was quiet, but his full intention was clear. He would brook no interference from anyone, including Carl.

"I've got no quarrel with that, Aden," Carl said. "Just, given what she's already been through today, we need to find a way to make it as easy as possible on her."

Aden nodded. "Totally agree. Here's what I'm thinking."

Aden laid out his plan to walk to the East River four blocks from the hospital, find the nearest marina, commandeer a boat, or bribe someone to take them, and then steer west across the Hudson River toward the Jersey side.

Carl's face grew pale then red then returned to its normal color. "Totally with you," Carl said, gritting his teeth for a moment. "There'll probably be police boat patrols and Coast Guard but whatever it takes to keep our girls safe, I'm up for."

Aden considered his son-in-law for a moment, then grasped Carl's shoulder. "Good for you, son."

When Alissa emerged from the bathroom in her street clothes, she found her father and husband clasped in a hug with the baby snuggled between them. They were obviously ready to travel.

"Ahem," she said, grinning from ear to ear.

The men separated, each attempting to surreptitiously wipe tears off his cheeks.

❧❧❧

Ten blocks from the hospital on Twenty-Third Street at the New York Skyports Marina on the East River, Aden found a small craft owner who'd cruised over to New York for the day and discovered himself in the middle of the largest terrorist attack in the world. The boat was besieged by people clamoring for him to take them across. Alissa sat holding the baby in the wheelchair, well back from the edge of the dock. Carl gripped the chair handles.

"I can only take six passengers," the boat owner shouted. "I'm going back to my home slip in Hoboken, nowhere else." He seemed to be selecting who he would save by some mystical process understood only by him.

Hoboken, New Jersey on the other side of the Statue of Liberty along the western shore of the Hudson River seemed like the right destination to Aden. He broke through the crowd and tapped the boat owner's shoulder. "I have cash," he said into the man's ear. "Two hundred bucks now and you get two hundred more from the near-est ATM machine when we land."

"You got it, man. Climb aboard."

Aden looked up and signaled to Carl to come ahead. The boat owner pushed people aside to allow them room on the pier to get to the boat. "I can still fit two more pay-ing adults," he declared to the crowd. "Cash only."

Aden and Alissa counted their blessings. *Sometimes greed works in your favor,* Alissa thought. She wondered briefly how Elena would have dealt with this man then shrugged. *Whatever it takes to keep Hannah safe.*

"Hey, honey," the boat-owner called to his red-headed wife standing on the Astro-turfed floating pier, one hand shading her eyes, the other on her hip, looking at enough black smoke billowing from mid-town up into the sky to make shade. "We'll eat good tonight!" He waved greenbacks in the air. His strawberry-blonde hair-piece flapped in the breeze like a flag. She giggled and waved her bejeweled hand at him. Her many bangles clanged together on her wrist.

Alissa worried briefly that her father would punch the man in the face, throw him off the pier, and take off across the river in the guy's boat. She hoped no one would end up in the water as the crowd surged around the boat. *Nothing to be gained*, she sent him telepathically. He seemed to relax a bit.

Carl carried Alissa and the baby onto the boat and set them gently down in a chair bolted to the floor in the middle of the boat. He pulled a life jacket from the pile on the floor under the built-in fiberglass seat and helped Alissa slip her arms into it. "Not the best, babe," he whispered to her as he knotted the lifejacket ties, "but something." Alissa nodded, exhaustion having caught up with her, and kissed his cheek.

Aden folded the wheelchair, which they would need again, and carried it and the bag of baby supplies onto the boat. Two men in suits leaped on board and took the remaining bench seats. The boat owner's wife finally deigned to board, expertly hoisting herself over the side onto the deck of the forty-footer without any help from her husband. She looked over at Alissa, Carl, and Aden. Her nose crinkled as if to say she could smell immigrant on them.

Whatever product she was using to spike up her hair glistened in the sunlight. This was her good deed for the year. Alissa guessed the woman now had bragging rights and a story to tell her bridge group about what she was doing the day terrorists brought New York to its knees.

Then the woman noticed the baby. "Oh my God, Gordon, get going, get going, there's a brand-new baby on board! Who knows what's going to happen next around here?"

Gordon, as if goosed by his wife's command, threw off the dock lines, jumped onto the boat, started the motor, and eased out of the marina into the East River. The crowd on the pier swarmed toward the next boat motoring toward them.

Out on the river, they saw hundreds of small boats heading west to New Jersey or north up the Hudson River. Either there were a lot of twisted tourists looking for a novel way to watch the chaos or people were finding their way off the island of Manhattan without walking. It didn't appear anyone was being stopped by either the police or Coast Guard. In fact, they didn't see any patrol boats at all. Maybe there were just too many private boats on the water at one time to manage. It bothered Alissa that the terrorists could get off the island in exactly the same way, but she couldn't think about that now.

Watching the Manhattan shoreline recede, Aden said, not for the first time, "You should all move to upstate New York near me, away from cities, danger, and early death." He sounded like a prophet, but she couldn't ignore him this time. Aden had always wanted them to live in a compound near him. It was time to reconsider the idea. Maybe the world had become too dangerous a place for them to be away from him.

Aden called Elena on her cell phone to let her know they were off the island. That annoying busy sound blatted from his phone before an automated voice told him "All lines are busy at this time. Please try your call again later."

No surprise there. Alissa and Aden looked back toward the city, black smoke still rising from mid-town, and prayed Elena was safe.

Chapter 14

HANA

Queen Peri reclined on a long bench covered in lion pelts raised on a platform above everyone else in the room. The queen's tunic, of a material much softer than Hana's, hung in gentle folds over her body, looped under her left arm, over her right shoulder, and was clasped together by a gold ornament that shimmered in the light flooding through arched windows. A thin gold rope entwined in her hair dangled brightly colored stones.

A braid of gold served as a girdle, and two more lengths were wrapped around her arms. Her dark, lustrous hair was piled on her head in a mass of curls, from which some strands escaped and trailed down her back and the sides of her face. Her skin was a lustrous copper color and her huge black eyes, accented by dark kohl lines, slanted upwards, away from her long, thin nose. She looked like a large bird of prey, a hawk or an eagle, ready to pounce. Hana shuddered involuntarily. She wished Danel was with her to explain what was happening.

Peri rose and walked around the room, her long arms raising and lowering like wings as if she were dancing to some music Hana couldn't hear, stepping first on her toes and then her heel. Hana wondered how long the queen had practiced this way of moving until it became natural. She instantly disliked the woman, which, she gathered from watching the matron's face respond to every twitch of the queen's body, was probably a very bad idea.

The queen's large eyes opened and regarded the girl and then closed slowly, as if she intended Hana to perform whatever had been asked in the time it took her to blink. She walked back to her seat. "Bring her to me," she commanded the matron. "Let me see the bird."

The matron took Hana by the shoulders, pushed her toward the platform near the queen's seat, pulled the back of Hana's tunic down to her waist and turned her back to the queen so that she could examine the blue mark on Hana's back below her shoulder blade. Hana felt the queen's warm fingertips on her skin, tracing the shape of the bird.

"Is this some kind of trick?" the queen asked the matron in a low whisper. "This, and the blue eyes?"

"It appears she was born like this."

"Let me see her eyes again."

The matron turned Hana back toward the queen, who leaned over, cupped Hana's chin in her hand, and tipped her face up for closer scrutiny. Peri peered into Hana's eyes as if to discern the mechanism that made them blue.

"Hmmm." The queen unfolded herself from her seat and paced back and forth in the chamber for what seemed like an entire season to Hana. She looked around the room at the people who normally attended the queen. They were all staring at her.

"Remove her tunic," the queen commanded. "I want to see if anything else is unusual about this child. Does she have a tail or feathers sticking out from her buttocks, perhaps?"

Her courtiers giggled at the queen's cleverness.

"She is a child, not yet bleeding," the matron objected, her voice low and meant only for the queen's ears.
"This is not appropriate in front of men." She waved her
hand in the direction of the male courtiers in the room.

The queen held up her hand to stop the matron's
voice. "Do as I command," she said, so quietly that Hana
could barely hear her, but then she flicked her hand and
all the men scurried from the room.

The matron removed Hana's tunic. Hana felt warm
air flow around her legs and up her back. A breeze lifted
the short curly hairs on her neck. Telling herself not to
quiver from fear, Hana kept her eyes on the mosaic on
the wall ahead of her. *Was this what her mother sent her
to this city for—to be unclothed in front of strangers and
examined?* She longed for her quiet village and the splash
of fish in the river.

She willed her mind to focus on the image on the
wall—a beautiful woman reclining on the back of a lion.
Men with spears walked before and after her. Her breasts
were also exposed. Hana took a deep, shuddering breath.
Perhaps bearing one's breasts is the custom in this place.
Perhaps what she was experiencing was normal in Sidon,
a ritual performed for the queen with all newcomers. But
she couldn't bring herself to believe that was true.

The queen walked around Hana in a circle as if
changing her perspective would reveal something more
about the girl. She touched Hana's shoulder and ran her
finger down her arm. "No feathers, I see." The female
courtiers tittered appreciatively. "Clearly she is not ready
for mating. She has no hips. We cannot even sacrifice her
virginity to Ashtart. The goddess would object."

The matron's head was bowed as she reminded the
queen of the arrangement with the Andulat elders. "It was
the king who demanded she be sent here, my queen. You

recall the priest's dream—that Zimrida would mate with the goddess made flesh and all the world's riches would be his forever." She looked up briefly to observe the effect of her words on the queen, who barely blinked her eyes in recognition of the agreement.

"You recall it was the king's courier who saw the girl when the gold crown was forged in Andulat. He brought stories of her beauty back to the court. The king demanded that she be sent to him after she had passed twelve harvests, or he would demolish their village and kill every member of their tribe."

The queen waved her hand and turned her face away as if to say that was enough information.

The matron offered one more fact. "The girl's family is connected to your royal house by third cousins. They begged for your intervention and offer her into your service in return."

Hana looked over at the matron. This was the reason she'd been sent to Sidon, to save her village from the king's wrath. Her parents must have thought their brave girl could bear whatever happened in order to protect the others in her tribe. Pride flamed through her, matching in strength her yearning to be home. She straightened her shoulders. She would be brave.

Peri waved her hand, as if her magic would cause the king to forget his desire for the girl. "I can manage the king. There are other girls who can be the king's concubines. We will wait a year. She will serve me, do whatever I ask her to do, and at the end of the year she will make the sacrifice to Ashtart with my son, the prince. She will be his first wife—a high enough honor for any tribe."

Peri broke off for a few breaths and glared at the matron as if to deter any comment or objection before it was voiced. "Whatever children come from that union will be in the king's house. Her first son will rise to become king. That should fulfill the king's demand. Keep her veiled. The king must not see her before then or I will not be able to keep my promise." The queen nodded her head, as if in agreement with her own decree. All her handmaidens nodded their heads in unison.

Peri held up her hand. "We will have done well by her family and those blue eyes will become part of our bloodline. What more can they ask?" She clapped her hands and the matron wrapped the tunic around Hana, took the girl's arm, and walked her out of the chamber.

"Where are we going?" Hana, deeply relieved to be out of the queen's chamber, stared around her in each of the rooms through which they walked. She realized they could go from the matron's chambers to the queen's without ever going outside into the sunlight.

"You'll stay with me during this year," the matron said. "It will be safer. You'll go to the queen's chamber when she calls for you." She let go of Hana's arm and looked at her. "The future that the queen has set for you is an honor. You must live up to that honor."

"If I was sent for by the king, how is it that I went to see the queen?"

The matron looked at Hana sideways. "You ask too many questions." Seeing that Hana would ask again if she didn't respond, the matron sighed. "I am of your tribe, child, as are the couple who brought you to me. The queen is the first child of our grandmother's sister's daughter. We hoped that taking you to the queen would prevent the worst from happening. The queen has her own reasons for keeping you away from the king."

"The worst? And what reasons?"

The matron shook her head. "You know nothing of our ways, apparently." She sighed. "Being a concubine, one of a hundred girls the king uses for his pleasure, is not to be your fate. You will one day be a queen your-self." She turned Hana to face her. "As for your other question, perhaps it works to your advantage that you are so naïve. The queen does not like the idea of being usurped by a foreigner as the king's favorite."

Hana shrugged and changed the subject, which made her head hurt. "Is that gold you all wear?" Hana touched the chain at the matron's neck, her curiosity overwhelming her sense of danger. "I've never seen it as thin as thread or braided in this way."

The matron laughed. "That's what you want to know? You are young. Yes, we make many ornaments from gold. Would you like one? It befits your status to have an arm piece."

"Yes, I would. I like the way it glows in the light." Hana again admired the walls in the matron's chamber, walking from wall to wall, trailing her fingers on the stones. "And I would like to learn how to do this," she pointed to the wall.

"What?" The matron looked mystified. "What do you want to learn?"

"To make those images from stones you have on all the walls," Hana said. "I want to do that."

"Mosaics? You want to make mosaics?" The matron clapped her hands and the man with the pointed hat appeared. "That is for artisans. Working with stones will ruin your hands. You are to be a queen someday, the wife of a prince who will become king, the mother of a king, the gods willing."

Hana felt uneasy at the idea of being a wife and queen. She looked away from the matron to hide her distress. She wanted to be home with her parents. A sudden fever of sadness shot through her. *Will I never see Andulat again?*

The matron talked to the man, then nodded her head and he disappeared through the archway. "I've ordered food and drink for you. I can't stay here all day and entertain you. I have other important duties. You should eat and nap. It's not possible to know when the queen will want you or for what. If someone from the queen comes to get you, go immediately. Don't dawdle or ask questions."

She took Hana's chin in her hand and looked into her eyes. "Be good." The matron started to walk briskly out of the room and then turned back. "Stay away from all men, especially the king." She left and came back into the room almost instantly. "And don't talk to anyone."

Hana wondered what the matron thought of as good behavior. She suspected that she was not capable of obeying her order. And why should she be afraid of all men?

ℰↄℰↄ

Hana stood behind Queen Peri and waved a large fan made of feathers. The chamber was shaded, the only light coming in through the archway to the courtyard. Thick white stone walls seemed to keep the midday heat at bay. Tables were laden with dates, figs, grapes and other fruit. Jugs of water stood ready if the queen needed to be refreshed. Hana wondered how many birds had been sacrificed to make the five fans that kept a constant breeze flowing over the queen's skin at the height of the day's heat.

At least there was some physical exertion to this task. Sometimes she was expected to sit at the queen's feet from sunrise to sunset doing nothing but looking at her adoringly or peeling the skin off grapes. She entertained herself by watching the sunlight glint off her own gold arm piece, making the serpent at the top wink at her. Sometimes she had to pin Peri's hair into its many curls, wrap the long gold chains around her, or clean the queen's fingernails. She thanked the wise lord that she only had to hand perfumed oils and soaps to others for the queen's bath or pass food to the woman who placed the morsel in the queen's mouth. Perhaps Peri didn't trust her. She was smart not to do so. The queen, as far as Hana was concerned, was more useless than straw left on the threshing floor after the grain was winnowed from the chaff.

Four other young women attended the queen as well. Being a servant rankled Hana—everyone was equal in her village—but these girls seemed to consider their servitude an honor. The other girls did their best to ignore her, as if she was invisible to them or beneath their dignity to acknowledge because she had not been born in Sidon. If she spoke to one of them, the girl didn't answer. None of them spoke to her unless the queen required it. For several full moons, their attitude toward Hana made her heart sore and something sharp stick in her throat. Soon she realized they were as useless as the queen and the sting of their rejection of her eased.

The queen, dressed in a sheer shift, reclined on a bed during the hottest part of the day, eating grapes from time to time, sipping water with lemon and honey. A hand-maiden massaged her belly and thighs with sweet smelling oil. Soft notes plucked by a musician came from a stringed instrument unfamiliar to Hana. She concentrated on the music but found that her mind wandered. Even the mosaics on the walls and floor were not enough to keep her interest anymore.

She had already figured out that some of the pieces were clay, some were stones like lapis lazuli or the black onyx of the rock at the mountain apex near her home, some were from shell fragments, and others were glass. Close up, a small section of the pieces depicted no understandable image. They were simply rows or circles of stones in gradations of colors. But surprisingly, when she stepped back, away from the wall, the whole picture made sense. There was so much she didn't know. How did the artisans know what tiny pieces to put where to form the image of a face or hand? What made them sure that when someone stood at a certain distance from the wall, the image would spring to life?

She kept herself busy with these speculations because she couldn't bear to speak the compliments to the queen that came to others so easily. She became tongue-tied and swallowed her words. When the queen demanded she say something, Hana felt like an animal startled in the hills by human intrusion, staring and silent. The handmaidens, however, had an inexhaustible supply of sweet words and kept up a day-long litany of flattery.

"Your thighs are round mountains shrouded in mist at dawn."

"Your breasts are the sun rising above the sea."

"Your feet step upon the earth as lightly as a breeze," intoned the third.

"Your womb holds the fruit of the world," warbled the fourth, not to be outdone by the others.

What did all that mean? Hana's thoughts about the queen were not pleasant and she knew not to speak the words out loud. *Your mouth has the sting of a viper.* She could never say that to the queen. *You use people for your own pleasure. You have the temper of an unloved child.* Hana understood without being admonished by the matron that this singularly selfish woman who was the king's wife controlled her life.

But how could this be her life, fanning a self-indulgent woman who did nothing but mate with the king, bear children, and order people around? As far as Hana could tell, the queen didn't even care for her own children. Nurses, teachers, and other servants were entrusted with that task.

The queen rehearsed a dance every day, saying she was planning to perform for the king that evening. She danced until her skin was shiny from sweat. While she danced, the queen's gaze turned inward, watching a story unfold in her own imagination. Her courtiers heaped praise on her. Even Hana conceded that Peri's dancing was pleasant to watch. The constant movement of the queen's arms was hypnotic, drawing Hana down into a well of longing. She shook off the trance and reminded herself that what she longed for was freedom.

This could not be the life her parents planned for her. Perhaps they had not understood the agreement their clan made with the queen's emissaries. Was she meant to dance for a king, lie on a bed, and have people feed her? The idea made her entire body revolt. She longed to be free, to wander outside in the open air, to watch the sea, to observe people in the marketplace. She had to find a way to convince the queen to let her study how to make stone pictures. She had no idea how to bring up the subject.

"Blue Girl," the queen said, pointing her finger at Hana as if she had read her thoughts. "Come here."

Hana put down the fan and walked to the side of the queen's bed. "Yes, queen." She knelt on the stone floor, her face lowered, more to hide her annoyance than to show respect for the monarch.

"I see you are miserable enough," Peri said. "That's good. The life of a woman is misery, even for a woman like me. It's important to learn that early."

Hana shook her head. Before she could stop herself, she said, "My mother wasn't miserable. She sang all the time and told stories. She laughed and hugged me."

Peri slapped her. Her long nails raked Hana's cheek.

Hana put her hand on her cheek. She had gone this far, why not go a little farther. The queen already disliked her. "I would be less miserable, if you would let me learn how to make the mosaics."

She raised her eyes and watched the queen's face. She had become as much of an expert on Peri's moods as the matron. She heard the other girls suck in their breath and then exhale in unison.

Peri studied Hana. "You are a simpleton," she said. "You have been here for three full moons and you have learned nothing." She flipped her fingers outward. "Yes, yes, go study chopping rocks into tiny pieces. Go ahead. Ruin your hands, wreck your posture, stain your neck and face from the rays of the sun. Thicken your arms. Get out of my sight. In a year, after your fingers are worn, and your knees are sore from kneeling on stone, we'll see how obedient you can be. Perhaps then you will be ready."

She waved her hand and a man appeared who took Hana away.

Chapter 15

ELENA

Standing with a rebuilt squad in City Hall Park in the square adjacent to the Brooklyn Bridge pedestrian walkway on the Manhattan side, within sight of the great swoops of steel cables above thousands of civilians trudging across the bridge, Elena quickly assessed the team she had to work with. Her people were tired and disheartened. All of them had lost colleagues today. Each of them had survived a near miss. Their city was being dismantled right in front of them, but they were also determined and running on grit. Grit would have to be enough.

No one was protesting in the square in front of City Hall today. No newly married couples posed for a friend's photograph of entwined, be-ringed fingers. No old people sat on benches beneath flowering tulip trees, resting from their afternoon walks before going on to the market. Throngs of people pushed toward the bridge, eager to get off the island, away from the terrorists. A wall of people crushed against police who were trying to keep some kind of order. They could no more hold back the ocean than control the chaos of people fleeing the city.

From where Elena stood, police officers were dwindling islands in a swirling sea of pedestrians.

"Here's the deal," Elena said to her squad, her voice as hard as the granite towers of the Brooklyn Bridge. "We're going to reconnoiter the bridge, both levels, end to end, red flag any and all explosives and anyone or anything else that looks suspicious, call for the bomb squad to dismantle any bombs when we find them, and move civilians off the walkway as fast as possible. The bridge is only a mile long. We can do this."

Her team nodded. There were no dissenters. This was their job right now. People's lives depended on them.

"Cantor, Fuller, you work with the officers already in place to stop any more pedestrians from starting across the bridge. Set up horses, turn people back into the square to wait. Calm them down if you can. You'll have your hands full doing that. Call for backup if you need it."

Mary Cantor flashed Elena a look of relief, but Elena didn't think she'd thank her later. This crowd of ordinary working people was an angry mob in the making. Even if nothing exploded on the bridge, people could get hurt as everyone tried to escape the city.

"The rest of you, we'll split into four groups of two. North, south," she pointed with two fingers at each pair, "east, west. Reconnoiter the entire bridge a.s.a.p. Stay on comms. If you see anything, say it."

Elena looked around her at the men and women who were going to run into trouble with her. Her admiration for them was at its highest. "If there's a bomb, get everyone the hell off the bridge, including you." She looked each officer in the eyes. "Stay alive," she ordered.

The squad quickly assembled their equipment and jogged to the bridge in a wedge, an attempt to clear pe-

destrians from their path that didn't work. Swarming
people were as intractable as stampeding cows. Competing news helicopters whirled overhead, violating the
FAA order to be the first network to get the story. What
was a fine compared to this footage?

Shouting into the crowd was useless. The squad re-
sorted to using their hands and arms, yelling, "Clear a
path, clear a path." Pedestrians surged around them instead of falling back. Elena wondered about Americans.
They always ran toward a disaster instead of away from
it. Their curiosity was stronger than their sense of self-
preservation.

There must have been two-thousand people on the
bridge at that moment and another several thousand
pressing in from the Park Row and Center Street entrance
near City Hall on the Manhattan side. Elena estimated
another five thousand surged toward the walkway entrance from all streets that led to it.

A regular walking commuter could cross the bridge
in less than twenty-five minutes but this was butt-to-belly
traffic with slower walkers clinging to the outside railings, terrified they were going to be accidentally pushed
over by aggressive New Yorkers determined to get to the
other side faster than anyone else. No one was observing
bike lane niceties. Bikers were wisely walking their bikes
across, but bike wheels and pedals made unexpected obstacles for an unwary pedestrian to trip over. She spotted
a few scooters and one Segway, its rider impatiently
waving his arms in the air. No one paid any attention to
him.

The arched granite towers of the bridge, standing
276 feet above the river since the structure was completed in 1883, were prime bomb targets. Footers anchoring
the four gigantic cables that held the spans in place were

another good target. The squad would start at these points and move out from there.

She called dispatch to get a message to the Chief. "We need more bodies at the Brooklyn Bridge for pedestrian control!" she yelled into her device. "Where's the bomb squad?"

Within seconds of beginning their search, the team located two bombs seated next to the cable footers with enough plastic explosives to take out the entire bridge and anything on it. They were rigged for timed detonation, with only minutes to go. This was a job for the experts. Elena looked up from her crouch to see the bomb squad vehicles at the beginning of the bridge on the Manhattan side. Eight men in heavy protective gear were running toward her. She rose and waved her arms above her head.

"Bomb! Clear the bridge as fast as you can!" she yelled into her comms device. She scanned the buildings on the Brooklyn side. There was no knowing where the bomber was or whether there was a secondary device that allowed someone to detonate the bomb remotely. Maybe the bomber was waiting for maximum effect, when more emergency responders were on the scene, to blow the bridge.

Her team fanned out across the bridge trying to turn back pedestrians who were entering from Manhattan and hurry people who might successfully run to the Brooklyn side. Elena had no idea if they would succeed before the bombs blew. People panicked. It was inevitable. They ran in all directions. They screamed. Some sank to their knees and wept. Some jumped over the railings into the river. Foolish people stopped to open abandoned brief cases and riffle through them. Above them, two rescue helicopters circled, making the sound of all hell breaking loose.

"We're dropping lines for your team to get off the bridge," Elena heard through her earpiece.

Crazy idea. "The lines will get tangled in the cables!" she shouted. Seconds later, civilians charged the lines, athletic young men climbing up the backs of others to get a higher grip. One helicopter swung away, ten people dangling from the rope. A man at the bottom of the rope fell off as his feet tangled with the bridge's cables.

Elena spotted a four-year-old girl in a little orange Mets jacket standing alone, screaming for her mommy. She ran to the child, scooped her up, and raced for the next dropped line snaking east toward Brooklyn in the middle of the walkway. Knocking to the ground two adults who were fighting for the same handhold, Elena tied the child onto the line and said, "Go!" into her mouthpiece. The helicopter rose and hoisted the child away.

"Evacuate!" Elena called to her team and jumped up onto the railing. Her fastest exit was the water below. A mile to the east, she saw the Manhattan Bridge blow. She leaped out away from the railing as the bombs blew the historic Brooklyn Bridge into a million pieces of shrapnel.

ୡୠୡ

Drums sounded in her ears, insistent, steady, pounding out a regular beat. Elena opened her eyes to shake off the thrumming, rolled to her side, and groaned. She rocked back to her previous position. *Every bone in my body must be broken.* Slowly, she raised one arm to begin assessing her condition, touching her head, face, neck, shoulders, chest. *My clothes are wet. At least this arm works.* She looked at her hand. *Blood.* She was injured.

She felt her head again, wincing in pain. Something had made a good size gash in it. Her head throbbed.

That drumming was the sound of her heart. If that was the case, drumming was good. It meant she was alive. She moved her other arm and winced. *That arm might be broken.* She lifted her head off the gritty surface she was lying on. Dizziness struck. She put her head back down, closed her eyes, and waited for the whirling sensation to pass. *I'm not completely paralyzed.* Sending instructions to her feet to move, she watched the toes of her shoes move back and forth. She listened again. Helicopters. Road traffic. Some shushing sound. Small motors. Horns. A long blat in the distance.

Where am I? I must have been in the river. I washed up here. She pushed herself to a sitting position to survey her legs and surroundings. *No bones sticking out of my clothing. That's lucky.* The river, crowded with boats of all sizes, flowed near her. A line of Coast Guard cutters blockaded every marina she could see from her prone position. *You're on the east side of the river. Why are all the cutters over there?*

Brooklyn. The name floated up to her consciousness. It was a relief to have a name for the place. *How on earth did I get here?* She looked to either side of her. The shoreline of the East River where she sat was littered with trash. She wasn't the largest object that had washed up here. A three-legged piano lay on its side ten feet from her, a refrigerator not far from that. *Remnants of Hurricane Sandy?* She rolled onto her hands and knees, wincing again, and stood, feeling for injuries in her legs and ankles. Her left leg was weak. It wouldn't bear a lot of walking. *Something torn, maybe a ligament.*

She looked down at her wet clothing. The insignia on her bulletproof vest indicated she was a police officer. *Lieutenant Elena Labat.* She felt no ownership of the name. *I'm glad I can read.* District and precinct designations were printed on her ID. That information meant nothing either. She patted herself, examined all her pockets. There was some electronic device on her shoulder she didn't know how to use. She had a knife, a gun, a flashlight, a taser. She was a dangerous person.

She looked for an easy path up to the road away from the small beach. A narrow dirt path that led to the sidewalk indicated many other feet had scrambled up and down that slope. If she used her hands, she could make it up the slope on all fours. She needed to get to a hospital. She took another look around on the dirt. Maybe there were more clues about who she was.

Spotting the edge of something round and half hidden in the silt near the toe of her shoe, she reached down. Dizziness engulfed her. She put her hands on her knees, winced from the pain and stood up, careful not to press on the broken arm. She looked at the object again without reaching for it. *It's a coin. Worn. Might be gold. Maybe it's my lucky day.* Carefully, she squatted, dug her fingers into the dirt around the coin and pulled it up. Thin and worn, the gold coin bore the image of a woman leaning forward with her right hand outstretched. *Looks old, very old. Maybe it's worth something.* She turned the coin over. Marks in a language she didn't know. She put the coin in her vest pocket and moved gingerly to climb up to the street above.

Hundreds of pedestrians moved in all directions. They looked afraid, angry, some almost as lost as she— eyes wide, mouths open, panting, cheeks tear-streaked. She backed to the wall of a shop building and waited to get her bearings, watching the traffic. She recognized nothing. Street names on the signs meant nothing to her. She had no map in her head of where she was.

Only way to get there is to start walking. Where have I heard that before? She moved away from the building and started off down one street, turned the corner to go right, and turned again at the next corner to go left. *I'll never get anywhere this way.* The dizziness had not abated, her arm felt like an arrow was stuck in it, her leg ached and felt weaker with each step. It wouldn't work for long. She saw ambulances blaring past her and walked in the direction they were headed. *A hospital, that's what I need.*

Two blocks away Brooklyn General Hospital loomed large, brick, solid looking. She hobbled into the Emergency entrance. The emergency room was crowded to the gills. All seats in the waiting area were taken. Gurneys of people lined the adjacent corridors. People sat or lay on the floor. She inhaled the sharp metallic smell of blood. At the intake counter, she stood at an open window until the harried woman on the other side of the counter, whose hair appeared to have been pulled in every direction, looked up at her.

The woman looked at her badge, wet clothing, blood oozing down the side of her face. "Yes, Lieutenant?"

"I'm injured."

"You and thousands of other people." The intake clerk was exhausted, all compassion drained away in the first five hours of this horrifying day.

Elena nodded, the movement making pain spike through her skull. She understood the woman. "I think I have a broken arm, maybe a concussion. I'm dizzy, nauseous. My balance is bad. Something is wrong with my leg."

"Yes. You're slurring your words. Sign in here." The woman pointed to a piece of paper on which fifty names were written ahead of hers. Many pages of names preceded the one on which she wrote the name on her badge.

"Take the clipboard, fill out the forms. We'll get to you as soon as we can. Sorry. Best we can do."

"Thank you." Elena accepted the clipboard, turned and looked around at the emergency waiting room. *No place to sit.* She hoped the triage team periodically swept through the waiting area to assess who needed help soonest. Noticing an empty spot on the floor in the hallway that led to examining rooms, she sat down and leaned against the wall.

The first entry on the form required her name. Her hand hovered above the space. She wrote in L-T. *My handwriting is really terrible.* She looked over the rest of the form. Except for being able to fill in E. Labat in the name spaces, she knew none of the other answers: not where she lived, next of kin, who to contact, much less her social security number, insurance information, or prior illnesses. She started to feel in her pockets for additional identification, something with her home address on it, something that might seem familiar. Her head clanged with a fierce headache and she was very sleepy. It would be a long time until they got to her. *Have to take severest cases first.* Her mind drifted. She remembered the coin she'd found in the dirt. *How old was it? So odd, the woman on the coin looked familiar.*

Elena fell into the dark, down comforter of a dream. She saw herself and Alissa, barefoot and in pajamas following their father as he pushed their mother's wheelchair with its giant rubber tires over the dune and down to the beach.

Stars were there ahead of them, glimmering above the night sea. They relished this rare treat—being allowed out on the beach after baths. The girls looked at each other, grinned as if they had gotten away with something, and held hands, marveling at how their skin reflected moonlight.

For days on end, their mother sat in the wheelchair under an umbrella at the water's edge, watching them play. They brought her their treasures, their exclamations, their salted faces to be kissed. Tonight, they all settled onto the sand on one blanket, their mother holding them close, and looked out at the dark ocean as the moon rose in its exquisite arc over the earth. Wind tangled their wet, black hair into curls and the steady breath of the ocean lulled them toward sleep.

One arm wrapped around each daughter, she spoke softly. "Long, long ago..." The girls leaned their heads against her and closed their eyes. This was how all bedtime stories began. Their bodies, trained from infancy, relaxed against her, listening half to her heartbeat and half to the sound of her voice. She was home and all of love to them. Their father sat behind them on the sand, his long arms embracing them all. He was their safe place, their touchstone.

"Before countries had lines around them on maps, before the shape of the world was known, before mirrors, cars, or even flush toilets—" The girls giggled. She continued, "—there were people who were as beautiful as you, as curious, inventive, and brave. One of those smart, brave people was a girl named Hana."

Alissa looked up. "Just like you, Mom."

"Yes, like me. Hana lived in a verdant valley between mountains near the sea in a land we now call Lebanon. Her tribe was called the Phoenicians and they founded their first city eight-thousand years ago."

Elena looked at her mother's face where all answers resided. "Mom, I can't figure out when that was from the number."

Her mother smiled. "I have trouble imagining it also. It was before stories were written on paper, when people were just learning to farm. They invented ways to make pots out of clay, weave cloth, and melt rocks of ore into metal objects. They made purple dye from spiny shells. They built boats out of cedar trees and sailed across the Mediterranean Sea, trading goods on all the islands and as far as Egypt and Spain. And here is the best part."

The girls raised their little chins to demonstrate attentiveness.

"They invented a way to write down the sounds of words."

Elena put on her serious face. "They were smart, then."

Her mother kissed the top of Elena's head. "Yes. They were smart."

"What tribe are we, Mom?" Alissa asked.

"We're from Hana's tribe."

"Wow," the girls exclaimed in unison. "Are we very old, then?" Alissa asked.

She laughed softly. "You are the age you are."

Elena snuggled closer and patted her mother's arm. "Are you very old, then, Mommy?"

"Oh, sweetie, I do feel as if I'm thousands of years old." She leaned her head back against her husband's chest.

Elena turned, looked at her father's face, and saw that under his smile he was sad. He tousled her hair. "Listen to your mother's story."

"So, Hana was a beautiful girl with blue eyes, the only person anyone had ever seen with blue eyes in all the cities and villages of Phoenicia, all across Canaan, and even in all of the islands in the sea."

"We have blue eyes!" the girls exclaimed together.

"Yes, you do. But then it was very rare. Perhaps there was another girl in Jordan with blue eyes and one in Anatolia, but Hana is the blue girl in our story. Because of her blue eyes, Hana was sent by her village as a gift to the king of Sidon." She sighed and leaned back against her husband. "Aden, I'm tiring fast. We need to go back."

Aden leaped up and rolled over the chair. The girls stood up in front of their mother. "Just tell us the end, Mommy, tell us how the story comes out."

Their mother reached out and touched their faces. Her voice trembled. "The end of the story is the beginning. Hana is the first of our line, the beginning of our family. Her courage is part of who you are, and you are part of a story that is thousands of years old..." She stopped speaking and slipped onto her side, unable to hold herself erect.

Aden scooped up his wife and gently placed her in the chair. He shook out the blanket and covered her with it. "Girls go ahead of me back to the house. Remember to brush off your feet before you go inside."

Alissa took Elena's hand and they ran ahead, stopping on the porch to slap at their feet. They ran through the house to their bedroom and leaped into twin beds where they waited under light covers for their father to come in and kiss them goodnight.

Lulled by the surf's constant breath, they waited until they fell asleep. Elena woke to red and blue lights streaming through the window, chasing across the bedroom walls, and her father wailing, "No, no, no, no..."

Her dream stopped and Elena felt herself drifting away on her father's sorrow.

Six hours later when the triage nurse got to her, Elena was lying on the floor unconscious. The form was empty except for the words "Lt Elena Labat." Hospital staff were so overwhelmed that day, they didn't report to the police that a Lieutenant Labat had walked into the hospital's emergency room. Then they were too busy trying to revive her. After she was stable, they were simply trying to keep her alive.

Chapter 16

HANA

The matron looked sternly at Hana when she returned to her chamber after having been chastised by the queen and banished from her sight, but she said nothing. Hana ate her evening meal of dates, cheese, a few morsels of goat meat, some bread, and an apple and went to sleep as soon as it was dark. In the morning, at first light, she was awakened by a hand roughly shaking her shoulder. For a happy moment, she thought it was Danel. Sleep passed and she realized it was a boy she didn't know.

"Come on, come on," the boy said, shaking her again, "we'll be late. The master will be angry. He'll set us the worst tasks."

"What could be worse than waving a fan over the queen," Hana said without thinking.

The boy looked at her through narrowed eyes. "Sweeping, mixing grout, sorting stones, you'll hate those jobs in a few days. When the back of your skinny, pale neck is burnt red from the sun, you'll wish you were back inside a shaded chamber swept by the breeze from a fan."

"How do you know where I've been?"

"Everyone knows who you are."

Hana put on her sandals, twisted her hair into a braid she fixed on the top of her head with a comb, put on her veil and followed the boy out into the street. The sky was a piercing blue. Light from the early morning sun struck the white surfaces of stone walls into gold. She breathed deeply. Briny air filled her lungs. It was early in the morning, before rosy rays of the sun spilled over the horizon. So few people were about, she could hear the susurrus of the sea ceaselessly sweeping the shore. She held her arms out and twirled, just once to let her joy make a small disturbance in the air. The boy looked at her in disbelief.

"No wonder they didn't keep you at the palace," he said. "You're crazy."

Hana laughed. "Maybe I am, but I am also happy to be in the open air, to be free. Walk on. I'll follow you."

They walked through the city and out one of the many gates, and then another few hundred paces to a large compound of many buildings outside the city walls. Clouds in the blue sky were stained pink from the sunrise. The sound of the sea was much stronger here. *I must find a way to go out on a boat.*

Hana's fantasies were interrupted by a gruff old man in a half tunic, white beard, and weathered face barking at her, "Girl, get over here and start sorting these stones."

"I don't know how," she said, thinking he would tell her or show her.

He pointed to a huge clay crock almost as tall as she was that was filled to the brim with stones made of every material, some as tiny as her smallest fingernail, some smaller. "You will figure it out."

It would take years to sort these, she thought, and she would be no closer to understanding how to make the mosaics than she was now. She lifted her head to protest.

The boy who'd brought her to the compound, whispered, "Silly girl, be quiet. This is an honor."

Hana opened her mouth. He put his hand over it. "You want to be an artisan? You do the menial work first. Be glad he didn't set you to sweeping. Sort the pieces by color. Each stone belongs to a family of colors but within that family are small differences in shade and tone. First sort them into color families, then make smaller groups of stones within each family that match each other exactly."

Hana shook her head. *Why wasn't she allowed to talk in this city?* "What's your name," she whispered.

"Abibaal," the boy said, "son of the first priest." He grinned at her. His black eyes twinkled. "You see, I'm in the same situation as you. I want to be something different from what my parents have chosen for me. They think they are punishing me," his voice sank to the barest whisper, "meanwhile, I love doing this."

"Now who's crazy," she said to him, but she was beginning to understand. She had yearned to do something. This would be doing something. Life was perhaps too easy in this city. People did not have to catch and prepare their own food. They did not have to build their own shelters or make their clothes. They had too much time on their hands and invented other, peculiar things to do with it.

"See over there the long boards with the bronze bowls set into them?" Abibaal took Hana by the shoulders and pointed her in the right direction. "Each bowl is for a different color stone. From there, the artisan will choose what he needs to make the design he has planned. When you are done sorting, put the stones into those bowls, one color in each bowl."

Hana walked over to the boards with inset bowls. It would take an entire cycle of the moon to sort that huge pot of stones into these fifteen bowls. But all she had was time. She might as well start. She looked around for something to scoop the stones out of the crock and found a small bronze bowl like the ones her father made to keep water cool. Its brown surface was scuffed and dented. She held it up and Abibaal nodded. She dipped the cup into the crock and with her other hand pushed the small pieces into the cup. Stones crunched and pinged against the metal. She looked around for a place to spread out the stones and saw that Abibaal was pointing to an area on the ground. This was going to be tiring but she would sleep well tonight.

Before the sun had reached the center of the sky, she had discovered that clay pieces could be several different colors, from red to brown to beige. Stone pieces could be white, or a variety of blues and greens, yellow, pink, red and black. Small purple pieces must have come from shells. Tiny glass pieces were white, green, and a thrilling green blue.

She had only skimmed the surface of the crock. Sweat poured down her face. She unveiled herself before she had sorted through the stones scooped up by the first bowl, wrapping her scarf around her waist.

By the time shorter shadows fell behind the columns that marked the entrance to the workshop, Abibaal brought her a piece of soft cloth to wrap around her head to catch the sweat and cover her neck. The skin on her arms had reddened to the color of clay her mother collected near the river. She looked around the workshop and hoped that there would be a rest period, food, and a shady place to sit.

She now had fifteen piles of stones on the ground. It was hard work, but her industry made her happy.

෭෨෭෩

Within six full moons, Hana was deemed an expert at sorting colors. Her fingertips were rubbed raw, the skin always peeling. Sometimes her fingers bled. Her legs had gotten strong from squatting and standing repeatedly all day. Her skin was nut brown. Red highlights shone in her hair.

The master moved her on to assisting the artisan who was laying out his idea for a large mosaic that would glorify the queen. "Since you're such a favorite of hers," the master said, "you should work on this project." He winked. Everyone seemed to know the story of her failure to please the queen.

A wall sized rectangle made of panels formed by hammering slender, grooved, cedar planks together lay on a set of tables. Abibaal had already created the base of the mosaic and the artist had sketched in charcoal an image of Peri dancing on the back of a lion. One of her legs was elevated and bent at the knee. Her arms were extended in those graceful gestures Hana had seen her perform. One of her breasts was exposed.

"To symbolize her great fecundity, which is a gift from the goddess," the artisan explained when Hana asked why the queen was revealed that way. A large feather adorned Peri's hair.

"That," Abibaal said, pointing to the feather, "will be a sparkling blue. It represents you." He poked her ribs with his finger.

Hana squealed and jumped away from him. "Me? Why does the feather represent me?"

"You are the blue bird that has flown into our city. The queen has captured you and made you her ornament. Everyone knows this."

Hana turned her face away from him. She would not give him the satisfaction of knowing the sorrow this explanation caused her. How could her mother have let her come to a foreign city to be someone's ornament? It made no sense to her. There had to be something else she was supposed to do.

"To work, to work," called the master. "We have no time to waste in silly chatter. This mosaic is due to be installed in the queen's house within two more full moons." He clapped his hands, and everyone set to work.

ട⁄ൟട⁄ൟ

Four full moons passed before the queen's mosaic was installed in the main palace chamber where she danced for the king. Abibaal told Hana that the queen had expressed her delight with the mosaic by kissing the master on his lips.

"That work was worth more than a kiss," Hana muttered.

"You understand nothing," Abibaal said. "The master will now get work from everyone who wants to curry favor with the queen. Her kiss is worth more than a pouch of gold and lapis lazuli. He will be busy for the rest of his days."

He was right. She would never understand the subtleties of how people behaved, but she had discovered that tiny stone pieces of four different colors made a person's eye magically appear from a distance of ten feet from the mosaic. Working close to the project, her eyes searching for the right color in the pots, she was lost in the puzzle of what stone went next to what, the gradients of color, that a single, tiny white stone in a circle of brown and black could make an eye look alive and alert, staring back at her from across the room.

Even when the artisan was cross and made her take apart everything she had done and start over she was content to be there in the workshop. She was not happy, not as she'd been as a child with freedom to roam anywhere in the small world she had considered to be everything, but she was satisfied with the work and appreciative of the people who taught her and worked with her. They weren't quite like the family she missed so deeply, or even like being with Danel—who she knew briefly but, for no reason she could understand, missed as much as she missed her own parents—but they were makers, people among whom she belonged, and that was enough for now.

Living with the matron was awkward. Every morning when Hana rose, readying herself for work, eating fruit, a bit of dried fish, and drinking ample quantities of water, she listened to the matron muttering, "Foolish girl, indulging herself in work that makes no difference to anyone, ruining her skin, destroying her own future."

In what was now their morning ritual, the matron took Hana by the arms and shook her slightly, held her wrists, turned her hands over and looked at her fingers. "Look at your hands, your fingertips! Look, look! Raw, completely shredded. Who will want you to touch them?" The matron ran her hands over Hana's arms and shoulders, along her calves. "Muscles, you have muscles like a man. Your neck is red. What man will want you in his bed?"

Hana suppressed the urge to say, "A brave one, I hope." She remembered most of the matron's questions were not to be answered. She did not want her mouth stitched.

"Well, go, go on then, ruin your life with hard labor. I have tried to talk you out of this."

Hana ran out of the chamber, out of the courtyard, into the street and caught up to Abibaal. He handed her a clean band of cloth for her forehead. She wrapped her head and followed him out of the city to the workshop compound.

Hana had learned not to travel through the city on her own, even to the market. It was safer to be with a male companion or the matron's servant. On her only lone foray to the market on an afternoon when the master was delivering work to one of his patrons, a strange man dressed in many colors sidled up next to her and put his arm around her shoulder. "Come now, little one," he whispered in her ear, "Your parents have left you all alone in the world. You should not be alone. It is too dangerous for someone as beautiful as you. Come with me."

She walked away from him and he grabbed her arm, pulling her toward an alleyway. "You'll like it with me. Many other girls are there. You will have friends." He clenched her other arm.

Hana pulled away from him as hard as she could, she squirmed, kicked him in the shins, and flung her arms in all directions. She looked around, desperate for help. She was in sight of the glass blower's booth. "Help me, please," she shouted.

The man in the many-colored robe ignored her struggle to get away from him. He wrapped his arm around her waist and hoisted her off the ground. She wrenched herself away and fell on the ground. He reached out a long arm and seized her by the hair, pulling her back toward him. "I have been looking for a girl like you, young, lovely, lithe, with spirit." He took her wrist, raised her arm, and whipped her around with his other hand, nodding to himself. "Do you know how to dance? Yes, yes, you would do perfectly. Come with me now and I will give you everything your heart desires."

Hana snatched her wrist away from his grasp. "My heart desires that you leave me alone at once!"

The glass blower had put down his long pipe. He wiped the sweat off his face with a cloth, stepped out of his kiosk, and glowered at the man. "Don't you know who she is?" He put his fists on his hips. "This girl is destined for the prince. You'd best keep your hands off her if you want to keep all your body parts. Go back to whatever land you came from."

Hana ran over to the glass blower and stood behind him close enough to smell his sweat. Fear fluttered in her chest like a trapped bird.

The man scurried off, looking back at her only once as if she were his homeland and he was leaving it forever. Hana thought she recognized her own homesickness on his face.

She waited next to the glassblower for a while, recovering from her feeling of helplessness and fear, examining the beautiful bowls, plates, glasses and beads in his stall. Periodically, she looked around the market, hoping to make sure the tall man had disappeared and wasn't waiting for her to walk home alone to attack her again. Her hand rested on a slender gold wire with a single blue bead. The bead glowed, reminding her of the sky and the sea.

"Do you want the bead, Blue Girl?"

Hana startled at being called Blue Girl by a stranger, attempted to say no, thank you, but the longing in her eyes must have been clear.

"Take it. It's yours. Wear it always. I will be able to tell everyone I saved the Blue Girl from that Canaanite and his harem."

She flashed the glassblower a smile he might value even more than his story, took the necklace and tied it around her neck. Her fingers found the glass bead and rolled it gently against her chest. "It feels perfect."

"It looks perfect," he said. "It goes with your eyes. Wear it always. Give it to your own daughter someday and she will give it to her daughter, and on and on. It will last forever. Now run home and don't come out alone again. There are many men who would steal you away for their own profit, or just lock you up so they can look at you every day."

Hana gave him another look of thanks and ran off, her ebbing panic turning to joy when she touched the bead on her chest. When she returned to her chamber, she took off the beautiful bead and put it in her leather pouch. It would be safer there, and no one would ask her questions about where and how she obtained it.

One evening on her walk home with Abibaal from the workshop, Hana spotted the fisherman who sneaked her through a crevasse in the wall into the city so many moons ago. She ran after him, crying, "Abirami, Abirami!" The old man seemed to have become deaf. He didn't stop or turn around and disappeared into the crowd walking toward the market. *Perhaps it wasn't him.* When she saw the old man, the thought suddenly occurred to her that he might be able to help her to escape. He knew about boats.

It wasn't the first time she'd thought about escaping from Sidon, but no plan ever made it past being assaulted by a strange man once she left the safety of the matron's house or the workshop. Her term at the workshop would soon be ended and then the queen would force her to marry the prince. She couldn't bear the idea of becoming his wife and enduring the lifetime of endless boredom such an arrangement promised. But if she ran away, where would she go and how would she survive? She needed someone to help her.

On their way home from the workshop, her clothes grimy with sand, rock dust, and sweat, she convinced

Abibaal to stop at Ashirat's house. She entered the courtyard while Abibaal waited at the doorway. Danel's father
was sitting on a bench talking earnestly to Ashirat. They
looked up when Hana entered the courtyard but didn't
smile.

"I—I wanted to find out if you knew anything about
Danel, if he's all right." Hana's words tumbled over each
other, a rockslide of sounds. "I've been worried about
him."

Ashirat looked her over with disdain. "Whatever
have you been doing, girl? I left you in the best of hands
and now you look like a disheveled, filthy laborer. And
you stink." She turned her face away to show her disgust.

"I'm learning how to make mosaics." Hana took in
the disbelief on their faces. "It's really wonderful. I love
doing it. The queen let me."

Still, they looked as if they could not believe their
eyes. "You should get a new tunic, child," Batnoam said.
"You look like an orphan. It is dangerous to appear lower
than your caste."

Hana nodded, crestfallen. *These people focus on the
wrong things.* "Have you heard from Danel?"

"Danel has been abducted, as we thought," Ashirat
said in her clipped voice. "The horse people traded him
to the sea people who carried him to the island of Alashiya and traded him to those barbarians. It took the entire
time you have been here in Sidon, an entire cycle of late
sowing and early reaping before their message reached
us. His new captors are demanding you as his ransom.
We've been to see the queen. It is useless."

"How do his captors know I even exist?"

Ashirat shrugged and Batnoam put his face in his
hands.

"The queen said no?"

"The queen said my son isn't worth one of your fingers." Batnoam's eyes glittered with unshed tears.

Hana looked around the courtyard, at the trees, the circle of stones on which she stood, at the simple mosaic on the wall. She was furious about the queen's assertion that Danel was worth nothing. *Could she leave this city? Without question.* "I'll go," she said. "I'll be Danel's ransom so he can come home to you. But you will have to keep it secret, so the matron and queen don't stop you."

Ashirat's face twisted. "You have no idea what you're talking about. It's impossible."

Batnoam stood, walked to Hana, and took her by the shoulders. "You understand, child, this is too dangerous, even if you survived the voyage. His abductors will most certainly sell you or do whatever they want with you. There's no guarantee that after they have you, they will let Danel go, if he is even still alive."

She looked up into his kind eyes. "Danel traded his life for mine. He didn't tell the horse people I was hiding in the grass. I will risk mine for him."

"Batnoam, we cannot accept this." Ashirat voice was quiet but stern. "The queen will expel us from the city, and we will spend our lives wandering in exile without even knowing if this girl has made the exchange. Or she'll have us killed. What the barbarians have demanded is inhuman. We cannot trade Hana for Danel. This is complete foolishness!"

Batnoam held up his hand. "The queen doesn't need to know we're involved. The palace will think Hana has been abducted. It's common enough. I will devise a plan. Go back to the matron's house now, Hana. I will come for you when I'm ready."

Hana looked back once and saw Ashirat berating her husband, her finger a drawn dagger. Batnoam was not looking at Ashirat but at Hana. His face beamed his gratitude to her.

Chapter 17

ELENA

Commissioner Mfume paced behind his desk. "Find Labat," he said into the phone. "Am I not speaking English?"
He waited for a moment then cut off the speaker on the other end. "I don't care what you've already done. She's either alive or dead. She didn't disappear into the ether. She was last seen standing on the Brooklyn Bridge before the blast. She would have been dumped into the river. The current would have pulled her somewhere. Have you scoured every inch of the riverbed on both sides of the East River?"

He listened for a half-second, scowling. "Did you call every goddamn hospital in the entire city, all the boroughs?" He paused for the blather on the other end of the phone and yelled, "I don't care about privacy laws. We're the police, goddamn it, we just saved the city from a bunch of madmen. Get them to tell you if she's a patient there or not. One way or another, her body is in the city and I want her found. Call me when you have her."

He hung up and walked to the window thinking when they found Elena Labat, he was going to give her a medal. Her intelligent assessment of the next wave in the

attack saved thousands of lives. Bomb squads were able
to find and disarm bombs planted on the George Wash-
ington and Williamsburg bridges and in the Holland and
Lincoln tunnels before they were triggered. Those bastards had certainly been way ahead of him. They had to
have been planning the attack for a year, maybe more. He
was relieved it was over and that the good guys had won.
But he had failed. The bad guys had killed hundreds of
civilians, the people he had sworn to protect, because he
didn't stop them soon enough. He would live with that
grief forever.

Mfume was due at the mayor's office for another ritual berating because quelling the attack had taken three
days. In the end, he was glad the Marines dropped in
from helicopters and stormed off Coast Guard cutters
from warships docked in the deep-water port, and damn
the politics, because he needed them to take back his city.
One-hundred-fifty terrorists were dead with the Marine's
help but Mfume knew there had been more bastards than
that. He had 385 dead civilians, more than 500 missing.
Walls of sorrow with photos and names of the missing
sprang up all over the city. He feared they would inevita-
bly become shrines to the dead.

The mayor let Mfume cool his heels in the reception
area, a sign to everyone that she was displeased. Mfume
didn't care. The mayor's bluster was theater. Somebody
had to be to blame. It might as well be him. When he was
finally shown into her office, the mayor didn't suggest he
sit. Instead, she started interrogating him without preamble. "When am I going to see your after-action report,
Commissioner?" The mayor used her sternest voice, the
one for putting down reporters at press conferences and
castigating cabinet members in front of their peers.

"We're assembling it now, ma'am." There was no
point in saying more.

"Can't I get what I want, what I need, when I want it?" The mayor fumed. Her perfect hairdo vibrated with her intensity. "I've got reporters nipping at my heels. The Governor is breathing down my neck. And then," she swept her arm in the direction of the window, "there are all those New Yorkers out there wanting to know what happened." She turned abruptly and stared at him. "In detail."

Mfume heard an echo of what he'd said to his own staff earlier. He ducked his head and suppressed a smile of recognition. "Yes, ma'am." He noticed she had removed all jewelry but her wedding ring and a black band she wore around her wrist. Her suit was black, her blouse white.

"And what are you doing about the missing officer? Her father is on the phone to me five times a day."

Mfume nodded. "I know Aden Labat. He's persistent. We're on it."

He didn't say that the loss of Lieutenant Elena Labat ate at him. He worried she'd been abducted, and they would receive a hideous tweet with a video showing her head being severed from her body. He imagined the image playing millions of times on electronic media across multiple platforms simultaneously. He tried to steel himself for this possibility, but he knew it would kill him if it happened.

An act like that could wreck the force, throw civilians into a panic, and make politicians eat each other's heads for breakfast on morning TV. Finding Elena's body, or better, finding her alive was critical to closure on this event for him

"Be on it faster." The mayor was nothing if not an expert at audible irony. She waved her hand in dismissal.

"Yes, ma'am."

Mfume walked through the mayor's outer office with his head up, as if he'd just received a commendation. Not until he got to the corridor outside the mayor's office, did he pull out his handkerchief and wipe the sweat off his forehead. He couldn't give two hoots about the damned after-action report, but he would find Elena Labat even if he had to do it himself.

Chapter 18

HANA

On a night with no moon, Batnoam shook Hana from sleep. She had no time to wonder how he had gotten into the matron's house past the guards. He allowed her a brief time to dress and make sure she had her few precious things—feather, dagger, scroll, bead necklace—before he whisked her out of the house. In the street, he put her in the back of a cart, piled rugs on top of her, and walked out of the city pulling the cart as if he were any ordinary merchant. He didn't have to tell her to be quiet.

The sound of the sea grew louder even though the cart rumbled over the unpaved path. Finally, movement stopped. She breathed easier with each rug that was removed until she was able to climb out of the cart and into the air. Nearby, the sea lapped the shore. The sky was full of stars. Some twenty feet out, a small boat bobbed on the tide. A sharp, briny wind cleansed her face. She could barely believe this was happening.

Batnoam leaned down so that he could see her face as he spoke. "This is dangerous, girl, more dangerous than anything you will ever do. You don't have to go. I will take you back and no one will ever know you wanted to leave."

Hana nodded. She had thought about this. *It is better to die free than be enslaved by the queen, or, even more horribly, be married to the prince.* She didn't say that to Batnoam, though. She wanted him to be sure she would find Danel and save him from his abductors. She wasn't being duplicitous. *I will find Danel.* She had made a pledge and would keep her word.

"How did you get me out of the matron's house without her knowing?"

"I paid the guard two gold coins."

Hana looked at him, taking in the seriousness in his face, the way his eyes held hers. "She'll know I'm missing at first light when she usually checks on me."

"You'll be far out to sea by then, with no trace of you. But you are worrying about the wrong things. I am telling you this is dangerous, and you can change your mind. You could drown in the sea if a huge storm overwhelms your boat. You could be killed outright by Danel's kidnappers. They are vicious. I'm told they have only one eye and great eagles are at their beck and call. They could sell you." Batnoam gripped her arms. "There are worse things than death," he said, his voice so low she could barely make out the words.

She had no idea what could be worse than death. She was already exiled from her home, separated forever from the people she loved. The ache of that separation was part of every breath. *What is left to grieve over?* "I want to do this. It's the right thing."

"How can someone so young and small know what's right?"

"Do you have to be old and large to know the truth?"

Batnoam laughed and quickly covered his mouth with his hand. Behind him, men boarded the boat. "This clear-sightedness must come with your eyes," he said. "The kidnappers have hidden Danel on an island across the sea, so our boatmen tell me, an island called Alashiya where they mine copper, a shiny ore your father must have melted down when he made bronze implements."

Hana nodded. "I know copper. We use bits of it sometimes in mosaics."

Batnoam shook his head and smiled briefly. "Listen. Enkomi is the name of the landing place on Alashiya where your boat will arrive. It is a three-day sail across open water. You won't be able to see land during the journey. I'm sending the fisherman who brought you into the city with you, for protection. He has already proved himself trustworthy."

Hana was relieved to discover that she would be with Abirami again, and then she shivered. It hadn't occurred to her that being on the sea meant that land disappeared. No matter where she had gone, she had always been on the land and could see its vastness if she stood at the top of a mountain. The land was everything in the world. How could it end? Not to be able to see the shore, at least, to see mountains from the distance where land met sea, seemed impossible. Batnoam must be wrong.

Abirami strode up to them and touched Batnoam on the shoulder. "The tide is right. There is a wind blowing to the west. We must go." He turned to Hana. "Hello, Blue Girl. I am glad to see you survived meeting the queen."

Hana wondered about the look on Abirami's face as he spoke. *Is that amusement?*

Batnoam wiped his face with his hand. "I have misgivings," he said to neither Hana nor Abirami but to the sky. He gripped Hana's shoulder, unsure whether to let her go. "Now I worry I will never see either you or my boy again." He started to say something else. Hana heard the words "ransom" and "barbarians" and then Batnoam pressed his lips together.

"I'll be safe. I'll bring Danel home to you." Hana put her hand on his arm in farewell and turned away from him. She walked into cool water that surged up across her legs, hips, and stomach. Perhaps she could be courageous simply by saying she was brave. That trick had worked before when she left her home alone and went down the face of a mountain. It would have to work now as well.

A man on the boat threw her a thick rope. "Wrap yourself in the rope and hold on," he called.

Hana thought of how Danel had secured her for the descent down the mountain's face. That seemed a life-time ago. She wrapped the rope twice around her body, tied a knot, held onto the lead with both hands, and called out, "Ready."

The man hoisted her onboard and she slipped out of the ropes, ran to the prow of the ship, and looked out across the sea. Now that she was onboard, she could see the boat was larger than it seemed from the shore. She had seen round holes in the sides of the boat as the man pulled her onboard. The center of the boat was lower than the platform along the sides. Three benches in the center supported six men who gripped long sticks that widened at the end. There were coils of rope and a pile of fabric. In one corner of the boat were huge clay pots with point-ed lids. She ran to examine them. One held water and in the three other pots were several kinds of foodstuffs.

There was no end to her questions about boats. As Hana ran from side to side, water drizzled from her clothes onto her legs. She was chilled but she didn't care. As far as she could see ahead, water undulated like thou-sands of black snakes in a cauldron. No moon lit a path across the water tonight. *How would they see where they were going?* She sucked in her breath. *What if this is a mistake?*

She ran to the side of the boat and watched Abirami climb up the rope, hand over hand, until he rolled over the side onto the deck. She waved to Batnoam the way she had waved to her mother. *I may never see him again.* That much she had learned. Journeys have uncertain futures, even if you know where you are going. Batnoam held his hand up in a salute, turned his back to the boat, and walked away back to the city.

"You must hide yourself, girl," Abirami said, as stern as the matron. "We don't want to distract the crew." He led her to a corner of the boat in the stern that was covered by a few planks of wood. "Crawl under there. Put this wrap over you. Come out only when I tell you. I will bring you food and water."

"But I want to see, to watch the water, to see the sun rise and set on the sea." She almost stamped her foot in exasperation.

Abirami shook his finger at her. "Not on this journey, not if you want to reach Alashiya alive. These men think I am your father and that we are going to Alashiya so that you can learn their weaving methods. They are traders, a rough group. It's best if you obey me and do nothing to make them think otherwise."

"Just one more question," she pleaded. "What are those holes in the side of the boat for? Won't the water get in through them? And what are those sticks with the wide ends the men are holding?"

"You are worse than a cat with a spindle of yarn," Abirami muttered. "The sticks are oars. The men use them to push the boat through the water when there is no breeze. They can also use the oars to steer, to make the boat go in the direction they want."

Hana sighed. *People always want me to be quiet and*

not ask any questions. Does that never stop? She pulled Abirami's wrap over her head and sat with her knees pulled up to her chin. "What if I have to…"

"I'll bring you a pot." He sat down on the planks above her, prepared himself for his vigil, and promptly fell asleep.

Hana listened to the steady wheeze of his snoring. The boat rocked as men called out instructions to each other to raise the sails. She huddled under Abirami's wrap and fell asleep as the boat moved steadily away from the shore and bore the sleeping girl out of Sidon onto a sea that sparkled as the rising sun painted it with every blue color light and water could conceive.

ဆာဆာ

Hana couldn't help herself. She had to see where they were going. *I must watch the sea in the daylight with the sun shining on it.* She stole out of her hiding place below the still-sleeping Abirami and walked over to the low rail nearby. Her blue scarf billowed out around her from the breeze. Men busy adjusting the sail paused to watch her. While she was sleeping, the boat had moved away from the land. Around her was a vast world of water, rolling and dipping. Batnoam was right. She could not see land in any direction.

She gazed at the many blues of the water, as brilliant as the stone in her mother's ring. A lighter vault of blue washed by drifts of white clouds was illumined by the sun above them. Even she could tell they were moving west.

But how could the men know they would arrive at land? For a few breaths she imagined they would sail endlessly across the water, never arriving anywhere. She would die on this boat. Breath caught in her throat. Fear made her legs weak. She clung to the rail with both hands, breathing rapidly.

"What are you doing, girl?" Abirami stood behind her. He wrestled her away from the rail and pushed her back toward the hiding place. "If you don't understand that you endanger yourself, think of what these men will do to me when they want to have their way with you? You must conceal yourself." He put his hands on his hips and glared at her.

Hana dropped to her knees and crawled back under the bench. She poked her head out. "I'm sorry, Abirami. I couldn't help it. I had to see for myself what the open sea was like." She pulled her head and legs in and put his wrap over her. "And I'm really very hungry."

"I'll find us some food. Don't move."

Abirami talked to the men in a language she didn't understand. He came back carrying two bronze bowls containing cooked grain, fruit, and fish. With her fingers, she broke off a piece of the fish and gingerly put it against her tongue. It was salty but not in a bad way. She put the morsel in her mouth and chewed. The fish was tangy. She followed it with an orange slice. Then she scooped up some the grain onto her fingers and ate it. It had been soaked in lemon juice and olive oil. "Not bad, Abirami. This food will be quite all right for three days." She smiled at him. "Thank you."

"You have food on your chin." He sighed, reached over and wiped her chin with the edge of his tunic. But he smiled, made himself comfortable on the bench, and ate his portion.

They quickly developed a routine. Abirami released her from her hiding place every so often as the sun and then the moon made its track across the sky so that she could stretch her legs, take in as much of the view as she could, and relieve herself. That night, the thinnest sliver of a moon hung high in a night sky filled with stars. Hana stared at the horizon a long time, her hands gripping the rail as the boat slipped through the water.

"It looks like a dream," she whispered. "How do they know where they're going, Abirami?"

"The stars tell them how to steer."

"But stars don't speak."

Abirami grumbled low in his throat. "The man who steers knows what to look for in the night sky, the same way you know where you are in the city because the matron's house is here," he pointed to one side, "and the artisan's compound is here," he pointed to the opposite side, "and here is the market."

Hana thought she detected amusement in his voice. "I think I understand."

"You know you don't want to go to the queen's house, which is there," he pointed to the large pots on the other side of the deck, "so you steer yourself away from it and toward the artisan's compound."

Oddly, his explanation made sense to Hana, but how did Abirami know she had been learning mosaics at the artisan's compound? *Were there no secrets in Sidon?* When she curled up under the bench to sleep for the night, she said, "Thank you for being my friend, Abirami." Even in the dark, she could see the creases on the old man's face ease into a smile.

In three days, as Batnoam had said, they made landfall in Enkomi, the name all the men shouted as the boat moved toward the rocky, white shore of an island. Hana crawled out of her hiding space to see what the commotion was about. In the distance she could see a white-capped mountain range with a forest spilling from its lower hills to a grassy plain. Closer to the shore, palm, date, and eucalyptus trees ruffled in the mild breeze, but mostly this cove seemed to be sandy hills littered with white rocks and some scrub grass.

Pillars of white rock jutted up from the sea on their approach to the cove. *It must be dangerous to arrive by boat at night,* she thought. The men sailed the boat as close to the rocky shore as possible, then dropped the sail, and rowed for a while. When she could see white sand beneath the water, five men jumped over the side to pull the boat by ropes closer to the beach. They waded through the clear blue water to greet a man standing in front of a thatched hut. Several smaller boats, like turtles hiding from enemies, were turned hull-side up along the shore.

Some distance away, a small village of ten dwellings bustled with women sitting on the ground making baskets or preparing food. Children ran between mud-brick dwellings with flat roofs. Hana felt a pang of homesickness. Beyond that village, as far as Hana could see from the boat, there were no other people or villages. Her heart banged in her chest. Batnoam was right. Danel was being held captive in a desolate land. *How would she find him?*

Hana and Abirami stayed on the boat as the crew took on more water and food. Soon, they were back on the sea, but now they stayed close enough to the shore that they could see the island on their right as they sailed. Their goal was Kty, a new city almost the size of Sidon, Abirami told her. They would arrive there before dark. Hana waited in her hidey hole under the bench. Suddenly she heard loud pounding of men's feet running across the deck. They were shouting. She understood none of the words. Abirami yelled and cursed them in several languages. She saw the legs of many men in front of him, struggling with him. She watched his feet rise up off the deck.

Abirami's feet beat the air like wings but hit nothing.

The man who held him must be very tall, she thought. Within seconds, she heard a yell, a splash, and then a brawny arm reached under the bench and pulled her out.

"Now, Blue Girl, we will see what all the trouble is about," declared a man who smelled so bad Hana turned her face away. He caught her face with one grubby hand and forced her to look at him. "Open your eyes," he demanded.

Hana looked straight into his face. The man gasped and let go of her. He stumbled backward then turned and talked to the other men in their own language. They seemed to be arguing.

"What have you done with Abirami?" Hana yelled at him, her hands clenched into fists, her body vibrating with fury. "Where is he?"

"If you run to the other side of the boat, you can wave to him as we sail away." The men laughed as if this was the funniest joke they had ever heard.

Hana ran across the boat and searched frantically for Abirami in the waves. She could see nothing. She ran to the bow, then to the stern. She screamed her friend's name, "Abirami! Abirami!" There was no answer but the slapping of the waves against the wood. She put her hands on her head and turned in circles. Her only friend in the world was gone.

"Don't worry, girl, we're not going to drown you. You are worth your weight in gold," called out the man who had confronted her, "and more again in lapis lazuli. We have plans for you. And if those plans don't work out, I may just keep you for myself." He barked with laughter at his own cleverness. "I think I would like to have children with magic eyes like those."

Hana couldn't speak. Fear closed her throat. She could barely gasp. Now that she looked closely at this man, Hana realized he looked nothing like the men of

Sidon or from her own village. His nose was longer than her father's, his brow and cheekbones were more prominent than Batnoam's and his chin was gigantic. He was taller than anyone she had ever seen, and his very height terrified her.

What had Abirami called the men? Were they Sumerians, Assyrians, Hittites? Those names meant nothing to her. Until she came to Sidon, she hadn't known that people were from different tribes or that their features varied greatly from her own. But it wasn't *how* this man looked that frightened her; it was how he was looking *at* her that made her quake. *This is what fish feel like when they are caught.* He gripped her by the arms again and dragged her to the mast.

"You'll not get away from us by following your friend into the sea." He lashed her to the pole and tested the restraints by inserting his finger beneath the rope that bound her midriff and pulling on it. "I know about you Phoenicians and I'm not taking any chances you will pull one of your magic tricks." Satisfied that she was securely tied, he ran his finger along her cheek and lower lip. "You are nearly ripe. It's a shame I won't get to taste you." He walked away from her, yelling orders at the other men.

Hana spit out the taste of his finger. *I am not fruit.*

By the time the sun began to set, they sailed into view of high white walls being built around Kty. Hana marveled at the walls as she tried to formulate an escape plan. She knew nothing of this island, she knew no one, had no resources, nothing to trade for her freedom. She was now in the same state as Danel, a captive. Her head dipped in sorrow. Neither of them would ever be rescued or see their homes again.

She felt a hand gently smooth her hair back from her face. *Is that you, Ouma?* Hana lifted her chin. She couldn't let herself be overcome by sadness. She had to find a way to escape. Strapped to the mast, she assessed the city as they approached it.

A great number of people were working on cutting and heaving white stones onto the walls, making them higher. *Did the king expect an attack by sea?* About the same size as Sidon, Kty seemed to have more temples. Hana counted five. *Did the people of Kty have more gods than the people of Sidon?* Why did they need so many gods? Yet, something about the place, the sea and the white stones against the vast blue sky created a stark beauty so different from her homeland that it called to her. It answered a question she didn't know she had asked. She tried to remember what anyone had ever told her about Kty. They had copper; they were master weavers. Ashirat said they worshipped the goddess Astarte here. Astarte was another name for Ashtart. A goddess meant priestesses. Perhaps there was a woman who would help her escape from these men. Hana had to think so. She couldn't believe that her mother, and Osnot, even Ashirat would have sent her out into the world to have her journey end in being the slave of these horrid, odorous men.

While she was thinking of an escape plan, the man who had tied her up cut her lose from the mast, picked her up in his arms, and threw her over the side of the boat to the waiting arms of another man standing waist high in the water. Jolted by the fall and carried to the beach like a sack of grain, Hana struggled against the man to get down.

The man laughed. "Feels good," he said. "Keep struggling."

Hana remembered the knife her father had given her. It was still safely in her pouch with her other treasures, tied around her neck and hidden inside her tunic. She pictured her father showing her where to stick the knife into a man's throat. She had a perfect view of the kill spot her father showed her. Perhaps that was the way to get free. She pulled the pouch out of her tunic and reached inside it for the dagger.

Chapter 19

ELENA

Her bed rocked like a boat on the sea. She clutched the sides and opened her eyes briefly, thinking she was still suffering from extreme dizziness caused by her head injury. In quick succession she saw small details that made no sense: curved wood, rudimentary pottery crocks, a sail of the coarsest cloth.

Where am I? What's that smell? Elena sat up slowly. She was at sea in a small wooden boat about the size of a cutter but with a sail and wooden hull instead of fiberglass. The sky was a clear blue. Gulls circled above her, calling. Nothing was as it was supposed to be.

Elena stood slowly, acclimating herself to the rocking of the boat under her feet. Men from an ethnic group she didn't recognize wearing strange garb rowed the boat close to the shore of a rocky island surrounded by clear aqua water. A young girl was lashed to the central mast. Elena's head whipped around. *Did I really see that? I'm dreaming.*

She walked closer to the child and reached out her hand to touch the girl's skin. The child was deeply tanned, her dark hair a mass of curls around her face. Elena swept the child's hair back from her face. The girl looked directly at Elena with eyes as blue as her own. She seemed achingly familiar. *Was that a look of recognition?*

A shock ran through her. *This girl—it couldn't be— this girl looks like my mother, my sister. How is that possible?* She took in the thick ropes wrapped around the child, the girl's exhaustion. Fury rose in her, clogging her throat, bringing blood to her face. *How dare these men imprison a child like this?*

Elena strode to the man who appeared to be the captain, pointing and yelling orders to his men. She tugged his arm to get his attention. He behaved as if she wasn't even there.

"Hey!" she yelled, using her most intimidating voice, her face close to his. "Hey, you release that child immediately!"

The man ignored her, continuing to bark his orders. What language was that? Some of the sounds he made were familiar. It sounded like a Semitic language, but she knew none of the words he was speaking. And why was he dressed so strangely? It took a little more time for all the pieces to come together: she wasn't in New York City, not even in the states.

Had she been abducted by the terrorists? Elena walked away from the man and looked more closely at the island they were approaching. Those white stone structures, they were new, some still being built. This wasn't a historic village being excavated by archaeologists. This was a city under construction. Laborers wore a cloth wrapped around their waists that reached only to their knees. Many of them were barefooted. It wasn't only a question of where she was. It was a question of when she was. *This can't be.*

The boat pulled closer to the shore. Elena stared at the large temple sited on a hill above the city. No cars, no buses, no bicycles, motor scooters, no electric lines, no cell phone antennas, no tall buildings. People pulled carts with wooden wheels. The air was amazingly clear. She breathed in deeply. She could smell something tangy on the air. Eucalyptus. Lemon. She turned around and watched the captain free the girl from the mast, pick her up, and throw her off the boat down to a sailor waiting in the water.

"Hey!" Elena yelled, running to the side of the boat.

The girl struggled but couldn't free herself from the man's grasp. Elena needed to stay with the girl. That must be the reason she was here. Every cell in her body was screaming at her, *she's your family! You must save her.* Elena looked for a ladder to get off the boat and found she was standing waist deep in water, the sea surging in gentle waves around her, keeping her a little off balance. *This is a dream but not a dream. I am somewhere else.*

She pushed through the water up onto the beach, staying as close to the girl as possible, her hand on the child's shoulder. She saw the girl reach for something in a pouch. Perhaps she had a weapon. The men formed a circle around them, although they still didn't see her. Elena looked down at her own body to make sure she was really there. She was wearing clothes Alissa might wear—leggings, a long shirt over a cotton t-shirt. *Did Alissa give me these clothes?*

She couldn't remember ever putting them on. She was barefoot. A plastic hospital bracelet on her wrist had her name on it. She had a vague memory of entering a hospital but nothing after that. She turned her attention back to the girl. Men were jeering at the child, that much Elena could understand. Covering herself in a blue scarf, the girl seemed terrified, but she slowly removed a short dagger from the pouch around her neck.

The man dumped her unceremoniously on the beach. Clenching the dagger in one hand, she jumped to her feet and hid the dagger at her side in the folds of her tunic. Before Elena could get her bearings, or think in what direction to run, the men surrounded the girl. The man who had talked to the girl on the boat said they were taking her to Ashtart's high priestess who would know how much she was worth.

"If you are lucky, she will take you for a sacrifice," he said, "and will pay us in gold for you." He threw his head back and laughed. He wiggled his eyebrows at her. "Maybe I will volunteer to help sacrifice you."

The girl shivered and drew her blue scarf around her so that it covered her face. She looked down at the ground. Her body was shaking; she stumbled as the men marched her up a sandy road that led to a large white temple on top of a hill.

Twelve tall columns held up the roof. There were no walls. The floor was decorated with a geometric mosaic—no images but lines, shapes, circles and spirals, black stones on white and tan. A tall statue of the goddess Astarte stood in the center of the floor. Elena stared at the statue. The artisan had made the statue as beautiful as any woman could be with her arms raised upward in welcome, long hair curling around her shoulders and breasts, her shapely thighs seeming about to move her body forward. Even her feet, her toes, and fingertips were beautiful.

This was what men worshipped, Elena realized. Beauty took their breath away, stirred something in them that they wanted to both cherish and possess. For a moment, she thought the goddess was whispering a secret to her. A voice in her ear she had never heard before was telling her to listen carefully.

The girl tore her gaze away from the statue and looked around. Paths led from the temple to other structures. Those might be living quarters, eating pavilions, weaving workshops. There must be many people here. "Goddess," the girl whispered, "please help me."

Elena's entire body galvanized itself to fight on the girl's behalf, each muscle remembering its training and experience. "I will save you," she said to the girl, "no matter what I have to do."

The girl bowed to the statue. "Thank you, goddess, I hear you." Tears welled in her eyes.

They stood in the entryway of the temple as a woman approached from a path that led to an adjacent building. She was dressed in a long white tunic of a nearly transparent cloth. Her hair was covered by a white scarf that draped around her shoulders. Around her neck was a thick gold necklace with a large blue stone at the center that sent off sparks of light as she moved. The woman walked up to the men, bowed her head slightly, which seemed to make them uncomfortable, and spoke to them in low tones. At first, Elena could make out nothing the woman was saying, but soon the words began to make sense and Elena could follow the gist of her speech.

The woman took the girl by the hand and led her away from the men. "I am Eirene, high priestess of Astarte, protector of women. The girl goes with me."

The men remained in the circle they had formed, looking a little surprised but still menacing. Elena assessed their situation. There were six men—muscled, stinking, and fierce—against two women. Three, if she counted herself. Their odds weren't good without any weapons. The priestess and the girl didn't look like they'd ever fought anything stronger than a harsh wind.

The leader of the barbarians leaned forward, threatening Eirene with his fist. "You pay us what she's worth first. Then you can take her."

The girl began speaking to the priestess. Elena leaned down to catch her words. "I am Hana of Andulat, the paradise found long ago after the world split apart and burst into fire. I have come with these men to find Danel, son of Batnoam, who was taken by the horse people on the plain outside Sidon. These men were paid to take me to his captors on this island but instead they threw my guide off the boat and now I'm alone. They intend to harm me. Will you help me?"

The girl had spoken so candidly, how could anyone not help her? Elena watched closely as the woman closed her eyes and appeared to be talking to someone who was invisible. At any rate, it was someone Elena couldn't see, just as these people seemed unable to see her.

"There are enemies of the good everywhere," Eirene said to Hana. "You obviously have your share of experience with this. As Astarte's high priestess in Kty, I can protect you for a while, but I cannot help you find your friend."

Hana shook her head. "Please, then, let me go free. Help me get away from these men. I can find my friend on my own."

"These men are no longer a threat to you. The goddess won't allow them to harm you. But now that you are here, I see the goddess must have meant for you to come to us for her own reasons." She scrutinized Hana's face, turned the child's hands over, examined at her fingertips. "You are an artisan."

"I'm only learning."

"The goddess has a task for you. When it is completed, then you can go free."

Elena could stand it no longer. *How dare this woman try to use the girl for her own purposes instead of protecting her?* "Don't worry, Hana of Andulat," she whispered in the girl's ear, "I'll find a way to get you free."

At that moment, the boat captain rushed the women, clutching Hana under his arm and lifting her off the floor as if she were no heavier than a bolt of cloth. Without thinking, Elena drove her fist into the man's throat. He gasped, dropped Hana, and staggered backward, his hands thrust away from his body to protect himself. For good measure, Elena swiped his legs. He fell on his back onto the stone floor, looking around, baffled. The other men jumped back, away from him, as if he was cursed.

"As you see," the priestess intoned, "the goddess protects her own."

Elena laughed, the first good laugh she'd had in a long while, and put her arm around Hana. She could protect the girl. It made her feel good to do it.

The men ran off, jostling each other as they pounded down the hill. Elena was certain the story about the goddess's hidden powers would spread wherever these people sailed their boat.

Chapter 20

HANA

The priestess led Hana to an austere chamber with a low bed, table, and stool. On the table was a clay pot holding fresh water. Hana put her dagger back into the pouch and washed her face and arms. The simple act of washing reminded her of meeting Osnot. Her heart ached. The meal she shared with Osnot seemed very long ago. She was a different girl now. Osnot might not even recognize her. She didn't recognize herself.

A clean tunic was laid on the bed. Hana removed her old one and was about to dress in the new one when Eirene said, "You will bathe first so that you don't soil the cloth with the smell of those foul men."

Hana nodded her agreement, pulled her blue scarf over her shoulders, and followed the priestess out of the chamber, down another stone path to a pool fed by a small waterfall that ran down the hillside. She removed her pouch of treasures, placed it on her scarf and stepped into the pool. The water was warm and soft. She lay back, lifted her face to the sky, and closed her eyes. Water soothed her body, sun warmed her. She was happy to float there, free of cares for at least a few heartbeats.

The memory of the men who treated her as if she were property, to be taken, abused, and traded at their will, clung to her. She washed her body hoping to eliminate the touch of their hands. The sense of losing control of her own body, the fear that someone else might steal away her freedom at any time, caused a throbbing deep in her abdomen. She had been rescued from peril this time by the goddess herself. Hana was still amazed at how a force she couldn't see threw the man to the ground. Never had she expected that any of the gods would truly save her, but to be safe, she had to learn how to protect herself. She needed to find someone to teach her.

Priestess Eirene broke into her reverie. "You are no longer a child. This is a good omen. The goddess will accept your blood as an offering for her protection of you."

Hana opened her eyes and lowered her feet to the bottom of the pool. "What?" She expected to see the priestess standing over her with a dagger. She looked down and saw blood spiraling around her legs in the water. She felt the deep throbbing pressure again inside her body, below her belly. She placed her hand there expecting to find a wound, but her skin was intact. Blood continued to flow from her, mingling with the water. She climbed out of the bath and stood on the path, watching blood drip down her thigh and shin to her ankle and onto the stones.

"What is happening to me?"

"The goddess has blessed you with fertility," the priestess explained. "You can now make the ritual sacrifice to her."

"I don't want to make a sacrifice." Looking down the line of blood on her leg, she was suddenly terrified that all her blood would flow out of her before she became a day older. "I can't remember what my mother told me. Will I die? Can the goddess make the bleeding stop?"

The priestess smiled and slowly shook her head. "You don't die. The bleeding stops by itself. Until you are an old woman, you will bleed for several days during each cycle of the moon. But now you can truly honor the goddess who saved you from those men. You will come fully into your womanhood by offering up your virginity on the altar of the goddess."

"Are you going to kill me?"

The priestess shook her head again. "No, of course not. For a prize like you, with those blue eyes, a prince will make a handsome gift to the goddess for the honor of taking your maidenhead. You will be ready at the next new moon when the sky is dark. Many will come to watch the ceremony. You will be famous."

Hana shook her head vehemently. "I don't want to be famous." She stamped her foot. "I want to be free to find my friend and go home."

The ceremony sounded painful and humiliating. She wrapped her scarf around her, picked up her pouch and clutched it. If necessary, now that she'd held the dagger in her hand, she knew she could use it. This priestess didn't look that strong. Then she remembered the small scroll. She opened the pouch, withdrew the small papyrus scroll, and handed it to the priestess with all the dignity she could muster.

"What is this?" The priestess scowled. She unrolled the scroll. Her face turned the color of ash, then fire. Her hands shook. In a tremulous voice she said, "It seems you are protected not only by the Queen of Heaven but by the great god whose name we do not speak."

She paced up and down the path for a while, leaving Hana standing on the stones, her blood spotting the white stones. "I must speak to Astarte. Go back to the chamber,

dress, eat and rest. I will send a novice who will teach
you how to wear the special clothing at this time so that
your blood does not stain the bed." She handed the scroll
back to Hana and walked off.

Hana put the scroll in her pouch and walked slowly
back to the chamber. The scroll had saved her from making a sacrifice. Those marks must have a great deal of
power. Her mother and father hadn't given the scroll to
her. They would have told her about it. Osnot, who worshipped the wise lord, must have tied it into her scarf.
Surely neither the matron nor Ashirat was powerful
enough to make marks on papyrus that would stop a goddess from taking what she wanted.

Was the wise lord more powerful than all other
gods? There were too many questions and no one to help
her find the answers, unless the wise lord would. She was
weary and sad with no hope of finding Danel or bringing
him home to his father. She abandoned the idea of ever
returning to her own village, even though she always felt
hungry for the place she was born, as if home had a taste
that she couldn't find anywhere else.

Inside the small chamber the priestess had designat-
ed for her, Hana wrapped herself in the garment as the
young girl showed her, put on her new tunic, ate some
bread and cheese and lay down on the bed. With her eyes
closed, it almost felt as if her mother was stroking her
hair and caressing her face. She fell asleep clinging to her
memory of her family.

Some time passed before the priestess woke her.
"The goddess has instructed me that your sacrifice will
be made in another way." She turned around a few times
in the chamber as if searching for words in its corners.
"On the temple wall you will make a mosaic of the goddess directing the seas and the stars. When you have

completed that task, I will give you all the help you need to rescue your friend and return home."

Hana nodded her head and said yes. There was nothing else she could do. It was better than being a sacrifice. "Will I have help? I need two people who can cut stone, make mud, and help me make clay tiles and sort colors. I will need to meet your other artisans so I can see images of the goddess. I need to see where you want the mosaic installed. We will need a workshop."

Eirene raised her arms as if to plead with the heavens. "You are a strange girl to make demands when the goddess has saved your life!" She whirled around to face Hana. "We have saved you from the barbarians, given you a place to sleep, food to eat, clothes to wear. You will do what you love to do. How dare you ask for anything else?"

"I'm sorry priestess, but a mosaic cannot be done by one person, unless you want it to take me all of my life. And then what good is your promise that I will be free to leave and find my friend when I've completed it?"

The priestess shook her head, but a smile briefly flitted across her lips and finally she relented. "You are a headstrong girl, but you reason well." She paced for a while and then stood with her arms uplifted, her eyes closed, her face to the sky. Hana waited. Finally, the priestess turned to her with a decision.

"Fine, I will introduce you to the artisan who made the statue of the goddess. He will understand you even if I cannot. I will make sure you have what you need." She walked out of the chamber, looking back once at Hana, as if to make clear that the only reason she was conceding to the demands of the girl who had been brought as a captive to the temple was because the goddess instructed her to do so.

Chapter 21

ELENA

Elena set herself the task of teaching Hana how to fight. With no idea how she came to be in this place, she worried she might be whisked away at any moment. She didn't want to risk leaving the child with no defenses. Luckily, she felt no hunger or thirst. There was no ache in the arm she sometimes recalled she had broken. Her legs were strong, and she was agile. Time seemed to be suspended, hanging somewhere in a clear blue sky above a sparkling sea.

Hana would have to learn how to wield her dagger, how to knock a larger opponent off balance so that she'd have the opportunity to stab him in the throat and escape. She needed to know when to run and when to fight. Her life depended on it.

Time set aside for morning prayers as the sun rose was the best time for instruction. All of the goddess's followers gathered on the floor of the temple and made obeisance to the statue. A dance as an offering to the goddess couldn't be unacceptable. She could talk Hana through each movement, whispering in her ear, taking her through them over and over until they were second nature. It would look like a dance to anyone watching, except that Hana's arms and legs would grow strong from the practice, her balance would improve, and she would grow confidence.

She walked with the girl everywhere she went, learning the paths through the city, observing everything. This was a Bronze Age city, she realized. The clarity of the air made her feel she had never drawn breath before. The sky at night was lit by millions of stars, so many more than she had ever seen, except maybe in an Afghan outpost. Now she'd made the connection, it seemed to her that these people lived in much the same way as Afghans did far from the major cities—no electricity, no plumbing, no motorized vehicles, no cell phone towers. Except that instead of rocks and spears, modern war lords now had rocket grenade launchers and automatic rifles.

Elena experienced an odd kind of ease in being invisible to everyone. She had nothing to prove, and yet everything was at stake. She had to protect the girl. If the child died, she would also die, and all her family as well. Hana needed to survive this experience and move on. There was something else she must do. The constant whispering in Elena's ear seemed to be calling her to go somewhere else. It pulled on her like distant music she knew but couldn't name. If only she could see the future, she could help guide Hana in the right direction.

But for now, her role was clear. Her task was to guard Hana from the many people who seemed intent on harming her. She was up to that, at least. As Hana raised her arm in a wide circle and lunged, the blue stone on her finger flashed in the sunlight and for a second Elena thought she saw her own mother standing on the marble terrace.

Chapter 22

HANA

Within a cycle of the moon from new to old, the goddess's worshippers had assembled everything Hana needed to begin work on a large mosaic that would cover three walls. She developed a habit of rising early and performing the dance of obeisance to the goddess with the priestess and the novitiates as the sun rose over the sea to the east.

During these prayers, she heard the goddess speaking to her, telling her how to add power and force to the thrust of her arms and legs. The movements seemed to open her heart to the wide blue sky and the rising sun. The sun's light engulfed her, pervaded her body, and caressed her skin. Something in the ritual calmed her, readied her for the day.

The goddess whispered in her ear, "Bide your time. I will find a way. You will be free." That was the chant Hana murmured to herself whenever she felt most imprisoned by her circumstances. All day, she felt the goddess's presence near her, protecting her.

Hana worked in the morning hours while it was still cool, chipping stone and making clay tiles. In the late afternoon, she took chaperoned walks around Kty followed

by a half-circle of five white-robed novitiates close behind her. Wherever she went in the city, she found images of Astarte in all sizes in stone, bronze, gold, wood, and
clay. In one, the goddess held snakes in her upraised
arms. A bird perched on her head. In another, she held
sheaves of grain. On another, Hana noticed with a start,
the goddess's eyes were painted a deep blue.

Kty was as busy as five Sidons, filled with people of
all descriptions, with sounds and smells so exotic she had
no names for them. Bearded men, small children, bald-
headed men, merchants, and artisans all inclined their
heads to her and murmured a word she didn't understand.

"What is this word they say?" Hana asked the novitiates.

They murmured together and the tallest said,
"Blessed one."

Hana shook her head. The world had strange people
in it with even stranger ideas. "Why do they say that?"

"Do you not realize you look like the goddess?"

Hana thought of the times she had caught a portion
of her reflection in a still puddle after rain or in the shiny
blade of her dagger. "I don't think so." Hana shook her
arms to release the absurd idea. "I look like myself."

The novitiates tittered. "You should be careful of
your arrogance," the eldest said.

In one section of the city, women walked about with
their breasts exposed, much like the images of the goddess. In another neighborhood, veils covered them completely, even their eyes. In some parts, the women had
elaborate headdresses in bright colors and in others their
hair was all the adornment they wore. Many women wore
bangles on their arms, and some wore them on their ankles and jangled when they walked. The veiled women,
Hana noticed, did not look at her directly but she could
feel their gaze, nonetheless. The bare-breasted women

had no difficulty laughing and calling out after her, "Hey Blue Girl, use me as your model. Wouldn't I make a beautiful goddess?"

One thing was certain. Here, as in Sidon, everyone in the market knew everything. Hana wondered how that happened. The stern novitiates around her were so un-moving she was surprised that breath passed their lips. But they must be the ones who were gossiping.

On an early evening walk, she spotted a small, brown animal with a long tail perched on the shoulder of the fruit merchant. She walked to the stall and asked about it. The animal chattered at her and jumped into her arms. The fruit merchant gave her a date to feed it. She held the date out for the animal to bite. It took the fruit in its two paws and fed it to her instead. Everyone around the stall laughed and applauded.

The next morning, Eirene told her not to touch those filthy animals. "Do you understand nothing? Those dis-gusting animals bear diseases." Hana stood with her mouth open, stunned that her innocent pleasures were under scrutiny. She looked over at her slender body-guards, saw the one whose face flushed and knew who she could not trust.

One late afternoon as the air was cooling with the descending sun, she noticed a small building at the back of the market tucked into the city wall. Painted on the stone near the door was the sign for life her mother had shown her. She walked through the open doorway and waited for her eyes to adjust to the dim light. Instead of cloth, carpet, jewelry, pots, or other goods, Hana saw dozens of scrolls of all sizes on one table and clay tablets laid out on another. Her hand went to the pouch on her chest.

A man with a long gray beard, a tunic of the same color as his beard, and wearing the same kind of head covering as Abirami came from behind a curtained area, approached her and bowed. "Yes, young woman, how may I help you?" He eyed the novices in their white tunics and scarves who surrounded her but said nothing to them.

Hana remembered then that they were not to be spoken to or looked at. To do so might risk a man's life. She could see he didn't quite trust the novices and she would be wise to follow his lead. Asking the women to wait for her outside the shop, she turned back to him. "What are all of these scrolls?" She gestured to the many rolls of papyrus.

"Business by kings and merchants must sometimes be conducted over long distances," he explained, his voice as deep as her father's. "For instance, if the king of Sidon..." The shopkeeper looked at her as if to say he knew where she came from. "So, if the king of Sidon wants to send information to the king of Kty and he doesn't believe a messenger will remember it correctly, he has his words written down on a scroll and carried by a messenger. I am a scribe. I write the messages on the scrolls so that they can be carried between the parties involved. I also read messages to people who cannot."

"Why don't the kings write their own messages?"

The man laughed. "They don't know how to write or read. That's why there are scribes."

Hana's cheeks burned with embarrassment. That was her problem. She couldn't write or read either. "I have a scroll with a message written on it. Would you be able to tell me what it says?"

"If I know the language, yes. Far to the east, they use a different writing system and I cannot decipher those messages. In some cases," he looked into her eyes as if he were deciphering a message written there, "I recognize some of the marks and not others, but I can piece the message together, the way *you* put mosaics together."

Hana was startled for a moment that he knew about the mosaic she was making but then remembered that everyone in the market knew everything that was happening in the city.

"Some languages," the man continued, "use pictures, as the Egyptians do. The Phoenicians have invented a new way of writing where the marks stand for sounds, or sometimes numbers so a farmer can tell a merchant how many bushels of barley he has sent him or how many goats he has traded. The sounds together make up words we speak every day." He looked at her earnestly. "Once you know the sound of the marks, you can read any message as if the sender were in the room telling it to you. Do you understand?"

She shook her head, no, but was heartened by his willingness to explain the mystery of writing to her even though she didn't truly understand what he was saying. Hana withdrew the scroll from her pouch. "Could tell me something about this?" She placed the small scroll in his palm.

He took the papyrus over to an oil lamp on his worktable and gently unrolled it. "You are not from here. Did I hear that correctly?"

"I'm from Andulat, across the sea to the east, where the land goes on forever. I came to Kty by boat from Sidon."

After some scrutiny of the writing, during which Hana held her breath, he looked up from the scroll. "It is in the Phoenician alphabet. I can read it. The mark of the wise lord is genuine, known only to his disciples. If you are the female referred to in the scroll, you are blessed and protected by the wise lord." He scrutinized her face. "Yes, I believe you are the one the scroll speaks of. But I think you know that already." He rolled up the scroll and handed it back to Hana. "How did you come by this?"

Hana put the scroll in her pouch. "An old woman named Osnot whose home is in the wilderness on the way to Sidon gave it to me."

"When was that?"

"More than two harvests ago. What does the writing say?"

"It says: 'Be sure the blue girl travels safely.' It is a command. The message bears the mark of the wise lord. Terrible things have been known to befall people who have not obeyed his commands. Have you shown this scroll to anyone else?"

"I showed it to the priestess at Astarte's temple. She protected me from the men who had abducted me. She said that because of the message on the scroll, I would not be sacrificed but that I must create a mosaic for the goddess."

The man stroked his beard, watching her. He seemed to be lost in his thoughts. At last, he said, "The scroll says nothing about the mosaic. Perhaps the priestess is worried you will replace her and has given you a task that will take you until you are an old woman to complete and so you will be unable to challenge her."

Hana laughed. "I have no desire to replace Eirene. Can you tell me how to sound out the marks on my scroll? I would like to study this writing."

As the sun sank toward the horizon, the man slowly sounded out each of the marks on the scroll and told her what they meant. She repeated after him, uncertainly at first, but gaining confidence as the sounds began to seem familiar. He opened a different scroll and asked her to read. She shook her head. "I doubt I can do that."

"Try anyway," he said, pointing with a stylus to the first set of marks.

She stuttered through several words and then looked up at him. "It's exhausting!"

He laughed and nodded his head. "It takes time to learn."

Hana thought of how long she had been away from home. The last thing she wanted was to stay on this island, but she wished she had more time to learn to read. Then the thought of Danel, lifted off the plain by the horse people and spirited away, struck her. She had not forgotten her pledge to his father. "I wonder," she stammered, "could you, would you know anything about a boy named Danel who was abducted and might be in this city?"

The scribe thought for a few heartbeats, stroking his beard. "I'm sorry. I know of no Danel. But with the protection you have, I'm sure you will find whatever and whoever you are seeking." He bowed his head.

Hana understood it was time for her to leave. "Just one more thing. What is your name?"

"Aryeh, my child. If I hear of a Danel in the city, I will get word to you." She opened her mouth to ask how he would know where to find her. He held up his hand. "Everyone in the city knows who you are," he said.

"Thank you, Aryeh. May only blessings befall you."

Aryeh bowed his head again.

She walked out of the building, blinking in the fierce afternoon light glinting off white stones. The sky was a brilliant blue. At the top of the hill with her entourage of white-clad women behind her, Hana looked out over the sea. If she were not captive here, she would admit that this was a beautiful place with wonderful people in it.

No matter what Hana saw in her walks through the city and its environs, her favorite image remained the statue in the temple, perhaps because there the goddess seemed alive. The statue talked to her. At least, it felt that way, sitting there, staring at beauty she had no words to describe. She wanted to bring that quality of aliveness to the flat mosaic of stones she was making. Hana began making sketches on the sand, trying to find the right way to represent the Queen of Heaven, as the priestess called the goddess.

The goddess ruled over the sea and the earth. She protected all who loved but especially women. If that was true, Hana should ask the goddess directly for her assistance. During her morning prayers, she asked for guidance. The goddess's first instruction, as far as Hana could make out from the whispers, was to make herself strong. The second instruction was to seek help from others. *Wasn't it odd that a goddess could not simply wave her arms and free her, return Danel to her, bring her home?*

Hana asked the sculptor who made the temple statue to be the master of her workshop. "I don't know what I'm doing," she confessed when she asked for his help. "I need your expertise."

Damasos nodded as if he understood her predicament and agreed to help her. "You're very young to be given a commission like this. You are either blessed or cursed by the goddess."

"Both, I think."

The man laughed and briefly put his hand on her shoulder. Suddenly overcome with emotion at being understood, she lingered near him for a while. He reminded her of her father, with his strong arms, dark beard, and silver hair. She watched as he stood before a large stone for a long time, looking at it from all sides before he drove his chisel into the rock with a hammer. He seemed to see an image trapped in the stone waiting for him to release it. There were days Hana felt she was an image trapped in stone also, but where was the artisan who could release her?

Watching the sculptor's hands deftly working the stone, Hana longed for home, for her father, the earthy smell of him and the feel of his strong arms lifting her in the air. She yearned for her mother's soft voice. She would never return to her village, never see them again. The sorrow in her chest was a pot of stones so heavy sometimes she stooped when she walked. She prayed to the goddess, asking for protection for Danel. When that plea felt empty and useless, she prayed to the wise lord in the way her mother had taught her, on her knees, her head covered and bowed, her eyes closed, hands folded together, the rocking rhythm of her body emphasizing each word of supplication.

"Always," her mother had instructed her, "no matter how heavy your heart is, begin by thanking the wise lord for all he has given us."

I'm trying. I mean to be grateful. I'm alive. I thank the wise lord for that.

Regardless of how she felt, she had to go on with the mosaic project. With helpers to cut and sort colored stones and shells, and other artisans to make new clay pieces for the background, geometric borders, and spacers, Hana had time to think about the entire project.

The background of the mosaic creates the space in which foreground marks mean something. She heard these words as clearly as if someone were standing next to her talking. Otherwise, the whole piece was simply a jumble of colored stones. If she could vary the background, perhaps she could make the central image more real.

Staring at the statue in the temple, she noticed that the scenery behind it blurred when she focused on the goddess. There must be a way to trick the eye into focusing on the main image.

"Perhaps," Hana thought she heard the goddess

whisper, "you could outline the central figure in some way."

Hana sent a boy to collect small bits of copper left over from the smelting process when the ore was mixed with tin to make bronze. Another she dispatched to scour the beach for shells with iridescent linings. She had no idea what she would do with those materials but having them at hand might spark a solution. "And bring back all the black stones you find also," she called after the boy as he scampered down the hill toward the beach.

Left to work on what the mural should be, how many panels, their size, the color palette, and what the panels would depict, Hana began to develop an idea of how to honor the goddess. Without intending to break her agreement with the priestess, she began sketching panels in the sand that showed life in her own village—women gathering food, men with spears, fish leaping from the river, sparks flying around her father at the forge as he beat the hot metal into shapes.

In her mind, a goddess who protected women also protected their families and activities. Only one panel in the center of the mural was devoted solely to an image of the Queen of Heaven. She was standing at the prow of a boat, her finger pointing to the stars in the heavens that guided the boatmen. Waves lapped against the side of the boat. A large fish leaped. The moon shone above her. To Hana, being at sea in the middle of night was the most perilous and thrilling experience. This panel depicted a goddess who led her people through the darkest times. The next step would be to draw in charcoal on the pre-pared plaster surface.

On an afternoon several full moons into the project, the priestess visited the workshop. She stalked over to Hana's sand drawings and stood above them, glowering. She walked in a circle around them, her hands on her hips. Hana had the distinct feeling that one of the noviti-ates had complained about her design for the mural.

"You were meant to make a mural glorifying the goddess," Eirene thundered, her face the color of a bronze coin. Her eyes threw lightning bolts. "This thing you have designed makes humans the equal of the gods. It is blasphemy!"

If she hadn't felt the reassuring hand of the goddess on her shoulder, Hana would have wept in frustration. "You don't understand," she explained as calmly as possible. "These images do glorify the goddess and all her works."

Eirene threw her arms into the air. "You are absurd. There are more people in this design than images of the goddess. They are the same size as the goddess." She paused to spit on the ground. "I don't know why I thought a girl could do such important work."

"But I can do it. I am doing it. This is what the goddess told me to do."

Eirene gave Hana a scathing look and swept out of the workshop muttering as she went, "As if this girl from nowhere knows what the goddess wants or hears her speaking."

Hana had no idea whether to keep working or stop. She continued to work, squatting now, to lay out tiles in intricate background patterns that seemed to push the foreground image toward her. She was pleased that her experiment seemed to be working.

The priestess came back before sunset with three burly men in short tunics and tattoos covering their arms. Their hands and forearms were wrapped with leather straps into which daggers were inserted. Their bald heads glistened with sweat. Hana had never before seen them on the temple grounds.

"Sons of Hercules," the sculptor said, warning her with his eyes to be compliant.

Eirene gripped Hana's arm with one hand and shook a finger in her face. "It doesn't matter what god protects you," she whispered in Hana's ear. "You cannot get away with this, this desecration—" She pointed to the sand drawings. "—this heresy. Now you will make the sacrifice to the goddess, and with the first man who comes for you, no matter who he is. We will get some value from saving you from those disgusting sea people. Even if the novitiates have to hold you down, you will take a man into your body. Your virgin's blood will stain the altar. Meanwhile, you will wait for your time in a cell. I hope you think about how you have destroyed your own freedom with your brazen imagery."

"But you said the wise lord protected me," Hana said. "Aren't you worried…"

The men took Hana by the arms, lifted her off the ground, and carried her away. She wrenched herself around, trying to escape their grasp, her legs flailing in all directions. Two men lost their balance, and spun away, holding their throats. But two held her fast and she could not get loose.

Helpless, she wrenched her head around and watched the priestess scrape away the sand drawings with her feet, leaving only the sketch for the central panel of the goddess, her arm raised to direct the heavens. Hana lowered her head and let the men drag her to the cell.

Chapter 23

ELENA

Elena watched Hana cower in the corner of a cell. She hadn't been able to get the girl away from the strong guards no matter how she threw herself against them or shoved or punched. They simply staggered and regained their balance. Desperate to find a way to break Hana free, Elena pushed at the stone door with all her strength. It didn't budge. Quickly, she examined every corner of the cell. There was no obvious way to help Hana escape. If she could only wrap her arms around her and help her materialize in a different place.

Her failure to save someone she loved, all too familiar, hung on her, pulled her down with its weight. She must concentrate. She must at least give the girl courage. She whispered to Hana, "You are brave, braver than you know. You will find a way."

The girl's face turned up, a look of shock and recognition in her eyes. "Mother?" she asked. "Are you here with me?"

Elena leaned over and kissed the girl's cheek.

A loud bang ripped through Elena's brain. Was that an earthquake? The world went from black as night, no stars, to bright light. She was somewhere else, not on an island with Hana, not home. Iraq. She was in Iraq. *Oh, God, not here. How did I get here?*

She rolled her head around on her shoulders to work out the tension in her neck. Sweat rolled out from under her helmet, creeping under her goggles, stinging her eyes. Sand swirled everywhere. It jammed their communication devices, seeped in under their clothes, and made a fine coating of silt on her scalp. She had never become accustomed to its ubiquity.

Wait. Wait. This is wrong. This is not where I'm supposed to be. Where is the sea? Where is the girl? I want to be with the girl. She closed her eyes, willed herself back with Hana, and opened them.

Elena blinked and forced herself to focus. *I'm still in Iraq.*

Ahead of the HUMVEE, five soldiers reconnoitered a reported IED. No matter how many times the squad was sent on this mission—to locate and explode improvised bombs planted everywhere a soldier might step or a vehicle might roll—the dread never abated. If she was honest, fear increased as the odds rolled up against them. Every time they returned to base safely, fate loaded the dice more heavily in favor of an explosion, death, dismemberment on the next mission. By the end of a tour, every mission was dread inducing. Even in her sleep, fear chased her.

On the rooftop nearest her, she thought she spotted the tip of a weapon. With one hand, Elena checked her medic supplies, feeling through the rucksack for the outlines of things that would stop bleeding, close wounds, ease pain. Morphine first, always. Wounds don't wait for the brain to pick a number from one to ten. In her other hand, she held her weapon, finger on the trigger. She had passed On Your Mark and Ready fifteen minutes before. She was standing at Go, on total tense, waiting to spring out from behind the vehicle to glue up a hole in her buddy's stomach or duct tape a soldier together until he could be airlifted to Germany.

Deep breaths didn't work. Anyway, she had decided what seemed like an eon ago that relaxing was a bad idea. Bad luck. Bad karma. Whatever anyone wanted to call it. Stay on tense. It was safer. You couldn't relax out here, not for the entire tour. No matter where you were. The enemy even blew up the DFACs, what her father called chow halls. There were no safe spaces. She cleared her head by force of will and waited.

Something's wrong with this situation. I'm not really here. This isn't right. It's the wrong time, the wrong place. I must get back. Elena blinked to clear her vision.

A young girl with blue eyes stood high on a white rock, looking out over a sparkling blue sea. In the next second, Elena was pushing against the stone door of the girl's prison. Every muscle and bone in her body strained against its weight. Slowly it began to move and once it rolled, she had it. She pushed it away from the opening and looked at the girl in triumph.

"Run, child, run," she yelled.

Another loud bang blew through her brain. *What is that sound?* Elena shook her head, forcing herself to concentrate on the scene in front of her.

A terrible rumbling from a blast ripped through her, like the sky ripping apart, a flash of light, a whirring, and then nothing, only blackness like floating in the deepest part of the ocean, falling and falling, drifting until her bare feet touched sand.

Chapter 24

HANA

The cell, built into a side of the hill, had a small window that looked out toward the sea. Hana had just enough room to walk ten paces in any direction. She stood at the window and dreamed of escape. She couldn't budge the heavy door the men shoved across the opening. There was no cooking hole in the top of the cell, which was made of the same stone that builders were using for the new city walls. Obviously, prisoners waited to be given food and water. It was another way to control them. It never occurred to Hana that someone might intend to starve her to death, or at least into submission. A new kind of fear turned in her stomach.

Examining the walls of her cell for crevices she could shimmy through the way she had done to get into the city of Sidon, she found markings she had at first ignored. They looked similar to the markings on the scroll she carried in the pouch hanging from a leather strap around her neck. The priestess hadn't confiscated her pouch. She still had the knife her father gave her. *I should have used it to get free of those guards.* She put aside her failure, resolving to use the knife in the future, if she had to.

Hana opened the pouch and extracted the scroll. Using a small, sharp rock she found on the floor that seemed to have been used to make the markings on the wall, she underlined the symbols on the wall that matched the writing on her scroll. She wished she could remember exactly what Aryeh told her about how each mark on the scroll sounded and how to put those sounds together to make words. She stepped back and stared at the wall. There was a pattern to the marks. Several of them repeated. If she could unlock their secret, maybe she would understand the message left by a prisoner who occupied this cell before her. She studied the scroll.

The priestess had muttered something when she looked at the scroll. Was it "give her safe passage?" Wracking her memory for the sounds Aryeh made in the order he had uttered them when he examined her scroll, Hana placed her finger on each symbol and made the sounds one at a time until the sounds became words to her ears. Before dark fell, Hana thought she knew what the message on the wall meant: *The sea gives safe passage to her who fears not the night.*

She couldn't be sure. In her desperation, she may have made up the message. Anyway, it didn't really matter. She couldn't get to the sea. She had already tried. The window was too small to crawl out, the door too heavy to budge, the walls impenetrable. The message seemed designed to inspire despair.

She sighed and sat huddled against the wall in the dark. Where was the goddess who spoke to her, who helped her? There was no clue on the wall about how to escape the cell. She would have to wait until they came to get her, and then she would break away from them and run. She would run like the wind.

She prayed to the goddess to help her as she had before. "A small earthquake might help," Hana suggested to the goddess, "one that would break down these walls." She slept and dreamt of a goddess as strong and tall as a man, a woman who would rescue her and help her find her way home. In her sleep, she imagined her mother stroking her head.

Sprays of pink and gold lit the dawn sky and streaked across the floor of the cell. Hana picked her head up off her knees, unraveled herself, stretched, and looked out of the cell window.

Her first thought was of Danel. She put it aside. She had failed to find him, and she couldn't do anything for him trapped in this cell.

The sea sparkled like the gem in her ring. Today its many blue colors didn't cheer her. Desolate, she turned around in the small cell and the light from the sun reflected off her ring onto the marks on the wall. Suddenly, she saw the message differently: *"Night brings safe passage to the sea. Fear not."*

The ring. The glass bead. The gold bracelet. She had things of value. She could bribe her guards to let her escape at night. The thought gave her hope.

That afternoon, a guard brought her a meal of dates, bread, and water. She drank almost all the water at once, gulping it so quickly that it dribbled down her chin.

"Be careful, Blue Girl," the guard said. "Your stomach will cramp. Eat and drink slowly. You don't want to be in pain before your sacrifice when the moon is full tomorrow. You will have enough pain during it." He laughed at his own joke, throwing back his head and slapping his knee.

Hana stared at him from the corner of the cell, her hand on her pouch.

"Don't worry," he said, the jeer lingering on his face. "I won't harm you. I've been told I'll be killed if I lay a hand on you. The king himself is to take your maidenhead. He's coming to inspect you today. No girl, blue-eyed or not, is worth my head."

"Please," Hana begged. "Please help me escape. I'll pay you. I have a valuable ring."

"Not on your life." He left the cell and shoved the door closed.

Hana felt that she couldn't eat a morsel, but she forced herself to put the food in her mouth, chew, and swallow. She needed her strength. She had to find a way to escape.

Before sunset finished, as the sky turned rose and orange and a thin rind of light green hung over the horizon, the door was thrown open and a tall man dressed in a fine tunic of several colors with many gold chains around his neck and a circlet of gold on his head strode into the small space. He took up all the air in the room as if it was his right to breathe first and everyone else must take their surfeit from what remained. The priestess followed him, fluttering like a distressed bird. Hana turned her back to them and stealthily withdrew her father's dagger from the pouch.

"Show me," the king commanded.

The priestess pulled Hana's tunic from her shoulder and swept Hana's long hair away from her back to show him the bird on her skin. Hana clutched the dagger close to her thigh. With her other hand, she held the front of her tunic to her chest. The king touched the image of the bird with the palm of his hand. He seemed mesmerized.

"Her eyes," he said.

The priestess took Hana's shoulders and spun her to face the king, lifting her chin so that she had to look directly at him. "Open your eyes," the priestess ordered.

Hana did as she was told. The king was not terribly old, she thought. For a few blinks, she regarded him as she would a subject she might make into a mosaic. He had dark, curly hair, a strong nose, full lips, and piercing brown eyes. He had the kind of face that could order people into battle, the kind of eyes that would stifle an objection.

"Hmmm," he muttered. "You are sure she's intact?" He put out his hand to touch Hana's belly. "I'm surprised no one has taken her before this."

"She has been protected, my lord," the priestess said.

"By whom?" he asked, now absorbed in examining Hana from head to toe.

The priestess muttered a response. The king clenched the priestess's arm and shook her. "Speak!"

"The wise lord, sir, the wise lord protects her."

He stepped back, away from Hana, looking at his fingertips as if they were on fire. "And will I not anger the wise lord by taking her? Even Astarte cannot protect me from El."

"I...Astarte...she." Eirene stopped talking and turned away.

"You have tried to trick me," he thundered. "You have tried to topple my kingdom with your heretical practices." His eyes were wild. He noticed now that Hana held a dagger. He seized her wrist and wrenched the dagger from her hand.

Too terrified to move or resist, Hana watched the king drag the priestess out of the cell by her hair, cursing her. Using Hana's dagger, he stabbed Eirene in the neck, exactly where Hana's father had told her to strike an enemy. Blood gushed from the wound. Hana sucked in her breath and stopped moving, stifling even her breath. She would be next, she was sure.

The king dropped the dagger and left Eirene crumbled on the ground. His guard stared at Hana for a few heartbeats as if to tackle her to present another victim to the king. "Leave her be," the king bellowed and strode away. The guard rolled the heavy stone door closed.

Hana secured her tunic and wrapped her blue scarf around her head. She would be ready for the first opportunity to escape. On the last turn of the scarf around her neck, the cell door slowly rolled open. There in the opening was her goddess, tall as a man, wild haired, and blue-eyed. Hana could see her as if she were as real as any other person.

"Run, child, run," the goddess yelled before she disappeared.

Hana lunged out of the cell, picked up her dagger and wiped the priestess's blood off in the sand. She gripped the dagger in her fist and looked around for which way to flee. Eirene's attendants rushed toward the priestess's limp body, lifted her off the ground and carried her into the temple. The ground trembled and shook.

Hana saw flames leap from the temple. From the city below she heard screams and yells. Men armed with spears and shields rushed by her but didn't stop. Within ten heartbeats, the sun fell into the sea and darkness enveloped the island. Hana pictured the words inscribed on the cell wall—*Night brings safe passage*—and gathered the courage to run down the steps toward the sea.

A man jumped in front of her, his head and face completely covered by his head wrap. Only his dark eyes were visible. Hana gasped, at first stepped back, and then lunged at him with her dagger. Her breath came in short spurts. Her body trembled. She swiped his legs at the knees as she had been taught by the goddess and threw him to the ground, leaping onto his chest.

It's not fear that makes me tremble. It's fury. She had seen the king kill the priestess. She knew how to do it. She pulled her arm back, ready to strike.

"I am Hana of Andulat," she yelled in as deep a voice as she could muster, "and I will be free."

The man flipped over and threw her aside. She staggered across the ground and down two steps, stumbling and falling. Stifling a sob, Hana pulled herself to her feet. The dagger was still in her hand. She held it in front of her, ready to strike at him again.

"Hana." The man's voice was a tense whisper.

"Yes, that's who I am." Behind her, steep steps ran down to the rocky beach below. She imagined turning and running away as fast as she could. But she had to fight him. She would rather die fighting than let this man take her.

"Hana, it's me, Danel." As he spoke, the man unraveled his scarf.

Chapter 25

ELENA

Alissa stood next to Elena's hospital bed as she had every day for the last three weeks. Her voice was hoarse with her constant entreaties to her sister, but she wasn't going to give up.

"Elena, please, we need you. You can't leave me. It's enough that Mom died. I can't lose you too. And Hannah needs her aunt. Remember you delivered her? Remember how beautiful she is? Please come back to me, please be here with us."

Elena's eyes fluttered. The fingers on her right hand twitched. She moved her head. Her eyes opened to slits. Alissa expelled her breath in a whoosh.

"Oh, my God. Elena! Dad, look!"

Aden gripped Elena's hand in both of his.

Spinning. The world is spinning. There's a bomb. A bomb! Take cover… Darkness, deep, soft, weightless. Sinking. Forever. But now light. I see light.

"Elena. Elena. Come back here. Elena."

I can't speak. My mouth is open. I have no words.

"Elena, my sweet sister, I need you. Do you hear me? I need you in my life. I can't do it without you. If you go away now, I'll be desolate forever. You must come back."

Elena heard weeping. *I'm falling away. No. The light, it arrests me, holds me.*

She opened her eyes and saw Alissa watching her. The small hospital room with its blue walls and white blinds louvered against the light from wide windows was familiar. *How long have I been here?*

"I will rescue you," Alissa whispered fiercely, her voice rough with unshed tears. "I will. I'll use whatever weapons I have." She swabbed Elena's eyes with a cotton ball dipped in distilled water, swabbed her lips, and took her hand. "Elena, please, oh please..."

"Hmmm?"

Alissa's breath caught in her throat. Urgent words rushed from her lips, "Elena, Hannah needs you. Hannah, the baby you brought into the world. Remember her beautiful blue eyes staring at you? She needs you to help her grow up, to be strong. She needs you to teach her and be with her. Where will she be without you? You can't let her go through life without you."

Elena stirred. She turned her head toward the sound of Alissa's voice. "Hana?"

Alissa stifled her sob. "Yes, Hannah, your niece." She lifted her daughter out of the baby carrier and propped her on Elena's stomach. "I'm putting your hand on her face. Feel how soft her skin is. Open your eyes. See how beautiful she is. She looks like you. She's got your fierce look in her eyes."

Elena's eyes fluttered open. "Oh."

The light was too much. Elena closed her eyes again. *There was a girl, a beautiful girl with blue eyes. She was standing at the prow of an ancient ship, the wind blowing back her long black hair. Stars rolled above her. She stood by the girl, who pointed out across the dark sea to the stars. She felt the boat move through the water and peace enveloped her.*

"Elena."

When Elena opened her eyes, hovering above her was an infant with wild, curly black hair, a cherub with huge blue eyes looking straight into her as if she knew every secret in Elena's heart. The child smiled, a wide, open-mouthed grin. Delight bloomed in Elena's chest. She reached out her arms and felt the child's soft body placed in them. She leaned her face toward the baby and breathed deeply. Was this what she'd been searching for, this child in her arms? She looked at her sister.

"Alissa?"

Alissa leaned in closer.

Elena whispered, "Dad?"

"Yes, my sweet girl, I'm here. We're all here." Aden riveted his eyes to Elena's face. Alissa wept soundlessly.

"Water," Elena said clearly.

John ran out to the desk on his crutches and told the on-duty nurse that Elena had revived. Alissa ran to get ice chips. Aden held the baby and stroked her head. "See how much she's changed since you helped bring her into the world."

"Dad," Elena said. Her eyes moved to focus on the baby. Hannah smiled at her and cooed. "Oh." Elena smiled. *This is what brought me back here, this child. I'm supposed to be here for her.*

A doctor rushed into the room accompanied by nurses and aides. They pushed everyone out of the room, administered a series of tests, and emerged from the room to tell the family what they already knew. Elena was out of the coma. They would now conduct a series of assessments to determine how much medical and physical therapy she needed. The family stopped listening. They only wanted to be with Elena, talking to her, holding her hand. To Elena, the doctors and nurses were flies, buzzing around her, something to be swatted away.

"Is it okay for her to hold the baby?" Aden asked the doctor.

"Well, that might not be a good idea at this moment," the doctor said. "At the least, she'll be weak and have some motor difficulty simply from being unconscious for all this time. There may be detriments due to the brain injury—speech, movement, memory."

Aden took his daughter's hand again. This time he was sure she smiled at him on purpose.

"Dad," she said.

He grinned at her and raised the head of the bed. Alissa wrapped her arm around Elena and placed tiny scoops of ice chips in her mouth. Elena pulled the child closer to her face and breathed deeply.

"So beautiful," she said, looking at Alissa. "You too."

Alissa put her head down on her older sister's shoulder. "Good to have you back, sis." She coughed to cover a sob and gave Elena a wobbly smile.

Elena's eyes roved the room as if looking for someone who wasn't there. "Hana?" she asked.

"She's right here in your arms, sis," Alissa said.

Aden and Alissa's eyes met, their faces maps of their alarm.

Chapter 26

HANA

Hana stared at the young man. His long hair stood in wild curls around his head. He was deeply tanned. His eyes burned. She gasped when she realized she knew that face.

"Danel. Danel!" she shouted for sheer joy. "I can't believe it's you. I asked everywhere for you. I thought you were lost. I thought I'd never see you again."

Danel grinned. "Oh no, I'm the one who's been looking for a way to free you," he said. "When Abirami found me and told me you were in trouble, I immediately began searching for a way to save you."

"You are free." She marveled at the words. "And Abirami is alive?"

"Well, of course I am, my girl," the old man said, stepping out of the shadows.

Hana's eyes spouted tears. Surely, she was asleep and dreaming this. "How is this possible?"

"I do know how to swim. Those sea people think they are the only ones who know how to keep their heads above the waves. I made my way to landfall at Enkomi, walked for three moons across this rocky island, and asked for Danel or the horse people wherever I found villages. By the next full moon after those Philistines threw me off their boat, I located Danel in a small village in the middle of the island. The horse people had given up on getting you and sold him off to another group of barbarians. Those captors were glad to take the pouch of gold coins Batnoam gave me for accompanying you." His eyes twinkled. "They were only going to sell you, after all. They got what they wanted with half the effort."

"Oh…" She put her hands over her eyes and then uncovered them and looked hard at Danel and Abirami. "I can hardly believe it." Hana thought she would cry and then she wanted to laugh instead.

She sobered abruptly and stormed at them. "Why didn't you come and rescue me from that horrible priestess? I was right here in Kty for six full moons. How is it you never found me? How could you leave me here and go out to sea without coming to get me if you knew where I was?"

"We heard of a girl with blue eyes who was making a mosaic for the goddess," Abirami began explaining. "We knew that must be you—who else has blue eyes? We thought you were safe enough and hoped we had time to figure out how to rescue you. We didn't know the priestess planned to sacrifice you."

"We don't have time for all these stories now," Danel said, his voice urgent. "The city is in chaos. The king's men are rounding up all the goddess's worshippers and killing them. There's talk in the streets of destroying all the images of Astarte. In their fury, they might destroy you as well. We must get you out of Kty right now."

Danel took Hana's wrist and ran with her down the steps to the cove. Abirami followed behind them as quickly as he could. Soon they were all standing knee deep in the sea, the waves pushing against them. "There's our boat," Danel pointed, "that beauty with the strong mast."

Hana noticed the pride in his voice. When the water was above their waists, a man in the boat threw a rope down to them. Danel climbed up and hoisted Hana on board. She breathed a sigh of relief when she saw Abirami's gnarled hands on the rail as he pulled himself onto the deck. All around her, she realized, men were stowing equipment and supplies, making the boat ready to depart.

"Have you been planning to leave Kty without me?" Suddenly, her throat was dry. Her stomach heaved. "If you hadn't found me…" She couldn't say the thought out loud.

"We tried to save you," Danel said. "We were turned back from the temple grounds repeatedly. In the market you always had those white ghosts around you and the guards around them." He made a face to imitate the novitiates' austere visages.

Against her will, Hana giggled.

"It was impossible, girl." Abirami's face aged suddenly. "You were always surrounded. There were more guards at the temple compound than we could overcome. We racked our brains for a clever plan. We needed gold to buy off your guards, so we took to the sea with goods to trade." He put a hand on Hana's shoulder. His words soothed her somewhat.

"We never gave up." Danel took her hand. "We knew eventually we would rescue you."

She looked at her two friends, her only friends in the world. "They could have killed me. The priestess was going to sacrifice me."

"We were terrified for you when we heard," Abirami said. "I prayed to the wise lord and Danel prayed to the Queen of Heaven. He said you would like that." His face brightened. "Our prayers were answered! In all the commotion, we thought we could spirit you away. And here you are."

She stopped her complaint mid-breath. They were all alive and together. She forgot her anger. If it was possible to beam joy into the air the way the sun beamed light, the people around her would be illuminated. Hana sighed. The burden of finding and rescuing Danel rolled off her shoulders. She felt taller. "Oh, I forgive you, as long as we are together from now on. But what are you doing on this boat?"

"I'm the captain of this boat," Danel said, barely keeping the boast from his tone. "Well," he looked down, "Abirami is the captain but he lets me give the orders." Danel winked at his wise friend. "He found a sound boat. You should have seen him thumping on the wood and bringing his eyes close to the seams between the cedar planks to determine if the boat was seaworthy. He even sniffed the wood for rot!" He looked at Abirami and laughed at the memory.

"It is a good, sound boat," Abirami said, "made of the trees from our home country."

"But where did you get the coins to buy a boat?"

Abirami smiled broadly. "I didn't give those barbarians all the gold Batnoam gave me."

Danel grinned at him. "We rounded up a small crew of good men. While you were thinking about stone pictures, we have made four trips from Tyre to Alashiya trading wood and purple cloth for copper, bronze, and other goods they make here. We make a small profit on each trip. Soon we would have had enough to ransom you from that priestess."

"An important man, then, after all."

"Look, you mouthy girl, just be glad it's our boat and we're not beholden to those barbarians who tried to sell you to the priestess."

"But how …"

Danel wiggled his eyebrows at her. "Always so many questions! You haven't changed at all. We have days for me to tell you all my stories." He put his arms around her waist, picked her off the deck, and whirled her around the way her father used to.

Hana clung to his neck and laughed. Her body could not contain all the joy she felt at being found.

Danel put Hana down on the deck. "But we must sail now before the king's guards set all the boats in the harbor on fire."

He issued orders to the crew. In a short time, the boat moved out of the cove and began its journey east across the sea toward Sidon. Hana stood by Danel at the prow and asked what they would do.

"We'll go to Sidon and see my father. Perhaps we will be able to stay in the city. We will make Sidon our home port and travel the world by sea, trading in all the foreign kingdoms across the world." He looked at her hopeful face. "At any rate, my father will know I'm alive. If we cannot live there," Danel looked over her shoulder to the east, his eyebrows furrowed with worry, "I will take you safely to your home. Or," he looked straight into Hana's eyes, "anywhere you wish."

Hana wrapped both her arms around Danel's waist, marveling at how much taller, and handsomer, he was than when she first met him, and watched the sea embrace the boat as they headed east across the water.

Chapter 27

ELENA

Elena sat in a wheelchair while her bed was changed. The heavy breath of the hospital's apparatus reminded her vaguely of the sea. She closed her eyes and rocked slightly, for the comfort of feeling her body move. By the afternoon, freed from IV tubes and catheter, she walked to the toilet with an escort. The cold seat on her thighs shocked her. Life awake was startling after her deep dreams.

That evening, the orderly brought her clear broth and Jell-O to eat. Never had she felt so hungry. Small green squares shimmied in her spoon and in her mouth melted to lime. With every bite, she imagined herself gaining strength and consciousness. Constant interruptions by hospital staff began to annoy her. She waited eagerly for each dear face that showed itself at her door asking, "May I come in?"

She smiled. "Dad, of course." He had been with her every day, but now that she was in his world, he had returned to the polite customs established when she and Alissa were teenagers.

When prompted, she spoke in short sentences, exhausted, as if she'd run a marathon, and remembered nothing of the day she was injured.

When Aden pressed for the story of what happened after the bridge blew, Elena shook her head slowly. "I was on a boat, an old boat with oars. There was a girl with blue eyes." She looked out of the window as if hoping to spot the girl.

"Her name was Hana," she told her father. "She needed my help. She was attacked. She's in danger and I'm not there to help her. I'm worried she'll be killed." Panic built in her chest. She wanted to leap out of bed and find her way back to the girl, but her legs wouldn't carry her farther than the door of her room.

"I'm supposed to be there with her. I'm supposed to protect her. She's calling for me. If I don't help her, I don't know what will happen to her. I don't know what will happen to us."

Aden turned his face away so Elena couldn't see his fear. He had his daughter back, but her mind was lost somewhere in an old story her mother had told her before she died. He understood Elena's anguish. She'd made a career out of her need to save helpless people. Now she had invented a fantasy of someone she could never save because the victim didn't exist. He worried his daughter would sink into despair if she didn't rid herself of the delusion.

Alissa handed the baby to her father and sat on the edge of the hospital bed. She took Elena's hand. "Something will happen to us? What do you mean, sweetheart?"

"Mom told us. You remember. Hana is the beginning of us. She's the first of our line. If she doesn't survive, we, we...we don't either." Elena's eyes strayed to the ceiling as if the vision of the girl she needed to save shimmered there. Her lips trembled. "Don't we disappear if she dies?"

Alissa turned her face to Aden. He read her sorrow

and worry. "Don't worry, Dad," she said. "I've got this. I know someone who can help."

തൈൽ

As she gained strength, Elena had flashes of what happened the day terrorists attacked her city—nose to nose with the skyscraper, the dead woman in a pool of blood and coffee on a marble floor, the despair on Sergeant Cantor's face, a small child in an orange jacket—but there were large gaps, as if her mind couldn't bear to know the whole story.

"Did we win, Dad?" she asked Aden one morning when he walked into her hospital room.

Aden grimaced. "Yes, if you can call it winning. We got the bastards. We took back the city. They gave you a medal at the memorial."

Elena grimaced. "Embarrassing."

"The President gave it to me to give to you." Aden pulled an expensive looking box from his backpack and opened it to show her the medal with its red ribbon resting on its black velvet bed.

Elena turned her face away. "I don't deserve that."

"More than five-hundred civilians died that day but thousands more would have if you hadn't figured out the bridges and tunnels were wired to explode. I was proud to accept it for you. I'm proud of you." He turned his face away so his daughter couldn't see the sorrow that overrode his pride.

She shrugged. The medal was too much responsibility. She couldn't live up to it. "What was the bad guy body count?"

Aden stood and walked to the window. "The Commissioner thinks fifty terrorists were involved in that action at the five sites they targeted. Our guys killed them, or they blew themselves up. Now there are armed National Guard troops patrolling the city and checkpoints are set up at all the tunnels. Traffic into the city is a disaster. Random security checks are routine in train stations, ferries, toll booths, and airports. People are skittish, paranoid."

"Who were they?"

"The terrorists were white supremacists from everywhere around the globe, including the U.S. They train in Russia. They have a website and a twitter account. And they're not done. At least, that's their claim, and I believe them. I bet they stand up an American sympathizer to run for president."

Elena shuddered. "Sons of bitches. What kind of strategy is that—kill innocent civilians just going about their daily lives, threaten women and children to prove you should be in charge of the world?"

She turned her head and followed her father's gaze out the window. "Where am I exactly?"

Aden grinned at her. "We're in an uptown hospital with a good reputation. And now that you're talking, I'm going to break you the hell out of here and take you home with me."

"Is John okay?"

"He took some damage, but he's healing." Aden looked into her eyes. "Anything going on there, with you two I mean? The guy's been steady. He's been right here with us as soon as he could get around on his own."

Elena laughed. "You're nosy." She tilted her head in a half-shrug. "On and off, but mostly off because…" she looked out of the window again, "because… war." The corners of her lips turned down. The world of things she couldn't say about her experiences pressed against her windpipe. Her father had been in Viet Nam. He knew what she couldn't say.

Aden changed the subject. He was still seething over the ineptness of the first hospital she'd landed in and the police department's failure to find her for a week. It was the longest week of his life, his fear that she was dead had rendered him incapable of speech for the time she was missing.

When the commissioner finally called to tell him where Elena was, he arrived at the Brooklyn hospital to find her in a coma. He had, according to Alissa's version of events, raised holy hell. His lawyer daughter was right behind him, feeding him the words that inspired dread in the people he was speaking to, but she stopped short of urging him to sue the hospital.

"It's enough that we found her, Dad." Alissa kissed her infant and murmured endearments to her. "We don't need to punish them. They kept her alive. Now we need to make her whole."

He had transferred Elena to a hospital that knew how to write people's names on charts and notify next of kin. And then they waited, one of them always by her bed around the clock. She'd been unconscious for weeks on end, breathing on her own, on an IV for nourishment, another infusion to head off a bacterial infection, and something to reduce swelling in her brain. That's all Aden understood of what he'd been told by the doctors. Most of the time, the rage in his own head drowned out the overly calm voices of health professionals.

But his daughter was recovering. He continually reminded himself of that. And now she was talking to him as if she cared about what was happening in this world, his world, the one he knew as reality. Coming home, he was sure, would heal her.

Chapter 28

HANA

Three days after they sailed out of Kty, Danel, Abirami, and Hana arrived at the same cove near Sidon from which Hana had left a full planting season before, smuggled onto a boat by Danel's father. This time they walked into Sidon through the main gate. Danel dispensed bronze and gold Kytian coins to the guards who marveled at the image of a muscled man wearing a lion's skin and carrying a club and a bow. Coins, Hana observed, were as good as citizenship in this city.

Within one-hundred paces of their entrance into Sidon, Danel's father came rushing toward them, his face, normally proud and aloof, alternating between laughter and tears as he made his way past people milling in the plaza.

He shouted to Danel, "Hello, hello!" and waved his arms in the air while still many paces away. He ran to his son and embraced him. He hugged Hana and threw his arm around Abirami's shoulders.

"This is a miracle. How did you make it back? Come, come, let's go to the house and eat. You must be hungry and thirsty. I can't believe you are really here.

The gods have blessed me." He stopped talking and hugged his son again, burying his face in Danel's shoulder. Danel grinned at Hana from his father's embrace.

"I heard the news in the market, but I could hardly believe it was true." Batnoam looked over at Hana and Abirami. "You found him and brought him back to me." His voice was thick with competing emotions. "The gods themselves must have helped you."

"Truly, it was Danel who found *me*," Hana said. "But yes, the gods helped me."

Brushing off her explanation, Batnoam embraced Hana again, kissed both her cheeks and her forehead, held her away from him appraising her, and then pulled her back into his arms. "You, my blue girl, have become a woman."

Hana blushed with pleasure at Batnoam's compliment. She stood taller, and began to think of herself as a woman, with a woman's rights, instead of a child. She looked at Danel and saw he was watching her.

Batnoam clasped Abirami's arm and looked into the old man's face. "You are a true friend, old man. Thank you for bringing them both back to me."

Abirami shook his shoulders and huffed, but his pleasure at being thanked showed in his face.

They made a small procession, walking through the city to Batnoam's house. The proud father called out to all the neighbors who waved at them, "Look! My son has returned. He is back with me."

But when they walked into the courtyard of Batnoam's house ready to celebrate Danel's homecoming, they found Ashirat surrounded by guards, their faces grim and determined, armed with daggers in their sashes and spears in their hands. The travelers' joy dissipated. Batnoam's elation disappeared as fast as rain hitting hot sand.

"They've come for Hana," Ashirat said, her voice flattened by fear.

"They're not getting her," Danel placed himself in front of Hana.

"The prince demands that the Blue Girl be brought to the palace immediately," a guard said, relinquishing his hold on Ashirat's arm. "You may escort her, but she is coming with us even if we have to take your life."

Hana put her hand on Danel's back and leaned toward him. "It will be all right, Danel. There are too many of them. It's not worth giving up your life to oppose them at this moment. We'll find a way. We've come this far."

Danel turned to Hana and took her hand. "I'm going with you. I won't be parted from you again."

They walked through the streets in a second odd procession, the blue girl and the son who had been missing, both so greatly changed by time and circumstances that it seemed to all who looked at them as if they glowed like the sun. They were surrounded by the queen's guard, with Abirami, Batnoam, and Ashirat following. Along the way to the palace, the neighbors, the glass blower and baker, the jugglers and the fishmongers, the artisans from the mosaic workshop, everyone to whom Hana had ever spoken who had heard that she and Danel were back safely in Sidon followed behind them and trooped into the palace to stand in front of Queen Peri and the prince.

Peri scowled when she saw them all crowd into her chamber. "What is this motley crowd doing here?"

Hana looked around at the room. Nothing had changed and yet everything and everyone seemed smaller and less regal. Perhaps the vast sea had changed her perspective. And where was the matron? Shouldn't she be here also?

"You wanted us to bring the Blue Girl to you, Queen," the guard captain said. "We have done so."

"You idiot. I wanted you to bring her alone, not with this group of fools."

"They insisted on accompanying her. You didn't order us to kill anyone."

Peri raised her arm and pointed to the guards. "Get out of my sight. Imbeciles."

The guards, who seemed to shrink several inches in size, scurried out of the chamber. The rest of the queen's court remained. The queen stared at Hana and Danel and they stared back at her. A juggler began tossing blue glass bottles into the air. Peri motioned to one of her handmaidens to fan her. The prince, in a multi-colored loin cloth, his chest gleaming with a gold breast plate in imitation of the Hittite king he admired, leaned over and whispered something to his mother. The queen's attendants whispered to each other.

Peri pointed at Hana. "Come here, girl."

Hana walked up to the queen. She stopped within an arm's length of the monarch, lowered her eyes, and then raised them again, looking directly at the queen. It was as insolent as she dared to be. Her stomach quaked. Not only her life but Danel's, and all these people's lives, depended on her behaving correctly and, as usual, she had no idea what she should do. Hana's shoulders relaxed as the idea flitted through her mind that the goddess who had helped her before might suddenly knock the queen to the floor. She smiled at her thought.

The queen did not smile. "I see your adventure has not made you ugly."

"Thank you, Queen, for the compliment."

The queen's lips puckered and then thinned into a straight line. "My son has already taken a first wife. We have no more need of you, unless he wants a concubine."

"I hope the prince and his wife are happy and fertile."

"You are still an insolent girl, I see." The queen
stood. She no longer towered over Hana. She stepped
back and walked around her, looking at Hana from all
sides.

The prince reclined on his chair, observing Hana
while his mother spoke. Then he rose from his seat,
tossed his long, black hair behind his shoulders, and
walked over to Hana. He removed her blue veil, undid
her tunic, yanked on the cloth and spun her around. The
throng in the queen's chamber gasped. Even his mother
was shocked at the prince's behavior.

Hana's heart froze. *I must fight!* But if she moved,
the prince might kill her, or Danel. Words stuck in her
throat. She wanted to thrust her dagger into the prince's
throat. She wanted to melt away into the air and never be
seen again. Without thinking, she flung her fist holding
the dagger into the air, like a warning or a declaration.
Sunlight streamed in from the courtyard and flared
through the blue crystals of her ring, flashing in the
prince's eyes.

He gasped and stepped back. "I'm blinded!" He covered his face with his hands. "What ungodly wizardry is
this?" he asked.

The queen stood to help her son. He brushed off her
hands. All whispering in the hall ceased. Danel took a
step toward the dais. Batnoam and Abirami seized his
arms and restrained him. Hana secured the tunic over her
body, returned her dagger to its pouch, and waited.

The prince staggered around her, one hand on the
hilt of the dagger tucked into his sash, the other grasping
for something to hold onto. He clutched Hana's hair and
pushed her to her knees. "I am not a scavenger," he
growled. "I will not eat after another man has opened his
prey." He turned his face in Danel's direction. "You
should be glad of this."

Hana didn't tell the prince his assumption was wrong. No one had ravaged her. She was intact, as the matron would say, and she would stay that way until she decided not to be. But it was safer for her that the prince assumed her virginity was already taken. The prince's own arrogance would defeat him. She only had to bear the humiliation he intended her to suffer, and she was strong enough for that.

The prince released his grip and turned his back to Hana. "Go out of my city. You may have thought I was not good enough for you but, in fact, you are no longer good enough for me. I care nothing for your blue bird and your blue eyes. They mean nothing to me. My line will be long and illustrious without you. Poets will be writing songs about me long after your entire tribe has turned to dust."

He waved his hand indicating everyone should disappear. "Be gone by sunset tonight," he commanded.

As an afterthought, as his sight returned, the prince flipped a gold coin to Hana, who caught it in her hand. "So you cannot say I sent you away without knowing your value," he taunted.

Hana looked at the coin in her hand. On it was the image she had imagined for the mosaic at Kty—the goddess Ashtart standing at the prow of a ship pointing to the stars. She must have seen the image in an artisan's workshop before she even arrived in Alashiya. *The goddess did save me once again.* Putting the coin into her pouch, she wrapped herself in her blue veil and walked back to Danel, taking his hand. More than anything else at this moment, she wanted to walk into the sea and cleanse herself of the prince's gaze.

Hana and Danel walked out of the palace, followed by their cheering retinue, retracing their steps to Batnoam's house and the celebratory meal Ashirat had laid out as soon as she heard from her neighbor that they survived their encounter with the prince of Sidon. On the way, Hana leaned against Danel and spoke quietly. "You are the one to whom I will give myself. You guided me over the wasteland, you sacrificed yourself for me, and rescued me from Kty. You are my truest friend."

Danel's color deepened, he grinned, and swallowed hard. His eyes sparkled when he turned to Batnoam. "Father, would you conduct the marriage ritual for us?"

Batnoam's face lit with joy. He pressed the flat of his hand to his heart and laid the other on his son's head. "It would be my honor."

In Batnoam's courtyard, Danel's father announced the joining of two families, two clans now united to make a new tribe. Danel walked three times in a circle around Hana, his arms outstretched, his chin high. His voice carried on the bright air. "I marry this woman," he declared to his father, his family and everyone assembled, "I marry this woman, I marry this woman."

In the center of the circle Danel made, Hana turned also, her arms outstretched, her hands brushing Danel's, and said more quietly, "I marry this man, I marry this man, I marry this man." They joined hands and Batnoam kissed them both on their foreheads.

While subdued well-wishers pressed Hana's hands, kissed her cheeks, and pounded Danel on the back, all Hana could think of was her real home, the lush valley of her childhood. This place, the city of Sidon, was not her home. She was glad the prince had exiled her.

"What happened to the matron?" she asked Ashirat, while the guests ate, drank, and laughed at each other's jokes.

"The queen beheaded her for losing you."

Breath rushed out of Hana's lungs. She closed her eyes. A kind woman was killed because of her. "But Batnoam wasn't harmed?"

"The queen knew nothing of Batnoam's hand in your departure. She was told you were stolen away in the night by the Philistines."

Hana put her hand over her mouth and shuddered. She turned away from Ashirat. Someone who had taken care of her was killed because she fled. The matron's death was too awful to contemplate. Sidon was a horrible place, run by a queen who thought ordinary people's lives had no value.

She was desperate to go home, to see her parents, to be held in their arms. Surrounded by all these people, she felt lonely and sad. Something was missing. She couldn't celebrate with them. She had completed the task the elders set her on, and although she was still alive, she surely had been sacrificed to the vanity of Sidon's royal family. She needed to be away from them. Only at home would she feel healed. She was glad she and Danel were being forced to leave.

When the guests had gone, Batnoam provisioned them and walked with them out of the city. Abirami would go with them, they had decided, and two of Danel's older brothers by Batnoam's first wife.

"There's strength in numbers," Batnoam said, his face broken by sadness to have found his son and lost him in the same day. "I will never see you again, never hold the child of your union..." He gave Hana a kiss on her cheek. "...but somehow I know that all will go well with you." He gathered Hana into his arms and whispered, "The wise lord is with you."

Danel and his father wrapped their arms around each other for the last time. Hana watched as Danel buried his face in his father's shoulder. She longed to do that with her own parents. *Soon*, she promised herself, *soon*.

Chapter 29

ELENA

Elena sat back in the wooden Adirondack chair on her father's deck and looked out over the multitude of colors in the rolling landscape. Half a mile away, in the crook between the hills, a small stream burbled toward a larger one. Six months had passed since she was blown off the bridge. It seemed like more, like eons, as if she had slipped into geologic time, her body turned to stone, the achingly slow movement of atoms in dense matter increasing her gravity.

This is the way of life, isn't it? We're always moving even when we seem to be still. Her thoughts rearranged themselves as they found their way to her consciousness—*maybe we aren't the water but are instead the riverbed, the rocks over which the water flows.* Restless, she threw off the plaid wool blanket her father had placed over her knees, put down the mug of tea, and walked off the deck, down the wooden steps and across the wide expanse of lawn toward the water. *Maybe if I get a closer look, I'll understand what I'm supposed to do.*

Her family was still treating her as if she was broken. Maybe she was still broken but she was impatient and sure there was nothing physically wrong with her except this persistent fatigue and headache. On the other hand, she couldn't bring herself to go back to policing, to waiting in the icy grip of fear for something unknown to blast her into oblivion. That was the wrong way, the way of death. Life was too precious for that. There had to be something else she could do.

When she thought about delivering Alissa's baby, she remembered being overwhelmed by the miracle of the child's birth. Is that what I want? Bringing another helpless child into a world that is violently tearing itself apart seemed to be an insane desire.

To make her father happy, Elena spent hours sitting in the office of the highly credentialed psychologist Alissa had found. She told the woman the story of Hana, who lived in an ancient, simpler world, a world without bombs and bullets but one still fraught with danger.

"She needs my help," Elena tried to explain to the psychologist. "She's my family—my mother said so—and she's in danger, and I'm just sitting here doing nothing."

She couldn't explain how her heart yearned for the freedom of the sea, for the unsullied world she had glimpsed. It was not that the ancient world was safer, but it seemed to her that one determined person might have a chance to survive it, to make something worthwhile happen. Nor could she describe how, by saving Hana, she felt she might save the world. Elena was sure if she could intervene in that time, the world might not be so wretched now. Although surely, that thought proved she was crazy.

"Do you still see Hana today?" the therapist asked.

"You know that's a ridiculous question," Elena said. "Of course, I don't see her now. She's obviously not from this time. I saw her when I was in the coma, but she's real and I know if I could get back there, I could help her."

"Can you hear yourself?"

"What do you mean?"

"How would you get back to a time that has already passed? Even if this girl did exist, you can't go backwards in time. There is only now, the present moment we are in, and the future."

Elena looked out of the office window at the parking lot below. She was sure the therapist was wrong, but she had no proof. Sun gleamed off the hoods of cars. *The world is so mechanized now.* She looked back at the therapist.

"How do you know Hana's time doesn't exist?" *Why am I bothering? This woman will never understand me.* "I belong there. I can make a difference there. Here," she spread her hands out, "I can't do anything useful. It's too late. The world has already gone to hell."

"What about your family here? The people who are alive. Your father, your sister. Don't they need you? Don't you make a difference with them?"

"Yes, I suppose, but it's not a life or death situation for them, is it?"

"Do you think you made a difference for the baby you brought into the world on the day terrorists attacked New York City?"

"Yes, yes, of course. I'm glad I was there. That was a miracle, but she would have been born without me."

"Don't you think you saved your sister's life by being there?"

"Oh. Maybe. Probably." Elena shrugged, as if to say that wasn't so much.

"What makes you think the girl you found in the old world is exactly where you left her? Hasn't her life moved on? Perhaps she saved herself."

The questions shocked Elena. Of course, the psychologist was right. Hana's life would've continued. That idea hadn't occurred to her before. But *she* didn't know what happened to the girl, and she hadn't participated in making it happen. Even though she had freed Hana from the prison cell, she had failed the girl in the same way she'd failed all those innocent people who died on the bridge that horrible day. She had sworn she would help them, and she hadn't done it. Grief sliced through her, leaving her breathless. Her throat hurt with shame as if she had swallowed rocks.

"I failed. I did nothing."

"Would going back to save Hana bring all the people who died on the bridge back to life?"

Elena shook her head. She wiped her face with a tissue. How could she explain that if she had saved Hana maybe there would never have been an attack on the bridge? "I think *I* would be safer there," she said instead of what she was thinking, instead of trying to articulate what was too complicated and deep to put into words— that she had been given one opportunity to change what the world had become, and she'd failed.

"Because the world here is a terrifying place?"

"Yes, exactly."

"Isn't that old world just as terrifying for Hana as the one in which we live?"

"It wouldn't be if I was there to help her."

"So, in that old world, you have superpowers, powers you don't have here?"

"You make it sound stupid and naïve."

"In the old world, where you are powerful, you can protect people and save their lives."

"Yes."

"And you long to do that."

"Yes," Elena whispered, "I long to do that." She reached into her jeans pocket and pulled out the gold coin, rubbing the image of the goddess with her thumb as if a genie could emerge and grant her wish.

"Is it possible that the young girl you long to save is yourself?"

Elena looked at the woman for a while and slowly nodded her head.

Chapter 30

HANA

Their small troop trekked across the plain toward the mountains in a straggling line feeling free and bold. Nothing could harm them. They had enough supplies to make it to Hana's home village and Danel had made sure to bring additional supplies for Osnot. He told Hana he had a sudden fear that no one had taken care of the old woman all the time he had been gone.

Hana held his hand and attempted to console him. "Surely your father sent someone else."

The escarpment they had to scale loomed into sight and they decided to make their camp by a stream running nearby. They would wait for the morning light for the ascent.

"It doesn't seem as high as it was from the top, the first time we did this," Hana said.

Danel smirked. "You were smaller."

Hana slapped his shoulder and laughed. She loved the freedom she felt with him, that she could say anything, ask any question, comment about anything and her words, or at least her saying them, would be accepted. Danel never told her to be quiet. Even if he didn't agree with her, Danel didn't make her feel she was foolish for thinking.

They made a small fire to keep them warm through the night when the air would grow cold. At dusk, they ate a meal of bread, dates, and cheese, drank sparingly of their water, and lay down to sleep. Leaning her head back against Danel's chest, Hana watched his finger trace the shape of a serpent, bear, and giant among the stars in the sky. He whispered to her how these great creatures would help him navigate across the sea at night and keep them safe. Then he pointed out the bright winking lights that outlined Ashtart, the goddess who protected Hana.

"You should thank her. It is astounding that you are still alive, not a slave of the priestess, or in someone's harem."

"I do thank her, every morning and every night. I look at the gold coin the prince threw at me and I think how she has helped me every step of my journey."

Before dawn, just as light began to glow in the east, Hana woke to gather their things and put out food for a morning meal. She woke Danel and he woke his brothers and Abirami. Gathered in a circle to eat, they heard a shrieking sound. Danel and Hana, remembering his abduction by the horse people several seasons before, jumped up.

Back to back, daggers in each of their hands, they looked around them. No thrumming on the ground from many hooves, no horses, no people running toward them from the horizon. The earth was not shaking. And then a swoop of wings, the graze of a talon, made them turn in circles and look up. Two giant eagles swooped down on them, pushed them all into a huddle, flew up into the sky, and turned to fly at them again. Danel put his hand to his forehead and looked at his fingertips. The eagle's claw had drawn blood.

"Cover your heads," Danel yelled. "Pick up rocks. Wait. Wait. Now! Aim at their heads."

All of them threw their rocks but missed the birds, which seemed to swoop down on them more quickly than the wind, but the spinning rocks flung powerfully into the air sent the eagles flying away, at least momentarily.

"Why are they doing this?" Hana yelled. "Did we disturb their hunting ground?"

"I don't care why," Danel grumbled. "We need to get to a shelter." He scanned the escarpment looking for a cave.

Time beat out as fast as the blood beating through Hana's body. Hand shading her eyes, she scanned the sky.

"They're coming back," Abirami called, spotting the birds wheeling in the distance and turning back toward them.

"I see a shelter," Danel yelled. "Follow me."

They left all their supplies on the plain and ran toward the depression at the base of the mountain that Danel spotted. It was barely a cave, but it was big enough for all of them to fit beneath the mountain's stone walls. As he ran, Danel pulled up heavy branches lying on the ground and tossed boughs to Hana, Abirami and his brothers, keeping one for himself.

"If they attack us, hit them with the branches." The men nodded. "Keep the branches up like this." He demonstrated, holding the branch above his head. "Make a screen in front of the cave."

Hana's heart thumped harder in her chest. She held the branch up above her head until she reached the shallow cave. Danel pushed her behind him. Jagged rocks pressed against her back. Shielding their bodies with spears of stiff branches, they were as protected from the birds as they could be. Hana kept her eyes on the sky, closed her hand over the gold coin in her palm, and prayed to the goddess to save them.

The eagles headed right toward them, flying low, screeching. She held her breath. Suddenly the air was a flurry of blue, red, and yellow feathers as hundreds of smaller birds swarmed the eagles, squawking at them, flapping their wings in their faces, pecking at them, turning them back, herding them away in another direction. The eagles came to a halt in mid-air, flew upward in narrow circles, tried to attack again and were repulsed a second time by swarms of brightly colored birds. Screeching, the eagles flew off, soaring into the sky, back to their nest high in the mountains.

Silent, the travelers watched. Even when all the birds were gone, they said nothing. Tentatively, Danel and Hana stepped out of the cave and looked at the sky. Small blue feathers littered the ground. He breathed in deeply and Hana took his hand.

"I think," his voice quavered, "you have a friend in the Queen of Heaven. I will never mock you again."

Hana smiled. She thought the colorful birds were protecting their own nests but said nothing. There were times when words were insufficient. She offered a prayer of thanks for birds that risked their lives to fight eagles and picked up one blue feather from the ground to add to the precious items in her pouch.

Chapter 31

ELENA

John Westmore drove up the rutted lane to Aden's house in the Catskills, expecting to find Elena and her father engrossed in a game of checkers, crowing over each other's bad moves, goading each other into disastrous choices in a Monopoly game, or reading out passages from very different books while soft jazz played on the radio. His last visit was the week before. Elena hadn't returned his calls since then.

He found Aden pacing in the living room. Elena lay on the couch with her eyes closed, a plaid blanket over her. Her face was pale yellow and sweaty. John waited a few seconds before he said, "Hey guys, what's up here?"

Elena didn't open her eyes. Aden looked away.

John took four long strides to the couch and felt Elena's pulse. Too fast and irregular, his combat training told him. Her eyes moved under the lids. She was alive, at least, dreaming perhaps. The color of her skin said jaundice. He felt her forehead and her cheek. She was burning up. *What the hell is Aden doing?*

"How long has she been like this?"

Aden stared at his daughter. "Three days. I thought she had the flu at first. She was throwing up. Then she said she had a severe headache and she couldn't move her head without her neck killing her."

"Did you call anyone?"

"No. Not yet. I don't know who to trust."

"Jesus, man. Did she take something?"

"I don't think so. One minute we were talking, the next she was like this."

"She needs to go to a hospital, right now. She might be unconscious. She needs IV fluids, a blood test to see if she's septic, other medical stuff to keep her going. Maybe it's meningitis, pneumonia, something that could be treated."

John heard the desperation in his own voice. He had been with Elena in Iraq and Afghanistan. He had been with her squad for five years on the police force. He had been with her in what she would call the Biblical sense but that wasn't why he felt so connected to her. Although he wouldn't use the word love—he was too much of a tough guy to think that way—that was the only logical name for his feelings toward Elena. They were more than friends who drifted in and out of each other's lives. He wanted—no, needed—to protect her. What he felt wasn't about sex and all that googly-eyed stuff about walking on air. She always had his back. She knew what he knew, had seen what he saw, thought the way he thought. If he didn't understand her, if he couldn't protect her, who could?

Aden waved his arm in the air. "She doesn't want to keep going." He sounded like a man who had lost everything.

"I'm just not going to believe that about Elena. She's too full of life and purpose."

"That's just it. She thinks she has no purpose. Even the baby doesn't work her magic anymore."

"Look, Aden, I can't let you do it this way." John turned away from Aden, pulled out his cell phone and tried to call for an ambulance. There was no signal on his phone. "What the—"

"We don't have cell service up here," Aden said. "Thought you knew that."

John looked around the house and found the landline phone in the kitchen. He called emergency dispatch and said he needed an ambulance immediately, he had an unconscious woman with a fever, "breathing shallowly," he added to increase the dispatcher's urgency. He gave Aden's address.

"It could be hours before anyone gets there," the dispatcher told him. "We had a fire in town. All units are over there. No telling how long that will take."

"Never mind," John said, keeping his fury under control. He hung up the phone and turned to Aden. "Where's the nearest hospital?"

"About twenty miles down the road in Livingston Manor. Lots of turns on these narrow roads between here and there. Besides, what do these doctors know? She's safer here."

John felt like decking Aden, but he checked himself. He knew what despair felt like.

"No, man, we are not waiting."

He scooped Elena up in his arms and walked out of the front door. On the porch, he turned around and yelled to Aden. "Hey, old man, come on. She needs you."

৩৩৩

Elena stood next to Hana and surveyed the plain ahead of them. She'd landed on the grassy plain with a thump that reverberated through her bones. Her feet were planted firmly on the earth. Tall grasses waved in the breeze. The sun blazed. Birds whirled across the blue sky. In the far distance she could see mountains jutting up into the clouds. She drew in a deep breath of untainted air. The world was beautiful, untamed, and full of possibility.

It had taken her days to find the girl, days of wandering in the darkness, a perpetual fog with no light. And then the landscape opened and here she was. It was such a relief to find her. Joy leaped to Elena's mouth in a laugh. She wanted to wrap her arms around Hana and swing her through the air.

Elena listened to the plans outlined by the young man Hana called Danel. Today they would climb the mountain wall and then cross the wasteland on the way back to Hana's home. Elena felt Hana's excitement building in her own chest. It would be good to be home. She seemed to see the village in her own memory, the thatched huts, the work areas for weaving, metal forging, pot making. A field of barley was ripening nearby. Deep homesickness throbbed in her stomach. They were going home where she was supposed to be.

She looked around at the small group of travelers and realized there were more people here she didn't know, six men of various ages, and Hana, who seemed to have grown as tall as she. How much time had passed since she was with the girl? In the months since the terrorist attack, two years seemed to have passed. Time was different here, it moved faster. She watched Hana with Danel and realized they were lovers. They laughed together frequently, taking every opportunity to lean into each other, putting their hands on each other's arms, clasping hands. Their faces seemed magnetically drawn to each other so that their lips could meet.

Elena felt left out and unneeded. Hana had someone else to help her, to be her companion. She had no right to these feelings. She hadn't really saved the girl, if she was honest. She had helped but Hana had saved herself. Other people had aided her. *Maybe you couldn't save anyone. Maybe they always had to do it themselves.* And yet, Elena's heart was hollowed out. She yearned to be useful and realized she was wishing for something dreadful to happen to Hana so that she could rescue her.

Elena caressed Hana's face and pushed her hair back. "I'm here, Blue Girl."

The girl looked up and smiled. "I see you," she said, the delight in her voice warming Elena. Hana turned to Danel. "The goddess is still here with me."

Danel put his arms around Hana and kissed her. "I'm glad. We'll need all the help we can get." They laughed as if the idea of facing danger together excited them.

When the girl looked back at Elena, the glow had left her face. "Oh, she's gone now."

Elena turned away. They didn't need her. Hana couldn't see her. They were young, strong, and determined. They could rescue themselves. A small clan on the move, they would migrate to somewhere else, somewhere she would never see no matter how she longed to do so.

With a sharp pang, Elena realized she didn't belong here with them. This wasn't her home, her time, her place. She had nowhere to go. She belonged nowhere. Without warning, the blackness embraced her again, and she fell, swirling around in it, her arms flailing, spiraling downward into darkness again.

Chapter 32

HANA

Before the sun reached the middle of the sky, they had scaled the rock face and began to walk across the desolate landscape of rocks and cracked earth that led to Osnot's hut. Somehow, the vast moraine did not seem as wide or as far as it had the first time Hana crossed it. Since Hana didn't need to rest, the group decided not to stop until they reached Osnot's shelter.

Abirami walked beside Hana, stepping carefully among rocks strewn in all directions and at all angles as if an infant god had tired of building mountains and abandoned the stones in disarray on the ground. "You came this way before?"

"Yes, on my way to Sidon, I walked this path with Danel. Well," she looked over at Danel and laughed, "it would be more accurate to say I walked *behind* Danel."

"You were right to tell me you were a brave girl all those many seasons ago when I found you outside Sidon's walls." Abirami looked around at the wasteland. "I think I might have sunk to my knees and wept. It looks like the gods despaired of all beauty here."

Hana put her hand on his arm. "It's not as bad as all that, Abirami. You and I have been through worse adventures than this."

The old man nodded and patted her hand.

They approached the spot where Osnot's hut should have been. Danel looked around, frantic, calling, "Old mother, old mother, are you here?" He raced in all directions, finally coming to rest next to Hana, his mouth drawn down at its corners, his eyelids heavy with tears.

Only a low stone outline of the dwelling remained. No one could possibly live here. Osnot was nowhere to be seen and planks from what must have been her hut lay strewn on the ground in all directions as if a funnel of air had churned through the shelter and thrown every stick of wood in a different direction. For a while they walked in widening circles calling for Osnot but even as they did it, they knew she was gone. She could not have survived such destruction, or if she had, she couldn't have remained there without shelter.

Hana, her heart heavy, stood in the spot where she was sure she had washed her face and hands when she first arrived in Osnot's hut. Danel searched for the spring from which Osnot drew cool water every morning. If it was still flowing, he would fill their water pouches. Hana knelt on the ground, remembering the rugs, the loom, the glass bowl, the old woman and her gift of marks on papyrus. Hana felt something in the air. *Perhaps it's her kindness that hovers like a blessing.*

"I think the horse people took her and all her possessions," Danel said. "That's the only thing that makes sense."

"Maybe the people in my village brought her down into the valley to care for her when she could no longer move about."

Hana didn't really believe what she was saying. Osnot was absent from the earth. "Perhaps people came after she died and took her things. Osnot wouldn't have cared about that. She told me she had completed her final task."

If she looked carefully enough, she was sure she would see Osnot in the night sky standing next to the Queen of Heaven.

ᏋᏁᏋᏁ

Water pouches filled, they decided to move on to the path that led down from the mountain to Hana's village. Her pulse quickened and her head buzzed.

"Your cheeks have high color," Danel said. "Are you sick?"

"Oh, no, Danel, it's the excitement of seeing my parents again, of showing you my beautiful valley. You will love it there. All colors of blue water flow in the river. It's alive with fish. We can lie in it and bathe and feel the grime of our journey carried away from us. We can even wash our clothes in it."

Danel smiled at her, put his arm around her shoulders and drew her close to him. He nuzzled her cheek with his nose. "We'll sleep on the riverbank under the stars and this time, because I know you know what I have taught you, you will show me where the bear and the serpent are in the night sky."

Hana laughed. "Yes! I will even show you where our old Osnot stands."

They had reached the crest of the mountain and could look down into her valley. Far below, her village appeared as peaceful as the day she left it. Tufts of smoke from cooking fires and the forge blew up into the sky and dissipated. Even this far away, Hana thought she heard the joyful shouts of children.

"There are so many trees," Abirami said. "Light sparkles off the river. I see why you called this paradise."

Hana nodded and began to run down the mountain, lost her footing, and rolled many times before Danel caught up to her, laughing, helping her up, and chiding her. "Take your time, blue girl, we will get there." She took his hand, stood up, and walked at a statelier pace down the mountain toward home. She almost expected her mother to be standing at the bottom of the last hill with her arms out, waiting to embrace her.

But no one was waiting at the bottom of the last hill, not even a child sent as a lookout to discover who was coming down from the mountain. "Something is wrong," Hana said. "Why haven't they sent anyone to meet us? Surely they saw us descending."

A ring of thatched dwellings still formed the core of the village. They passed the pot-making area where a woman was placing new clay vessels into the earth for firing. The woman looked at them cautiously and turned her face away. In the weaving workshop women were stripping flax to be made into thread and woven on their looms. Anxiety grew in Hana's chest. No one waved to her as if they knew her, or called out to them as strangers, or approached them—odd behavior from a friendly clan. Something had happened.

Hana broke away from her friends and raced toward her old home, calling out, "Ouma, Aba! I'm here. I'm home. Where are you?" She stood, breathless in the opening of her old dwelling and looked into the darkness, waiting for her eyes to adjust.

"Ouma, are you in here?" She took a step into the house and waited to be embraced, her breath in her throat, her hands shaking with excitement. Something was wrong. The smell, the scent of sage and wild berry was absent.

A young woman rose from the floor and walked to Hana. "I don't know you, my dear." A child clung to her skirts. Her voice was kind, but it was not the voice Hana was longing to hear. "My husband and I live here with our child. Who are you hoping to find?"

Hana strained to keep the tears from her voice. "Alyssa the storyteller and Hammurabi the metal maker, don't they live here anymore? Are they somewhere else in the village?" She turned her head to look around at the other dwellings.

The kind woman shook her head. "No, they are no longer here."

Hana turned away, stumbling on the flat ground. She felt dizzy and lost. Sorrow and fear thickened in her throat. Danel put his arm around her. "Come on. We'll find the elders. They'll know the truth."

In the center of the village, an old woman walked up to them. Hana searched her face and tried to remember who the woman was.

"You are welcome in our village," the old woman said. "Strangers are always welcome. Please come into my home, wash, drink, and share my food."

"You are so polite," Hana exclaimed, suddenly re-membering the woman's face. "Don't you recognize me? I'm Hana. I'm from here. This is my clan. Andulat is my home. You are the elder who sent me to Sidon."

The woman reached up and took Hana by the arms. She pulled Hana down toward her and looked into her face. Hana watched as recognition dawned.

"Yes, of course, the blue eyes. How could I not know you? You are the girl we sent to the king so he would leave us in peace. I'm old now, my sight is nearly gone, and I forget everything I knew at least once a day."

The old woman's cheeks and neck turned the color of
fired clay. "I didn't expect you to return."

Hana jerked her body back away from the woman.
*They sent me away to become the king's concubine and
never expected to see me again. How could my parents
have gone along with such an arrangement?*

"It is long ago," the old woman said. "Perhaps my
memory of what was to happen has faded." She placed
her hand on Hana's arm. "Come sit with me and tell us
all your adventures."

By the time they were settled on the floor in the
woman's dwelling, others from the village had crowded
in. A young boy climbed onto Hana's lap and stroked her
cheeks with his fingers. "Blue eyes," he said and giggled.

The old woman held the boy's hands and lifted him
off Hana, putting him down on the floor. "Shoo, shoo,"
she said. The child waddled away and the elder turned
back to Hana. "Now I recall that one of the king's soldiers spotted you when he came to collect a gold crown
from your father. We were told by messenger that we
must send you to the king of Sidon or everyone in the
village would be killed and our homes burned to the
ground so that no trace of us was left in the world."

Stung that the elder had no remorse about sacrificing
her to the king's whims, Hana hid her anger by drinking
deeply from the water the woman offered. She wiped her
chin with her hand.

"Perhaps I was meant for the king, but other things
happened instead."

"Have you run away? Are you going to bring the
king's wrath down on our heads again? We've been
through that already, in spite of sending you to him. It
was horrible. Strong men with weapons came. They beheaded four men in front of their wives and took away all
of our beautiful, young girls. They burned our grain

storehouse. We were not the same after that. The people became afraid and listless. They lost hope in the future."

"When was that?"

"Two planting seasons ago."

Hana could restrain her fear no longer. "Did they kill my parents? Is that why they are not here to greet me?" She closed her eyes so that when the woman answered, the response wouldn't hurt as much. Danel took her hand.

"Oh, no, my dear," the old woman said. "Your parents pined for you and would not eat or drink. By the fifth full moon after your departure, they had made themselves sick with worry. We tried all our remedies and prayers, but nothing helped. They would have died from grief and remorse. Before the harvest, we sent them away so that their sadness would not infect the entire village. Several of the strong young men and women went with them to seek a new home in another place."

Hana put her hands over her face and moaned. She rocked, trying to comfort herself. She tried to be glad that her parents were alive. Danel wrapped her in his arms and pulled her head down on his shoulder. He whispered comforting words into her ear.

But Hana could not be comforted. "I'll never see them again. They've left and I'll never be able to find them. How can I bear that?" She looked imploringly at the old woman. "Did they leave anything for me, something that would tell me where they've gone?"

The elder sat with her head to the side. "Your mother said something about following the sun across the sky as it moves from morning to night." She shook her head. "I'm sorry, that's all I recall."

Danel wiped Hana's face with his hand and kissed her forehead. "I have no words of consolation, Hana, no magic or potions that will ease this for you but tonight when we look in the sky, perhaps we will find your parents there among the stars as well. Or, maybe along our journey our paths will cross, and you will be reunited."

Hana stood. "I can't breathe." She ran out of the dwelling and down to the river. Sitting on its banks with her feet in the water, she waited. Maybe the goddess would show her where her parents had gone if she was quiet enough. She moved her hand to shoo away an insect and the blue stone in her ring flashed. The world became still. In the air before her, her mother appeared.

"Go forward on your journey, child, go out on the sea and seek us. We are following the sun to its resting place."

"Ouma?" Her mother's image rippled on the air. "Ouma, don't leave me."

But her mother was gone. Hana put her head down on her knees and wept.

Danel conferred with Abirami and decided there was nothing more to do in Andulat. He walked to the river and sat down next to Hana.

"It's time for us to go back to the sea. Being at sea will give Abirami and my brothers something to do that is useful. Otherwise, I think they'll get into trouble. They have already asked girls from your clan to accompany them. And," he looked down at her, "it will be easier to follow the sun toward the night on the water."

Hana pictured the endless movement of the water, its deep blues and greens, its black roiling surface at night. The sea might comfort her. But she could not be just a passenger. She had to have purpose for her life, something that equaled the sacrifice she and her parents had made.

"What will I do? I'm not good at doing nothing. I won't be only a passenger on your boat." She looked up at him. "I must have a life that means something."

Danel laughed and sat down on the riverbank next to her. "You will find your purpose, but meanwhile, I will teach you to pull up the sail, how to row and steer, how to fish from the bow, to navigate by the North Star, and any other thing you want to learn. We will sail the known world, as far as the sea takes us. We can find a boat in Sarepta. Abirami says it's a few days from here. We'll walk along the coast. That will be easier than going back the way we came."

"If there was an easier way to get here, why didn't we go that way in the first place?"

"You wanted to see Osnot. She lived in the wasteland. There is only one way to get to her—the difficult way."

For a moment they were both quiet, thinking of the old woman who brought them together. Danel's excitement about going to sea made her smile.

"Sarepta has everything, Abirami says, pots, cloth, even small images of your goddess. With the coins Abirami made from selling our boat in Sidon, we'll take on timber, glass beads, and cloth, sail to Alashiya and pick up copper, gold, and maybe other goods. We'll trade at all the islands across the sea. You won't believe how many islands there are. We can travel to where the sun falls over the edge of the earth at night and wherever else there is to go. Are you brave enough to go to sea with me?"

"Yes," she answered without hesitation. "Can we search for my parents?"

Danel grinned. "Yes. That's settled then."

They gathered their small clan together, and after three days of walking, found a boat and supplies in Sarepta, including enough food to last through several full moons, extra clothing, and jugs of fresh water, paying for everything with Hana's gold coin.

Abirami managed the purchases, telling Danel and Hana they would be taken advantage of because they were too young to bargain well. They grinned at each other and shrugged. In addition to what they expected Abirami would acquire, he bought fur pelts and woven blankets. "It gets cold where we're going. You will be surprised," he told them.

They nodded at him and let him do what he wanted. He was part of their family, their own elder. "Everyone needs a purpose," Danel told Hana. "You taught me that. Abirami's is to watch over us."

The trip back to the cove at Enkomi where Abirami had been thrown overboard was uneventful. This time Hana passed the three sunrises on deck, freely breathing the briny air and feeling the wind blow in her face. She stood at the prow at night and pointed out the starry figures in the sky by which Danel navigated, hoping she might find guidance there about her parents but neither the goddess nor the wise lord whispered a word.

At Enkomi, Hana walked through the weaving workshop set up in a stone dwelling at the small port. She studied the clay and bronze bobbins that held the weavers' thread taut as they moved it through the loom. *How did people think of these clever uses for items she might have discarded?*

She thought of all the marvels she had seen on her short journey so far—chariots, wheels, and horses used to pull them, huge chiseled stones, boats, statues, mosaics. Her travels had revealed how ingenious people were. Had she had remained in the village where she grew up, following the same traditions as her parents she would never have known that people were capable of such inventions.

As a gift for her attention, one of the weavers gave Hana a narrow, hooked bone used to tamp down each strand of yarn woven into the tapestry. She added the bone to her pouch of treasures she now wore hanging from the blue sash around her waist.

From Enkomi they sailed west away from the island, steering clear of Kty, with the rising sun at their backs and a calm sea ahead. Danel had heard from men at the port in Enkomi about a sacred cave in a place called the Pillars of Gades, a rocky promontory that guarded the entrance to a greater sea few sailors dared to enter.

"If you make a sacrifice in the cave there," Danel told Hana, "the goddess will take away your sorrow. That's what they say, anyway."

She looked at him oddly, her mouth pursed.

"No, no, not that kind of sacrifice. There is no blood involved. You freely give the goddess an object you cherish by throwing it into the water in the cave. That's what I heard."

Hana thought for a while, looking out at the sea, the wide blue sky domed above them, piles of white clouds on the horizon. Relinquishing her sorrow felt the same as abandoning her parents. Was she brave enough to do that? She felt the weight of the blue stone her mother gave her as she began her journey and rolled the ring around on her finger. Light leaped from the stone. Perhaps if she sacrificed the ring, she would find her mother.

She nodded. "I can do that."

ভঙ্গ

They sailed west across the sea, following the setting sun, not knowing what they would find or how long it would be until they came upon land. Six times the sun sank into the sea ahead of them before they came to a rocky island that, from a distance, looked similar to the one they'd left behind in the east. For a while, Danel and

Abirami worried that they had gone in a circle, pushed by winds and tides back to where they started.

Hana, standing in the bow, called out, "The trees are different. There are more of them. The central mountains are higher. There are more, smaller islands nearby. This is a different place. It's not Alashiya."

Sailing south around the island's jagged coastline, they spotted a cove that would give them safe harbor. They could see a small settlement of wood and thatched-roof huts on an abutment above the shore where a river vented into the sea, and higher on the hill, a temple or palace was being built, cut into the rising mountain.

"There must be fresh water," Danel said.

"And food," Abirami added.

Hana smiled for the first time since they left her village. "It will be good to put my feet on the earth."

They pulled into the cove and discussed who should stay with the boat. Island people began gathering at the shoreline, waving their arms. Some waded into the sea.

"Look, Danel," Hana called out. "They look like us."

Danel insisted he and Abirami should be the ones to venture on land first, in case the people were hostile, and Hana should stay on the boat with his brothers and the other women.

Hana reminded Danel that he was the one who knew how to sail the boat. "If we lose you, we are all lost."

Danel nearly growled and shook his head. Wings of his long, black hair flapped his face. "Then keep your dagger in your hand," he muttered. "Let no one take you."

In the end, Abirami, Hana and one of Danel's brothers went ashore. Danel paced the deck, waiting for them to return.

Before the tide changed, they were back, wading into the water out to the boat. Danel hoisted Hana up onto the deck. The men climbed up the rope ladder. Hana's cheeks were flushed with excitement.

"They don't speak our language, but we can make ourselves understood. Abirami can understand some of their words. They are a welcoming people. I didn't see any weapons or guards. They are building a palace for their king, who now lives in the north, and they have invited me to meet him."

"I would expect they did," Danel said, his voice hardly more than a harsh whisper. "I don't want you to do that. It's dangerous. There are more of them than us. They can take you away from me."

"Oh, no, they are kind. They treated me like a goddess. They wouldn't harm me."

Danel turned to Abirami. "What do you think of this idea?"

Abirami appraised both their faces. "It is wise to be cautious but also friendly. They have fresh water and fruit, vegetables, dried fish. They did seem to think that Hana, with her blue eyes and gentle manner, is the goddess. They exclaimed and bowed. They offered her gifts." Abirami smiled, as if to indicate he thought the strangers might be right. "What Hana really wants to do is look again at the images she saw on the walls, large fishes leaping above a blue sea. Another..." He looked over at her for the word.

"Fresco, I think was their word for it," Hana said. "They paint on their walls when the plaster they apply over the stone is still wet."

"Yes, a fresco. It shows an image of a tall bronze man holding many fish from a bountiful catch. She—" He looked at Hana and she nodded to him, "—she wants to examine how the images are made."

"Of course, she does." Danel was forlorn. "I guess I won't be able to stop you, but I can go with you so that they know you are mine."

Hana pursed her lips. "Yours?"

"Yes, you know what I mean. You are my wife. You are not a virgin. They cannot use you for a sacrifice."

Hana thought that was not what he meant, but she knew that he intended to protect her, and for that impulse she cherished him.

The next day, after many instructions, they left Danel's brothers in charge of the boat and made the expedition to the place the local people called Gortyn. While Danel and Abirami haggled with the locals over fresh supplies, Hana, accompanied by the brother's wives, went from chamber to chamber in the palace to examine frescoes.

An artisan told her a story of a great rumbling of the earth, fire and ash raining down, and a huge flood destroying all the villages along the sea. Life, he explained, was uncertain. Their paintings were a way of appeasing the gods, of acknowledging how little power they had, and offering their gratitude for the abundance they had been given.

Hana watched amazed as the master artisan outlined a new fresco on a wall in one of the palace's many chambers. Within a few strokes, she realized he had placed her at the center of the panel with men on either side, their hands raised to the sky, praising her and bowing. She sucked in her breath when she noted that he intended to depict her with her breasts exposed. Her humiliation and terror when the prince of Sidon snatched off her clothing flashed through her body.

Her hands shook with the memory. She exhaled into the realization that this was the way the goddess was always shown. *Oh,* she thought, *I understand. Abundance, milk, even life, flows from women.* This depiction was the artist's way of glorifying her.

Hana bowed to the master and smiled. *What gift do I have to give him in return for this deep compliment?* She opened her pouch and pulled out the blue glass bead on a gold thread that she had been given by the glass blower in Sidon. The bead, the only glass object she had ever owned, was precious to her. She kissed it and placed the bead in the man's hand.

The artisan's eyes glowed. He sank on one knee and bowed his head. He remained in that position until well after she had left the workshop.

เอะเอ

Two full moons later, after stopping at two more ports to trade the goods on board for other materials, refreshing their own supplies, and giving the small clan an opportunity to roam around new cities for a few days, Hana and Danel found the edge of their known world.

They stood in the bow, the boat dipping and rising in the waves, and saw a white mountain rising from the sea straight up into the sky. Between the mountain and the land to the south, the sea surged in both directions across a narrow strait. They clutched each other's hands as the boat rocked.

Danel steered their boat closer to the mountain on the north side of the strait. "They say this is where the cave is." All of them leaned on the rail, training their eyes on the coastline.

Danel's brother, from his perch high on the mast, spied a dark opening in the rock close to the beach. "I see it, I see it! I see the cave. I see it. It's there." He pointed.

Hana gripped the rail of the boat, her breath coming fast. No one knew what was beyond this point. Perhaps the water poured off the world in a waterfall just beyond her vision. The tide might sweep them out into the large sea to their deaths. Perhaps there was no other land but what they could see around them and they would be lost in the vast sea. The strait was so narrow they could see the landmasses to the south and north at the same time.

The people who lived on these lands were unknown to them. No one had spoken of their customs, whether they welcomed strangers or demanded tribute before travelers could pass, or worse, killed them where they stood.

Hana looked around at their small clan. "There's no sign of people or a settlement on the beach. The tide must sweep in when the moon is full."

Abirami was excited, the color high on his cheeks. He took deep breaths to calm himself. "I have imagined this but never thought I would see it."

Danel steered the boat toward the cave. They lowered the sail and rowed. "I worry the rocky shore and the high swells of the sea are a danger to our wooden hull." He pulled the boat in as close as he thought was safe, trying to prevent the craft from being dashed on the rocks.

"We can't go in closer." Danel looked around at Hana. "If the boat smashes on those rocks, we will die here. Only birds and flowers live here. There is no one to give us aid."

Hana and Abirami huddled together while Danel watched the waves, the direction of the boat, the wind, weighing all the factors that could cause a catastrophe. A fish they had only seen before on the fresco in Gortyn leaped into the air, its sleek body in an arc, and splashed back into the sea. Droplets of water sprayed from its fins sparkled in the sun.

"Did you see that?" Hana whispered to Abirami. "A large blue fish jumped up into the air."

He nodded. "It's a good omen."

Hana put her hand on Danel's arm. "Danel, if the fish can swim here, we can swim to the cave. There must be a place to stand inside it. The opening is large, and the sea doesn't fill it. There will be a way to make my sacrifice to the goddess."

Danel shook his head violently. "I can't let you do that. What if you drown, what if that large fish eats you? What if you fall and crack your head on the rock? What will I do then?" He gripped his hair and stalked around the deck.

Hana watched him for a while and then put her hands on his shoulders the way he once did to her. "Danel, you can let me. Abirami will come with me. We'll help each other. I will make my sacrifice and we will swim back to the boat."

"You headstrong girl, you are always getting in trouble. Do you think that old man can save you?"

"I think the goddess and the wise lord will save me." She kissed his cheek. "They have so far." She looked at him. "And you, of course." His face lost its fierce look.

She kissed his lips and handed him her pouch. "I am leaving my precious things with you. Guard them as you would me."

Within a few heartbeats, Hana and Abirami were ready. Danel clutched the pouch to his chest, his face showing the fear he couldn't speak. His brothers rowed the boat as close to the shore as Danel dared. Hana and Abirami slid down the rope into the waves. Danel stood at the bow and watched them bob in the sea and then strike out with long arcs of their arms slicing through the water toward the cave. A blue fish leaped up from the sea and swam along with them to the shore, light-filled drops of water spraying the air around them.

Danel held his breath, ready to dive into the water, until Hana pulled herself up onto the beach. Abirami followed her. They walked gingerly across the pebbled beach, the stones seeming sharp under their feet, making short work of the distance to the cave opening. They looked into the cave, looked back, waved, and disappeared into the darkness.

For Danel, waiting in the boat, Hana and Abirami were gone the length of his entire life.

ೞೞೞ

Hana and Abirami entered the cave cautiously, expecting it to be dark, anticipating people might be inside. Instead, the cave was empty and flashed with light. Hana looked around, astonished. The walls of the cave were blue, as blue as her eyes, and glowed from light reflected in the water in a small, calm pool in the cave's center. Light sparkled like stars against the blue walls as if the entire vault of heaven had descended to earth and was enclosed in that small space. Hana opened her mouth to remark and then realized she knew no words that could express her awe. She looked at Abirami's face and saw her own joy and astonishment reflected there.

There was enough space to walk around the pool of water in the center. Near the entrance, a sign was carved into the stone wall, a mark that to Hana signified a dwelling with lines going straight up and two lines crossing those.

"This looks like the sign for home that my mother taught me, only marked twice."

Abirami nodded. He was absorbed in examining a stone axe, shards of clay pots, and a sharp cutting tool. "People have been here before us. I think those marks are intended to claim this cave as a clan's home at some point."

"But there's no fresh water here."

"Perhaps they rest here for a while and then climb up the gentler slope on the east to that flat plain far above the cave." He pointed east. "From there they can follow the direction of the North Star on foot."

"Look how spears of light stream through the opening and illuminate the pool." Hana sighed. "I think I hear my mother singing to me."

Abirami smiled at her. "Go ahead and make your sacrifice."

Hana stood by the cave wall and removed the ring from her finger. It was heavy in her palm, as if all her mother's hopes for her, the entire story of her family, resided there.

A quake in her heart made her knees tremble. How could she let go of the only emblem of her mother's love and faith in her? How could she let go of her clan and their story? What was she thinking, imagining she could throw the ring into the water in this strange place and never see it again? Her body filled with tears at the thought. She grasped the ring in her palm and closed her eyes.

"Mother, what should I do?"

Wish for me, my darling girl, wish with all your heart to be reunited with me.

Hana took a deep breath, kissed the ring and tossed it into the water. "May the gods help me find you, Ouma." She closed her eyes and prayed to the wise lord that her mother was safe with her father in a beautiful place.

The ring turned over and over on its way down into the waves, and with each turn, light flashed from the stone as if it was sending her a message. Her prayer echoed in the cave.

☙❧☙

When he saw them emerge from the cave, Danel's heart lightened. He grinned and waved both arms. If the energy he felt surging through his arms and legs could leap from his body, he would have made a bridge of the air from where they stood to him. Hana and Abirami waved back. They jumped into the sea and swam back to the boat.

Dripping wet, long tendrils of hair wrapped around her arms, her blue eyes blazing, Hana began to babble about the wonders of the cave.

"Wait, wait, you're talking too fast," Danel said, putting his fingers on her lips. "Get dry, put on warm clothes and then tell me."

When they were both wrapped in fur blankets, Hana told them what she and Abirami found in the cave at the end of the earth.

Danel smiled and shook his head. Now that he had them back safely, his fear had dissipated, and he could be generous. "You two are certainly adventurous. I am almost willing to believe anything you tell me."

Hana shook her hair loose from the blanket around her. "The cave was the most beautiful thing I have ever seen."

Danel looked over at Abirami, who nodded, his old eyes wise and warm. Danel smiled, took Hana's hand, and kissed her palm.

"And I think it taught me how to direct the eye to the object in a mosaic. It's something to do with how light reflects off certain things."

He nodded. "Of course, I understand now. You are going to make mosaics wherever you go. That is your purpose."

That evening while the sea was calm, they took a meal on deck, and set off for the island of Tamaran. Danel had been told by a sailor at the last market where they traded goods that the island was on the other side of the strait, north across the unknown waters.

Hana stood at the prow of the ship suspended in darkness. Lights flickered above and below her as the night dark sea, illumined only by the moon and stars, parted along the moving bow. Wind and water shushed her. Eventually, she sank into sleep on the deck and dreamed a goddess was watching over her.

Chapter 33

Elena stirred in her sleep, woke, and lay in the dark. Moonlight filtered through the sheer curtains at the window. She listened to the house creaking in the wind. She had been dreaming she was on a wooden boat, the night a dark cloak around her.

"Hana," she whispered into the dark. No one whispered a response.

She turned her head on the pillow. Beside her John moved in his sleep, snoring lightly.

She had fully recovered from the meningitis that, undiagnosed, had wormed its way into her brain after her skull was fractured. The disease had burned all the rage from her and left her empty. She knew this much: she could no longer put on a uniform and pick up a weapon to kill someone. Maybe she couldn't change the world, but she could change what she did in it.

In the grip of death, she had chosen life even when she didn't want to. She had held onto life as if it would save her. *We continue. We persist, maybe until we get it right.* That was the gift she brought back to the world, even if no one listened. To her family's complete surprise, she enrolled in midwife training.

Sometimes, when her beautiful niece looked straight into her soul with those deep blue eyes, Elena felt connected to Hana, the girl from the past whose life seemed so real when she was in the coma. She would never be with her again, never co-exist in Hana's time in that beautiful, untainted world. Deep homesickness for a place where she had never really been swept through Elena's heart, constricted her throat, and cramped her stomach. She shook herself to lose the feeling. How could she long for a place she'd never been?

Slipping out of bed, she walked barefoot into the living room and stood at the sliding glass door, looking out onto the slow-motion roll of waves swishing across the beach. John was too good to her, to bring her here where she could take long walks on the beach and listen to the hypnotic sound of the sea. He had her back. He knew what she needed. The sea, the endless stretch of moving blue water all the way to the horizon, was healing her.

She opened the doors and walked down the wooden stairs, across the dunes, and down to the beach. Her bare feet sank into sand glistening with moonlight. The moon made a path across the water.

She walked to where the barest fringe of waves caressed her ankles before receding in a swish and stood there for a while watching the sea and the moonlight until something tickled her toe.

Looking down, she expected to see a sand crab nibbling her skin. There on the sand was a ring. She reached down and picked it up. The ring had a gold band worn thin—by time, by waves and sand—and a deep blue stone that by some miracle had not been swept out of its setting.

She cupped the ring in her palm. The full moon climbed higher in a sky brimming with stars and moonlight flashed off the stone. She slipped the ring on her finger and looked out at the night dream sea.

THE END

About the Author

Ginny Fite is the author of the Detective Sam Lagarde dark mystery thrillers *Cromwell's Folly, No Good Deed Left Undone*, and *Lying, Cheating, and Occasionally Murder*, the thriller, *No End of Bad*, three books of poetry, a book of essays *I Should Be Dead by Now*, and a collection of short stories, *What Goes Around*. She lives in Harpers Ferry, West Virginia.

Made in the USA
Lexington, KY
30 October 2019

Sept. 28 2019